THE CHURCH AT PARKERS WHARF

Louise Gorday

The Church at Parkers Wharf

Cover image: By Lglswe - Own work, CC BY-SA 3.0, https://commons.wikimedia.org/w/index.php?curid=11009908

ISBN 978-1983965517

Printed in the United States of America

For Ray
The love of my life and a great father
Your support means everything

To M.J. Carr
Thanks for making me a better writer

Also by Louise Gorday

The Pickle Boat House

Bayside Blues

The Clockwise Carousel

Contents

CHAPTER ONE

Black Widow

January 16, 1919

Prentis Gant swung the black Model T coupe onto Main Street and glided past the graying warehouses with their identifying numbers painted in red above the doors. Past small, colorful beach cottages in shades of peacock blue and salmon pink, and on beyond the edge of the amusement park that defined the bayside town of Nevis, Maryland. A sharp right put him and his companion, Jackson Dwyer, onto One Notch Road. There were probably half a dozen roads in Nevis named *Some Number* Notch Road. One-notchers always had a church on them, and this particular one led to Saint Peter's. Jackson knew it well. He had worshipped there as a child, a youth, and a young man, but when his love for the bottle eclipsed his love of the Lord, he stopped going altogether. He hadn't attended in years.

Jackson closed his eyes and pressed back in his seat. "Aren't you the least bit concerned about what might be barreling the other way? Isn't there a hairpin curve up here somewhere? Slow down!"

"Took that out four years ago. Relax. We're barely pushing twenty-nine miles an hour on the flat, and I'm fixing to slow down."

The flivver rounded a sharp curve, and a white clapboard church nestled in a grove of evergreens came into view. The road was congested, a tight squeeze past wagons on the left and Model T Fords to the right.

"They giving away money today?" Jackson asked as Prentis crept through the bottleneck. He studied the cluster of mourners gathered in the churchyard at the bottom of the hill, near the low stone wall that enclosed the cemetery. "Stop!" he blurted out, fumbling with the door handle.

Prentis stomped the brakes and muttered an oath as the car jerked to a halt. Jackson flung open the door and stepped out, his left foot still on the running board. "Who?"

"Archibald McClelland, I suspect." Prentis squinted to get a better look. "Yes, I believe that's his widow burying number two. He didn't last much longer than his brother. 'Course, William was quite a bit older."

"Camilla," Jackson murmured, looking at the matron standing nearest the casket. Dressed head to toe in black mourning garb, she had the figure of a dumpling. Although he couldn't see her hair, he knew it to be gray with a few streaks of brown still running through it. She had been a sweet, svelte thing when they were young. But then, thirty-some years ago, he had cut a dashing figure, too. He sighed. Funny how time molded bodies like clay but left the feelings etched in granite.

"Don't worry about her, Jackson. Sitting on all that land out there, Camilla McClelland won't be wanting for suitors, even if she is the most opinionated, overbearing woman this side of Washington. If what I've heard is true, she'll be moving fast. Archibald was gambling it all away, and she probably needs a flush of new money to keep it all afloat." Prentis plucked at the back of Jackson's coat. "We need to hustle."

Galloping hooves and rumbling wheels shattered the quiet of the sacred place as a buckboard appeared, bouncing along the road that connected the caretaker's cottage to the main road. It shot past the grave sites and streaked toward the cemetery entrance.

"Fire, you reckon?" Prentis murmured.

"Hope not," Jackson said, checking the tree line for smoke.

He jumped the low cemetery wall and jogged toward the barreling wagon, waving for him to stop. "Sir! Why the rush through here? This's a *graveyard*, for Pete's sake."

The wagon slowed to swerve around him and continued jouncing along toward the main street. "Sorry, Mr. Dwyer," the driver yelled over his shoulder. "Don't you know? Prohibition just passed. Best get your drink while they're still pouring. Nevis be dry as a bone tomorrow." He flicked his whip and rumbled on. When he reached the street, he turned left, bouncing and weaving down the potholed road toward town.

"Did he say Prohibition passed?" a male voice called out from the burial group.

"Yes sir, I believe he did," Jackson called back, and almost before he could close his mouth, the crowd of mourners dispersed, men dashing for their horses, cars, and wagons. Within seconds, they had floored, lashed, and goosed their various conveyances after the wagon, and a minute later they were out of sight.

Prentis shook his head. "Never underestimate the power of panic and an uninformed populace. Reckon they don't know it isn't supposed to go into effect until twelve months *after* ratification? We'll still have that lousy two-percent around till *next* January."

Jackson laughed. "Apparently—unless there's something we don't know. In which case, seems we should get ourselves to town while *they're still pouring*."

Prentis put the car in gear and looked back at Jackson, who remained rooted to the turf, staring across the field. "Remember what I said about keeping you out of danger? As your closest friend, I think—"

A whoop of excitement cut him off. It came from the graveyard. Transfixed, the men watched as the bereaved Camilla McClelland danced about, not directly *on* her deceased husband's grave, but waltzing nonetheless among the tombstones, locked in the embrace of another woman dressed in black. The dancing was brief and ended as suddenly as it started, with the women doubling over in laughter. Then Camilla straightened up and gazed toward the road, her black crepe-covered hat sitting just high enough on her head for Jackson to see her eyes. For a moment, their eyes locked, hers blazing with satisfaction and defiance. A pang hit him in the chest: longing, hurt, and regret all exploding within him like ice chips from a six-prong pick. He groaned under the weight. Time had not tempered two souls linked in an apparently endless dance of desire, rejection, and heartache. Jackson broke out in a sweat and looked away, unwilling or unable to contend with her. He would never see forgiveness in those intense brown eyes.

"Get us out of here, Prentis," he said, returning to the car. And then, unable to help himself, he glanced her way once more, only to be rewarded this time with a smile and ever so slight a movement of her gloved hand. Was that a *wave*? "Wait! Stop, Prentis! She waved at me."

"Hell no," Prentis said, unleashing the full power of the Ford. "You've spent the last how many years cleaning yourself up to catch that woman's eye, and what's it gotten you? A bunch of buildings to look at, and you're still not satisfied. That woman'll be the death of you. Black widow if ever I saw one."

The T roared down the notch road, leaving behind temptation and a low rooster tail of dust. Jackson could still feel the woman's presence, and after all these years, he could still hear her voice ringing in his ears. *You'll never amount to squat, Jackson Dwyer. Never. Nothing.* He shook his head and watched the world whizzing by.

"Prentis?"

"That's me," Prentis said, again pushing twenty-nine miles per hour and apparently trying to squeeze out a few more.

"I can't do it."

"Doc says he can't hang on much longer. Not my business, but don't you think you might regret it later?"

"I regret everything later. Drop me at the courthouse. He wouldn't expect anything less."

CHAPTER TWO

Big Shoes to Fill

As the steamboat docked, the sandy-haired fellow in the passenger lounge pulled his knapsack from the luggage rack and slung it down onto his seat. "This one yours?" he asked the young brunette standing next to him, the escaping tendrils of her wilting bun pushed haphazardly behind each ear. She nodded, and he pulled down a small blue valise, noting the *FMB* monogram written in gold right below the leather handle. "Here you go, Miss . . ."

"Good luck, Mr. Shoemaker. I think you'll like it here in Nevis."

"Oh, I don't want to put down roots in a small town," he said, wondering whether the *B* stood for *Brown*. "Eighteen months at the most. Catch a few headlines, make a name for myself. Then I'm back to Philly."

Her sweet smile faded, and he wanted to kick himself in the knickers. He should have figured out her name and determined where she'd be staying, *before* making a complete ass of himself. He adjusted his ill-fitting tweed suit, grabbed his felt hat, and followed her down the steamship's gangplank. "I don't suppose you need any assistance in getting home?"

"Someone should be here to meet me," she said, searching the crowd that had turned out to meet the *Chessie Belle.*

"I can wait with you, if you'd like." He took her suitcase.

"I think I'll be all right," she said, taking it back. "Everybody knows everybody in these boring small towns."

"Fanny!" A man elbowed toward her through the throng of disembarking passengers.

"Daniel!" Fannie threw herself into his arms, and he lifted her up in the air and spun her around before setting her back on her feet.

He held her at arm's length. "Can't believe you're back," he said, wide-eyed in a lovesick-puppy sort of way. "You won't need to be going back, will you?"

Fanny shook her head.

"Can I buy you lunch?" He took her suitcase and pulled her away from the train.

"I can't, but you can walk me to Betty's if you like."

Tate Shoemaker sighed and watched them chattering away as they flittered off like little lovebirds. He dropped his bag at the end of the pier and looked around him: an empty boardwalk—understandable in the January chill—bayfront businesses catering to vacationers drawn to the water; and a battered fishing industry whose heyday had come and gone. This quaint burg was going to be sheer misery. He understood why his father had left the place and fled to Philly to make his name in the newspaper business. What he saw might be impressive to a small-town girl, but this would-be Coney Island couldn't touch cities up north.

He crossed the beach and trudged up Bayside Avenue toward downtown and the office of the *Evening Star.* He had received directions from the duffer who offered him the job, and they were precise: *Pass Main Street, but if you reach the train depot, turn around. If you make it back to the beach, start over and pay more attention.* Apparently, actual street numbers didn't mean a great deal around here. Already, he was beginning to see why.

He didn't need a number. The newspaper, with its striking white and blue marquee displayed prominently out front, occupied prime real estate. Inside, there was a flurry of activity at the front desks, and the smell of ink and machine oil hung heavy. His spirits lifted, and he felt a burst of energy as he knocked on the door of Riley Tanner, editor.

Tanner thrust a meaty hand at him. "Tate Shoemaker? Great to have you, son. If you're half as good as your old man, you'll do fine here. Jumped at the chance to have another Shoemaker. Only advice I got is, play it straight, play it fair, and don't play on company time." Tanner patted him on the back and pushed past. "Got a fire to put out, so I'm going to hand you off to Buck Hooley, assistant ed. He'll find you a place and get you started." He ran a hand over his bald head, pushed a pencil behind his ear, and shuffled off.

The building was all one room. Tate followed the silent Buck Hooley to the opposite end of the newsroom—about as far away from the excitement as one could get and still be in the same building—and unpacked his Corona portable typewriter, a fistful of pencils, and a couple of empty notebooks. Anything else, he would have to earn. He gazed up front to where Tanner stood and where all the action was. How close to that could he get in six months? With one big story, he was betting, dead center.

CHAPTER THREE

Legacy

Jackson batted away misty plumes of breath and stared at the barn-board warehouses separating the bay from the amusement park—a hundred and twenty, last count. Dwyer's Oyster Packing, the whitewashed one trimmed in dark green, was his. Nothing grand about it, but in a waterside community like Nevis, location was everything, and this little gem sat right next to the steamboat pier. In his youth, he had almost frittered it away. Then he decided to straighten up and fly right—a good woman could have that effect on a man. What best use could he put it all to now?

The black Tin Lizzie skirted the shoreline, and his stomach fluttered. He watched the Ford pull over and park, grinding away at the dockside gravel and his sense of refuge. Prentis got out and joined him at the pier railing.

"Gone?" Jackson asked.

"Yes. 'Bout an hour ago."

Jackson bit his lip and nodded.

"If you must know, he went peacefully."

Jackson snorted. "Did you come out here to help me purge my soul?"

"No, not really." Prentis stamped his feet, hunched his shoulders against the damp cold, and pulled his neck scarf up to cover the bottoms of his ears. "Waterfront never gets old, does it?"

Jackson shook his head. "No, sir, it does not. Not every man gets to see his success staring back at him. But building a business and keeping it successful . . . Diversification—that's the ticket now."

Prentis bobbed his head. "Getting right down to business, are we?"

"The world keeps turning." Jackson pointed at the row of warehouses, nautical chandleries, and sailor dives. "Maybe I should try to buy out some of these along here. Like Millman's Glass and Varnish. He's barely making it, and no money to do any improvements, but I could invest a little capital and make something of that. *Any* of these in here, actually. If you don't tie up all your cash and can wait out the lean times, waterfront's never a poor investment."

"I hear ya. I never could understand why these owners didn't sell out when the Bayland partnership moved in and started the amusement park. They could have gotten top dollar. Like you—why didn't you sell?"

"Because when you're young and stupid, you always have something to prove," Jackson said, laughing. "I'm not the type to flash the cash around. I needed something big and imposing—like a building."

"Yeah, you were pretty young and stupid, no argument there. But then, we all were. You wear success very well, so you can stop trying to impress now. I'm only a politician, but let me inflict on you a piece of unasked-for advice. You can send the dredgers and the bugeyes out all you want, but making a good living in oysters will soon be a thing of the past. Even Loring Packers in Solomons is having a rough go of it."

"Might sell those, too," Jackson said, his breath puffing out as if he were smoking a hidden cigarette.

"What happened to your oyster shells?" Prentis asked, nodding at the far side of the packing house. "Find some shallows to dump 'em in?"

"Got tired of filling in and extending the pier. No profit there. Micky Cann tipped me off to some Aberdeen farmers who use it to lime their fields. Sold and shipped the lot of it by rail late last week."

"I like it," Prentis said. "A smart man never lets an opportunity walk on by. Although, I'm pretty sure that even with your *big building* over there, you've got enough stuffed in your mattress to do whatever the tarnation you want."

"Oyster crackers—that's the thing. I'm going to corner the market on the complete Maryland oyster experience, Prentis. Nice little picture of a smiling oyster on the front of the package. *Ollie,* that's what we're going to call him. *Ollie's Oyster Crackers.* Ship 'em to Balmer and south as far as Virginia Beach. Then I'm going to repackage them as Ollie's Chowder Crackers and ship 'em up as far as Bar Harbor and corner that market, too. Diversification—that's the key."

"You're going crackers?" Prentis chuckled. "Why, the possibilities sound endless. Have at it. Give birth to Ollie and make him a celebrity. Be happy and succeed at everything you want. Nobody deserves it more than you. But you might want to wait a bit and let things settle. You could change your mind."

Jackson shook his head, suddenly engrossed in the packing house, where a brawny dockworker in a blue apron worked a heavy chain to roll up the broad metal door of the delivery bay. In a thick Eastern Shore accent, he called out to a second worker. They maneuvered the second man's laden cart to the loading dock and began lifting off bushel baskets.

"How they look, Smitty?" Jackson shouted to them.

"Good size *ersters*, Mister Jackson," the first yelled back. "They be shucking soon. Come see yourself."

"Might do that." Jackson turned to Prentis and said, "You have no idea how wonderful it is to see business as usual. Last night, I dreamed about crazed, ax-wielding suffragettes chasing me along the pier. Carrie Nation went on a tear through my building with an ax and near chopped it to the ground. Lucky I'm still standing."

"Hmm," Prentis said. "My nightmares usually involve beautiful women. Unfortunately, my wife's usually there, too. Listen, Jackson, I'll try to keep the suffragettes and all other dangerous distractions away from you. And those properties . . ." He glanced back at the warehouses. "I suppose I could make some inquiries. No one needs to know who's asking. Be glad to do that for you."

Jackson shook his head. "That'd be nice, but you're right. Maybe we should hold off for a bit."

Prentis cleared his throat. "There is another reason I came looking for you."

Jackson watched his friend examine the paint peeling on the railing, noted his rapid breathing, the clench of his fist. *How seldom people ever changed.* "Of course there is."

"We can chitchat all day, Jackson, but in the end, we still need to have *the talk.* I need to know whether you're serious about running for mayor. And you have to give me an answer *today.* The empire is going to someone. May as well be someone I like."

"Criminy," Jackson said, hanging his head. "The old man's corpse is still warm." He thought a moment and then, eyes narrowing, looked at Prentis. "And all this encouragement coming from the kid who had to win every footrace, school competition, and spitting match by whatever means required? Tell me again why *you're* not interested."

Prentis flipped a chip of paint free from the handrail and snickered. "Oh, I'm tempted, but I prefer the relative anonymity of the town council, where I'm less of a target. I prefer to pull strings . . . like yours."

They both ducked as a white gull—something dangling from its beak—swooped in over their heads and landed on a nearby post. "So it was you who decided I'd make an adequate sacrificial lamb? My mother thanks you. Clearly, no one on the town council wants to stick out their own neck. I guess there's something to be said for hiding in a group."

"Oh, there are others," Prentis said, watching the gull swallow a wiggling fish. "Teddy Lumpkin and R. J. are like pointers on a fresh scent, and the council's splintering, waiting for me to anoint someone. It doesn't matter which of them I throw in with. They're both incompetent. I'd end up doing all the work and getting a big, fat empty thank-you. No, the mayor would have enjoyed seeing *his* success staring back at you—like a big building."

"Chance Dwyer was the most corrupt politician Nevis ever had—an insufferable bully and a sot. A hard man to love, and I'm not sorry to be out from under his thumb. I don't want to follow in his *esteemed* footsteps."

Prentis nodded. "I understand, but you're in the unique position to capitalize on what he built in Nevis. If you don't, nothing's going to change, and God knows what the town will look like in another ten years. Don't tell me you're not the least bit interested. Don't you care about Nevis?"

"Pshaw. Watching him waste away this last week, I've done nothing but think about Nevis—its fished-out fishing industry, an amusement park that relies so much on liquor at a time when the drys in this country are pushing hard to make it illegal. You should dream about Carrie Nation—who looked an awful lot like Camilla McClelland, by the way—demolishing your cannery with a big old felling ax."

"See? You're already thinking mayor thoughts." Prentis pulled a notepad from his breast pocket and began scribbling. "Where's your car?"

"Home. I hopped the train and walked down from the depot."

"If you'd like, I can take you back over to the house to say good-bye."

"Uh-uh."

"Well, then, where can I drop you? I don't like you wandering around by yourself right now."

Jackson smiled. Prentis had some good qualities. "The dedication of the new post office would be fine."

"Oh, you don't need to bother with that. I'll call someone else on the council. Nobody expects you to be there."

Jackson pulled his hands out of his coat pockets and blew on them. "You're only as good as your word." He pointed to Prentis's car and started walking.

"I know better than to argue. Give it your all, and even if you do mess up, I'll clean up, smooth over, make nice for anything that doesn't come out right. You speak from the heart, and people like that. In spite of the cold, I imagine there's a big crowd just dying to hear you speak."

"Yeah, it'll be big because everyone'll be expecting a train wreck."

"We haven't had one of those since 1901. A shipment of ponies or some such when they were building the park. Not to worry. No ponies this morning." Prentis checked his pocket watch. "And hypothermia will be setting in if we don't go now."

Jackson climbed into the car and examined his red, chafed hands. "Did he ask for me?"

"Yep."

A low hiss escaped Jackson's lips. "Prentis, he's gone and I'm not sorry."

Prentis shifted the car into gear and it lurched forward. "Welcome to the human race."

"Yes, but I'm the only one who called him 'father.'"

"Aw, hell, if that's the worst you ever called him, you did better than the rest of us. Let's go."

When they hit Main Street, Prentis pulled into Neely Merkle's Ford lot and cut the engine. They rolled to a stop.

"Car trouble?" Jackson asked. "Let's leave it and walk. I hate being late." He opened his door.

"Engine's fine. It's *you* I'm worried about. You're a big boy, so I'm not going to give you any lectures about Camilla. What I do want to say is that no matter what you want—Camilla, dancing crackers, or anything else—it'll be easier to achieve with position and power than without. Sounds shady, but it's something they could chisel on the bottom of the statue in every town square in the country. Say yes to the mayoralty. It's a ticket to everything you might want: respect, Camilla—you could even shine up Chance's legacy. Trust me."

"I do trust you, and if I gave you a yes, I'd certainly need your help to succeed. But I don't know. . . . There are other things. . . . I'm tired of doing what's expected." He looked at the car lot and zeroed in on the two shiny red Indian motorbikes parked up close to the building. "Maybe I should buy the finest machine he's got, and drive it until it runs out of gas—someplace no one will ever find me."

"You're not the type. Besides, its freezing in Appalachia this time of year. And one of those bikes won't get you a hundred miles on a full tank."

Jackson sighed. "I suppose I could do some good. But if I were to commit to the mayoral race, you'd have to find another place to perform, puppet master, because I'd be my own man. Nobody pulls my strings. The office of mayor would become respectable again. Dad's cronies, including some on the council, shouldn't think nothing's going to change. If you find that to be a conflict—and as I seem to recall, you were always in the thick of things, money changing hands . . ."

"*Shh!*" Prentis slid down in his seat. "I do the best with what God gave me, but I don't claim to be a saint. Can't you stop overanalyzing everything? Just enjoy the prospect of being mayor in this charming burg and forget all the other headaches? Running off won't make you any happier than staying. Use your authority to make Nevis the best little bayside hamlet it can be. Win the runoff and you'll have what's left on the current term to decide whether you want to make a career of it. Play your cards well and don't rile any of the big dogs until you're elected to a full term. A little back-scratching isn't going to destroy your moral fiber. Then do whatever you want to them. Nobody's asking you to be something you're not. But I do think that once you're in there, you'll never want to go back.

"But, Jackson," he continued, "here's the thing. Don't waste energy questioning my motives. I'm the last person you need to be worrying about. If you'd been paying closer attention, you'd know how much trouble I've kept this little town out of. I've done nothing these last five years but clean up your father's legal messes. No one will ever watch your back like I will. I'd never do you dirty. With what I know and your wholesome reputation, this should be a cakewalk. You'll have women hanging all over you. Pick a nice one and let that merry widow McClelland be."

And therein lay the difference between them. Prentis had always loved power and position, but not Jackson. He had spent his life watching its destructive effects up close. Then again, maybe this could be his big opportunity to impress—a means to the end of a long journey. He gave the shiny red motorbikes one last look and clicked his door shut.

"Yes. The answer is yes. Work your magic and make things happen, but no strings. I'm sick of strings and attachments. And read my lips, Prentis: no more women."

Prentis slapped his arm. "That's my boy! A word of caution, though. I'm not going to kid you. With Prohibition bearing down on us, our future mayor may very well be forced to navigate a carefully plotted course between the wet and the dry advocates. I know you don't drink, but you may have to find enough middle ground to please both sides. Think you can handle that?"

Jackson nodded and stared down Main Street. He could just make out the federal flag flying above the courthouse. Was he a fool for committing more time to the insane politics of that place? "Do you think the voters will realize this election is in the bag?"

"Well, when there's no opposition running, it'll kinda be obvious," Prentis said with a laugh. "Which reminds me: Even when I unify the council, you're not going to be running unopposed."

Jackson arched an eyebrow and studied Prentis's sober expression. "I'm not liking this already. Who?"

Prentis pulled on an earlobe. "Don't get upset. We can handle it. Haven't had a chance to verify, mind you, but I heard Lemuel Browning was filing papers to run."

Jackson belly-laughed. "Lemuel can't stagger up the courthouse steps unaided, let alone sign his name."

"Thought you'd like that," Prentis said, grinning. "Your father doesn't get to flip over in his grave even once before everybody and their one-eyed mule decides they can handle the office. Actually, there are several contenders who were lining up their ducks before . . .well, before. Expect Buddy Tanner to throw his hat in, and a yet-unnamed representative of the local suffragette league."

"Those women. They can't vote, but they've just got to meddle."

"You're right about that. And I'm done preaching at you, but someone else wants a word."

A car pulled up on Jackson's side and Rankin Baylor, a close associate of Jackson's father, climbed out and tipped his hat. "Prentis. Jackson, sorry about your father. There won't be another one like Chance."

Jackson nodded and hoped not. "Heading to the dedication?"

"Right." Rankin leaned past Jackson and looked at Prentis. "And?"

Prentis gave him thumbs up. "He said *yes.*"

"Excellent!"

"Wait!" Jackson said. "How did you know . . ."

"Plain as the sun at midday that you'd follow your Dad," Rankin said. "And, of course, you *are* the best candidate. Late last week, Chance asked me to set up a blueprint for your campaign and show you the ropes." He leaned back in his car and pulled out a packet. "We don't have to sit down with it right now, but I thought you'd like to look it over before we do."

Jackson turned to Prentis. "Is that what *we* want?" he asked, an incredulous look on his face.

"We'll talk," Prentis said, and he reached across Jackson and took the envelope. "Got to go, Rankin. We're late." He placed the envelope on the seat between them, and took off.

Jackson sighed heavily and picked up the envelope. "Dad's last gift. You knew about this? I was that much of a sure thing?"

"Yes," Prentis said, not venturing a look in Jackson's direction. "I didn't want to upset you and complicate your decision. Get rid of the stuff, if you don't want it. But don't think Rankin is just going to disappear. We should at least hear him out."

Jackson tore the document into bits. "This wasn't the type of help I was hoping to get from you. *You* get rid of him and then maybe I'll trust you again."

"Challenge accepted," Prentis said. He tossed paper shreds out the window, and they rode the last blocks in silence.

As they approached the new post office building, Jackson pulled his hands out of his coat pockets and blew on them again. Nobody liked to shake a cold hand. "So, this morning's speech—it changes from Jackson Dwyer, grieving son, to Jackson Dwyer, newly announced mayoral candidate." Jackson glanced at the remnants of the envelope still in the car. "I don't know if I'm ready for all this, Prentis."

"Of course you are. It's in the blood."

Jackson's hands stopped chafing. "Don't ever say that again, even in jest."

"Sorry." Prentis downshifted to let a sheepdog amble across the road. "If you want, we can use the train story. People love a heart-warming story in political speeches."

"Pass. All people want and need is an honest man, and if you want to stay on the mayor's good side, you'll never forget it."

CHAPTER FOUR

The List

Inside the anteroom of the mayor's office, Jackson pulled his winter coat off and flung it onto a ladder-back chair near the door. Eleven months had passed since he accepted the challenge of creating a new administration, and he continued to bask in the glow of a luxuriously long postelection honeymoon.

"Ahem." The prim gray-haired woman sitting at the reception desk tapped her pencil.

"Sorry, Missus Hasson," he said. "Sure am going to miss you." Being careful not to look her way, he picked up the coat and hung it neatly on a metal hook near the door. No doubt, she was flashing him the smile—the one like his mother's that made him feel ten years old again. Still, better than the glare of a disapproving father.

"Of course you are, dear. No one else will be able to keep up with you. Best have someone in here before I leave, so I can teach her the right way to get things done. Heaven help her if it has to come from you."

"I'm trying. If you can keep my interruptions to a minimum this morning, I might just find someone."

"The Nevis Society of Suffrage and Human Rights, the *Evening Star,* and a persistent gentleman who wants to discuss general business opportunities," she said, reading from the memo pad next to her phone. "Shall I make appointments?"

"No, Missus Hasson. I seem to be all booked up today. Arrange a talk with the *Star* for midweek next. The ladies will have to wait until my schedule loosens a bit."

She eyed the calendar with all its empty pages and flipped forward to next week, which was as devoid of meetings as this one. "Do you want me to tell you what you really need?"

"No, ma'am," he said over his shoulder. "Maybe later—after some coffee." He closed his office door and joined Prentis at an oak table shoved against the double window on the far wall. The streets below them were quiet, the weather bitter cold and uninviting. He glanced left down Main—north, toward Second Street—and wondered when the spring flowers would be poking their heads up toward the sun.

"You do realize you'll never find another one like her," Prentis said with a chuckle.

"Yes, and thank you, God." Jackson slapped a writing tablet down on the table. "So, tomorrow, the first day of Prohibition, and purgatory. I need to discuss with you the Baltimore mayors' meeting."

"Table that a minute, Jackson. The last of the papers for you to sign on your father's estate."

Jackson scribbled across the bottom. "Give it all to charity."

"They'd be set for life," Prentis said, sliding the documents back into their envelope. "Legally, it's all in your name now. Do with it what you will."

"Thanks for handling that for me. I owe you."

"I'll remember."

"There is one more thing you could do for me: help me keep my name out of it so they don't hike up the price. How about looking into that little yellow bungalow that sits on the corner of Main and Second?"

"What? You're not going to stay at Maidstone? I'd be glad to take that lovely manor off your hands."

"No. I just want the bungalow."

"Give me a house number," Prentis said. "I'd hate to surprise you with the wrong one."

"Number Eighteen. You know it. The one with all the red flowers in the spring. Tulips for miles along that street."

Prentis frowned. "Sounds lovely, but there's no street in Nevis full of flowers. You're talking about old Jake Glynn's place? That's the only house on the street that has any flowers. I think he's passed. Jiminy, Mr. Glynn was an old guy when we were nippers. Don't know if it's for sale, though. If not, I'll find you something similar. We can plant as many flowers as you want—hell, put up a greenhouse and have 'em all year."

Jackson thought for a moment. All he could picture was the father's deep voice and the young boy laughing as they sat on the stoop together, surrounded by giant cupped flowers—red ones that danced in the bay breeze. "No, just that one."

Prentis pulled out his ever-present to-do list. "I'll see what I can do. As for other—and no doubt more profitable—real estate ventures you've expressed interest in, there's been some movement on the waterfront. It's been a couple of months since we made some offers, so I decided to make another go of it. Sent the new guy, Robert from accounting, around to see who might be itching to sell."

"Holy moley. That's the only guy you could dig up to send? If they think the town's buying up property, the price of real estate will skyrocket."

"Relax. Nobody's ever expressed even a glimmer of interest except Danny Millman. And guess what? He's softening a bit. I think he might sell if the price were right, but he didn't name that price. Evidently, he has a serious sweetie and wants to marry her, start a bunch of little Millmans."

Jackson's eyebrows shot up. "Make an offer."

"Sure, but you'd better make it a good one. Robert got the impression he might already be entertaining an offer from someone else." Prentis pulled two Cubans from inside his vest, gave one to Jackson, and started looking around. "Cutter?"

Jackson handed him a flat metal cigar cutter adorned with the proud silhouette of an Indian in full headdress. "And?"

Prentis looked over the piece. "*Indian Motorcycle . . .*" He used it and handed it back. "Father's?"

Jackson nodded. "That and his address book—the only things I kept."

"Nice. To answer your question, there is no *and*. Robert couldn't gauge whether Millman was playing it shrewd or really was looking at another offer." Prentis tossed his match into a nearby ashtray and said, "Why the puzzled look, Jackson? It's a simple process. Make him a good, fair offer and focus on this liquor mess."

Jackson waved a hand at him. "Pshaw. When I tell you about the mayors' meeting, you'll see that there is no liquor mess. But Danny boy fielding multiple offers for a business that's going nowhere? That has me intrigued. If he really does have an offer, why didn't he come back to us with a counter? Local buyer?"

Prentis shrugged. "I can't answer these questions, Jackson. Give me a good number, and it'll be a done deal."

"Two hundred above whatever's already been thrown at him. And get me the name of the other buyer. Nothing goes on in Nevis that I'm not privy to."

"Consider it done. Now, tell me why life isn't messy."

Before Jackson could respond, there was a knock at the door and it opened a crack. "Files," Mrs. Hasson said, and she entered with an armload of manila folders and black notebooks. "Sorry to intrude, but I want to know everything is in its proper place before I leave." She tucked the folders in a file cabinet in the corner and put the notebooks on the shelf above it. "This should lock," she said, tapping the cabinet. "Would you like me to order a new one?"

"No, thank you, Missus Hasson. Just get things in the right places. I'll have your replacement handle it." Jackson carefully propped his cigar in the ashtray and waited for the door to close behind her. With a roll of his eyes, he said, "Mayors' meeting—it went well. Heavily attended, by the way. Everyone's scurrying around like Rhode Island Reds with their heads chopped off. I'm not sure why. We knew there was a good chance nobody would ride in on a white charger at the eleventh hour and stop this ridiculous experiment called Prohibition. The consensus is that everybody will keep their head down and follow Baltimore's lead. That means loose enforcement. In other words, *wet.*"

"Yeah, but we're much closer to Washington, and they're going to be dry. Maybe we should follow its lead. Wet might get you jail time."

"Get a clean sheet," Jackson said, sliding the tablet toward Prentis. "We need a comprehensive list of the pros and cons of staying wet."

"You put too much to paper. It's going to get you into trouble some-day. Please tell me you'll let her buy you new furniture, or at least keep this under lock and key."

Jackson pointed to the file cabinet. "Lockbox."

Prentis drew a vertical line down the middle of the sheet. Across the pro column, he scrawled *"Fundamental right to the pursuit of happiness,"* saying each word aloud as he wrote. He gave Jackson a defiant look.

Jackson laughed. "Yeah, that one can stay."

"Your turn."

"If you can manage to squeeze this one above," Jackson said, pointing at the first entry. "And it's something of a question, too. How dependent is the Nevis economy on the German beer concessions in Bayland amusement park? My guess would be, quite a bit. And what about all these Nevis brewers? Can they rely on their farms to get 'em through this nonsense?"

"If no park beer, does Nevis tank? Germans starve?" Prentis murmured, scribbling in the two as separate entries in the con column before beginning the next: *"Suffragettes make life hell on earth."*

"As long as I'm mayor, women aren't going to have any say in the way this town is run, and that includes telling us what we can drink." Jackson continued to stare at the paper a moment. "Con," he said, pointing at the column. "It's never good to stick out in a crowd."

Prentis gave him a quizzical look.

"Talked to Mayor Broening's representative late yesterday. The Baltimore breweries are all but shuttered, and all those good folks are out of work. They're thinking that without liquor, the restaurant and theater business may be down as much as twenty percent, and they're already predicting bread lines. If we become an imbibing oasis, feds are going to take notice. Nevis doesn't need the retribution."

Prentis scribbled in the paper margin, leaving a neat trail of connected ovals. "Having a dry town might sound good in theory, and we'd keep a lot of mothers and wives happy, but we both know our efforts aren't going to stop the liquor. If you're desperate for a drink, you're going to make it in the basement or the bathtub, or pay someone who wants to make it for you. We simply don't have the local manpower—or the willpower—to enforce the Volstead Act."

"Even though it's a good test of states' versus federal rights and responsibilities, I still don't like the illegality of nonenforcement," Jackson said. "Maybe we should drag our feet a while. We might get some relief from the major breweries. Anheuser-Busch and Pabst are regearing to produce beer at point-five percent alcohol—the limit under Volstead."

"That would be the 'near beer' I keep hearing about, but trust me, Jackson, it's more like water with a little horse piss thrown in for the suds."

Jackson looked out across the bay. Weak sunlight had managed to fight its way through the gray. He suspected that the day after Prohibition, it wouldn't look any different.

"Enforcement?" Jackson mused, blowing a smoke ring, then leaning in to send another one through the first. "Mayor Broening said, and I quote, 'Prohibition and Mr. Volstead's Act be damned.' He's not lifting a finger on enforcement. Residents can do as they please. Governor Ritchie hasn't issued any public statements so far, but the consensus among the mayors is that Broening is following his lead, and the various Maryland jurisdictions will be allowed to vote on their own local option to stay wet or go dry. Much as I'd like to follow the letter of the law, I think we should maintain a unified political front and follow *Balmer's* lead—no local efforts to enforce the Amendment. Enforcement would be a bear, anyway. Half the town already knows how to make beer. The other half will be firing up stills all over those woods. I'd at least like to keep these people safe from jake-leg moonshine."

"Agreed." Prentis gave his arms a stretch and then added *keep locals safe* to the pro column. "Even so, the con would be that it'll still be illegal."

Jackson wandered over to his desk and pulled a stack of memos from under a round glass paperweight. He sat down again and swung his feet up next to the telephone. "Let's call it 'going underground' until wiser heads in Washington prevail. Fact is, the majority of Nevis voters don't want to go dry. And it doesn't make sense, anyway, if every town around us is tapping a keg on Saturday nights. I'm liking this job, and keeping voters happy and safe will ensure that I keep it. If the suffragettes don't like that, let 'em move up to New York or out west to Kansas, where they can vote their little hearts out."

There was another knock on the door. Jackson muttered something unintelligible. "Later, Missus Hasson."

Prentis smiled and then looked contemplatively out the window, toward Maple Street. "Don't know about moving the women out, though. There's a cute little thing named Alice down at Seventh and Maple. I'd sure hate to see that go."

"How's the wife feel about that?"

"Thelma's not well. We have an understanding. I'm discreet—"

"And she gets to remain under your roof and die in peace? Tarnation, Prentis, how can you live with yourself?"

"I do love my wife. And if I had the money, I'd take her to see the specialists at Johns Hopkins." Something drew Prentis's eye to the foreground below the window. "That enforcement-be-damned policy may work fine in Baltimore, but they don't have one important piece that we've been avoiding: *him*."

Jackson walked back over. The only person on the street was a blue-uniformed policeman, standing on the corner. "Chief McCall may be a drinking man today, but tomorrow his world will be as dry as ours. He can be quite ornery when he wants to be."

The cop had his coat collar up and his dark cap pulled down tight over his ears, nightstick at his side, .38 Smith and Wesson in a shoulder holster, and blackjack in his hip pocket—and his copy of the penal code left conveniently at home. Jackson had seen him in Kelly's saloon with a row of empties lined up before him. Their interactions had been few and generally formal.

"Been working on that, actually," Prentis said. "I sense he's a practical man who understands the art of negotiation. When the time is right, we'll come to an accord. I don't see him being a long-term problem."

"You know I hate that," Jackson said. "You handle it." He picked up the list. "I think we need more information about what happens to Bayland with the squeeze on liquor. See what you can find out about their beer concessions. If we buck the feds, I'd at least like to know everyone I'm sticking my neck out for."

"I'll make it a priority. But do you really think they'd send a couple of us locals up the river for allowing a little booze to flow through here?"

"Looks like we're gonna find out." Jackson folded the paper into thirds, tucked it in his vest pocket, and walked back to his desk. "My gut feeling is that if we mind our own business, keep things low-key, and don't send the booze anywhere else, we'll do all right. I think it's the best compromise we can make. Now, off you go. Dig into the how all this affects the park's interests."

"You passing up Kelly's this evening? You don't have to drink to let the boys know you feel their pain."

"No, I'll be there," Jackson said. "With a big fat stogie and bells on, tolling as I go. But not for appearances' sake. I'm going to miss Kelly's. Whatever will we do with ourselves?"

CHAPTER FIVE

The Nevis Gentlemen's Club

Jackson took a luxurious puff of his cigar and watched Prentis elbow his way through the crowded saloon to the long back-corner table—the one shrouded in the thickest blue-gray haze. Kelly's was packed, with less than twelve hours left before the popular watering hole, and all the others like it, shuttered its doors—a casualty of Prohibition and the Volstead Act.

Prentis had scarcely removed his neck scarf and unbuttoned his coat before Kelly put a beer in his hand. "Gonna miss this," Prentis said, and took a long pull. Putting down the half-emptied stein, he said, "What is the charming Missus McClelland going to say when she finds out you're in here?" he asked Jackson.

Jackson pulled the cigar out of his mouth. "I see this isn't your first of the evening. Don't be starting trouble—I haven't had a drink in thirty years. And furthermore, I'm not interested in what Camilla thinks. 'Nuff said."

"You don't say? No spark? No hand waves or invitations to survey the *lower forty?*"

"Shut up."

Prentis laughed, and a few of their nearest neighbors joined in. "Okay. Whatever you say. And guess who I saw sitting on the steps of the diner as I passed? Young Jack Byrne. The she-devils are meeting again. Probably going out of their delicate minds celebrating the town going dry."

Kelly leaned in and served another round. "That young-un's got his nose into everything. Caught him in here one day trying to sneak a drink. You should pull him aside later, find out what they're planning. Appeal to his manhood."

"*Pfft.* I merely have to up the ante," Prentis said. "Last time they had their little hen party, he said they paid him a nickel to sit out there and not let anybody inside. Anybody got six cents? That should do it."

Murt, a skinny fellow, a little tipsy and always eager to please an authority figure, popped up at the end of the table and said, "Consider it done. Everybody ante up and I'll go find out." He pulled his hat off and passed it around. "Six cents," he said when he got it back. "I shall return shortly." He sucked down the rest of his beer, climbed over his cousin Wilbur Hill, and half brother Chad Miller, and disappeared into the crowd.

Wilbur, the local Methodist preacher, was a man of few words when he wasn't proselytizing. He frowned constantly as if he were busy solving all the world's problems. Jackson thought him a decent, amiable fellow, although when he loosened up and sneaked a few, he was a crier. He turned his weepy eyes up to Kelly. "How are you to get along? Selling this place?"

The expression in Kelly's eyes changed from their usual peevishness to something gentler. "Doesn't belong to me," he said, glancing around the saloon that had been his livelihood for twelve years. "What's left of the Budweiser and Michelob beer is mine, but Messrs. Anheuser and Busch own the rest, lock, stock, and spitoon. "Building belongs to the railroad. They can rent it out, for all I care, or close her up until people come to their senses and invite me back."

"Wha-a-at?" It was Pops, the shriveled-up, silver-haired geezer in a red bow tie and misshapen bowler, who generally hung around the saloon until the missus came to fetch him home. "Whatcha gonna do now, leave town?" he said.

"Nope. Born and raised in Nevis. I'm staying right here. I've had a year to prepare and I've got plans." He caught Jackson's eye and gave him a wink.

"Just thinking about it makes me feel pa-a-arched," said Pop, lifting his half-full glass to Kelly before draining it.

Wilbur wiped the foam from his upper lip and said, "We all feel for ya, Kelly, but once this town dries out, it could be a long time before it's wet again. Where we gonna drink until the lawmakers get back in their right mind? I hate the thought of running all the way up in the woods to Flanagan's every morning to wet my whistle."

"Better watch those backwoods boys and their corn shine," somebody else chimed in.

"Flanagan's okay," Pops said between sips. "Don't trust anyone new to the art. Only Flanagan. Never killed nobody or even blinded 'em."

"Always a first time," someone else said.

"Don't you worry about your whistle, Wilbur," Jackson said. "While you boys been drowning your sorrows, Kelly's been figuring things out." He looked around. The crowd had thinned a bit. Some would probably be back before midnight for one last pull, but now was probably as light as the crowd would get. "Draw close," he said, motioning them in with a flutter of his fingers.

Conversation at the table died away as the men waited on the particulars. Just for effect, Jackson took another look around. He let them linger quietly, insecure in the silence and more apt to value and protect the secret he was about to share. After all, he had a reputation to protect. These weren't casual, take-it-or-leave-it drinkers, and Jackson saw fear in their eyes. They were in the moment, and nobody gave much of a damn about anything but the brew in their hand, and the next one heading their way. "Mr. Gant is only going through this once. Anybody that misses out gets left in the dust. Fill 'em in, Prenty-boy."

Prentis looked at Pops and, in a voice just loud enough to be heard if they leaned in and didn't breathe, whispered, "Speakeasy."

Pops's face fell. "It's all right, we ca-a-a-n take it. Spit it out. Right boys?"

Everybody nodded.

"*Speakeasy*," Jackson repeated, more slowly this time. "A secret bar where everyone can get beer, maybe spirits—haven't thought that part through yet. The only way you can get in is with a password: *The Nevis Gentlemen's Club.*"

The man to Jackson's right, wearing a red flannel shirt and looking like Paul Bunyan in the flesh—emitted a low moan. It was Nate, the butcher, whose legendary unkempt beard had given rise to the phrase every housewife in Nevis had angrily muttered at one time or another: *free Nate with every plate.* "The Nevis Gentleman's Club," he repeated, stroking the beard. "Dang it all, that's good. Sign me up. We gonna make our own?"

Prentis tipped back in his chair and called Kelly over. "Kelly, I think it's time to share. Tell 'em what you've got planned. Is this town going dry?"

Kelly put down his tray and walked over, a big grin creasing his face. "Hell no. Some silent partners and I been stocking up for months. I moved my whole storeroom to another location. Give me a week to get situated. It'll be different, but as good as here."

"Not so bad, right, fellas?" Prentis asked. "Just a few administrative matters to take care of before Kelly starts giving out memberships, location, things like that."

"But, but, but, isn't that illegal?" Pops asked. "Chief McCall won't like that a bit."

Jackson said, "Don't you worry about a thing, Pops. Come tomorrow, we can't make, transport, or sell it, but if everybody plays nice and keeps it all on the q.t., nothing in the law says we can't have a drink."

"Leave it to Jackson to figure it all out," somebody said."

"You're smarter'n all the rest of us put together," said another. Keep this town wet, and you can be mayor for life."

Jackson held up his hands in protest. "Let's give most of the credit to Kelly. He's got the biggest stake in this. We're just trying to do what's fair and right." Jackson loved the adulation, but he preferred to distance himself from activities that, at the very least, skipped along the edge of illegality. Who bought trouble?

"Where is this speakeasy and what's the password?" Nate asked. "You know you can trust us, Jackson."

"Soon enough," Jackson said. "Right, Prentis?"

"Yes sir," Prentis said, waving his empty mug in emphasis. "Of course, you fellows do realize that Kelly can't just let you drink for free. Why, he's stretched himself financially thin these last months. He's got to recoup his investment. You understand."

"We'll pay for it like we do now," Nate said.

"Which would be illegal," Prentis said. "No, the Nevis Gentlemen's Club, henceforth to be referred to as the *Club,* is going to be an upper-crust, classy place with a monthly membership fee—no sale of beer or liquor. You gentlemen see if you can keep yourselves out of trouble for the next week or so. By then, things should be up and running. Right, Kelly?"

"Exactly. Shut up, be good, and you'll get in. Talk this around town—especially to the wife, girlfriend, or one of the gals at Sally's place—and you'll be wetting your whistle in the bay." He picked up a bottle from the tray he had set down. "To the new place. May the liquor be just as good and just as cheap as it is now, and those lunatic teetotalers clueless about where we're hiding the stash."

"Hear, hear."

"Jackson? Mayor Jackson?" Murt's voice boomed across the crowded saloon. His chat with young Jack Byrne had been a quick one. He pawed his way around tables and chairs pushed askew by the night's overexuberant crowd and reached the back table, sucking wind and holding his side.

"Long breaths, Murt. We'll wait."

Murt took three deep breaths and said, "You've got a target on your back, sir. Those crazy women are gonna run you outta office."

"They're gonna shoot 'im?" Pops asked, his voice cracking. Wilbur's tears began to flow freely.

Jackson looked at the old man and shook his head. "S'all right, Pops. Nobody's shooting anybody. Jack tell you that?"

"Yes, sir. Heard the whole discussion with a bigwig lady from New York. Said either this town supports the Amendment, or your days in office are numbered. Either that or they'll die trying. And they don't seem shy about taking others with them."

"Camilla McClelland there?" Jackson asked.

"Everybody with an interest in sending pain your way was there."

"Jiminy," Jackson muttered. The Eighteenth Amendment wasn't even in effect yet, the list not a day old, and already his priorities had begun to shift. He could probably keep the feds away from Nevis, might even protect himself fairly well against the ghost of Carrie Nation herself with a hatchet in each hand. But standing against the full and well-directed wrath of one Camilla Agnes McClelland was something he hadn't been able to do in thirty years. God knows, he had tried. Maybe that flick of the hand wasn't a friendly wave after all, but a trigger finger limbering up for target practice. He glanced over at the full bottles of Anheuser that Kelly had left in the center of the table, and pulled one over.

Prentis leaned across the table. "Is she really worth it? Nothing would make her happier."

Jackson wrapped his hand around the bottle, feeling the cold dew on the glass. He muttered something else under his breath and set the bottle down. "I'd best leave well enough alone," he said, rising. "See you tomorrow, bright and early."

Prentis took a pull on the drink. "Don't count on bright *or* early."

Jackson said his good-nights and worked his way toward the door. The room was bustling with ebullient noise and motion, much like the time the newspaper published the wrong price for the mercantile's ice cream and Mr. Tanner was obliged to all but give it away. Jackson had no doubt that by the end of the night, the goodwill among the revelers would be reduced to fistfights, broken town windows, and a few sleeping it off in bunks down at the Nevis jail—in other words, just another Saturday night. He had almost made it to the street when he was hailed by a man quietly drinking by himself.

"Not staying to toast at midnight?" the man asked.

Jackson chuckled and shook his head. "Father Aloysius McGee! As you are aware, I never touch the stuff. Does Father Piper know you're out drinking?"

"Oh, I wouldn't call one Anheuser *drinking*. And yes, he does. The agreement between us is that as long as he doesn't have to bail me out in the morning and stays out of the sacramental wine, all's well between us." He put his glass down and said, "If you don't mind, I'll walk a piece with you. My wagon is hitched down at the post office—away from the rowdiness that I suspect will soon be spilling out of here."

Father McGee was an easy man to talk to. As town confessor, he knew the darkness in every man's heart, but his easy smile and lighthearted banter lulled the unsuspecting into forgetting that he could call them on their sins at any moment. Tonight, however, the priest's mood was subdued, and they walked along in silence past the shuttered Merkles Leather Repair Shop, the town library with its oversized Corinthian columns, and Spitler's Auto Supply. Three more lampposts, and they would go their separate ways.

"Something you wanted to discuss, Father?" Jackson asked, pulling out his cigarettes. To his surprise, McGee reached over and bummed one.

"We all have our vices, Jackson."

"And what, exactly, is so troublesome that it drives you to one of yours tonight? I won't tell a living soul," Jackson said, making the sign of the cross over his heart.

"There's an appealing irony there," the priest said with a laugh. He took a long drag on the cigarette. "It's not so much an unburdening as it is having a discussion with the right person."

"The mayor thing?"

"Mmm. I believe we need to discuss liquor."

"Why, yes, of course. It's on everyone's mind at the moment. I'm sure you're aware that sacramental wine is exempt from the restrictions under Volstead. Are you worried about having non-Catholics show up for Holy Communion on Sunday?"

Father McGee looked startled. "Oh, no. Well, maybe a new face or two, but nothing we can't handle. No, my concern is for my parishioners." He took a puff. "How well do you know your Bible verses, Mayor? Do you recall Isaiah twenty-five: four?"

36

"I think I was absent the day we talked about him."

"Quite possibly," McGee said with a smile. "'For you have been a defense for the helpless, a defense for the needy in his distress, a refuge from the storm, a shade from the heat . . .' That's what it says. The Germans in this town earn their living by brewing. They are a proud and a stoic bunch as a rule, but I hear some of their concerns, see the worry in the eyes of the quieter ones. Mr. Volstead is not their friend."

"Trust me, Father, Volstead is *no one's* friend. And I wish I could undo all the evil that's been done in the name of God and saving people from their vices. Unfortunately . . ." Jackson gave a halfhearted shrug.

"I understand completely. And I would imagine that you've dedicated quite a bit of your time recently to these new prohibitions."

"Yes. There is nothing we can do about the federal laws. It seems they are here to stay. As you know, I say that as someone who abstains from the bottle."

"I . . .well . . . Lord forgive me, how should I put this? I know a pastor at Saint Vincent de Paul in Baltimore. His parishioners are politically well connected, and he tells me that, um, enforcement there will be rather lax." He ran his index finger around the inside of his Roman collar. "Local options. The enforcement. People have needs," he blurted, losing his customary composure. "How strictly will these laws be enforced in Nevis?"

Jackson halted in the cone of light beneath the last lamppost. "Father, are you suggesting you want to bootleg?"

Father McGee looked him square in the eye and said, "No." But there was a fiery light in the man's eyes.

Jackson smirked. McGee was a peacemaker, but when necessary, he could come out swinging. He and Father Piper were as different as night and day. He liked the feisty little priest. Father Piper, not so much. "Good. I'd hate to see the revenue men haul you in. Truthfully, Father, as I understand the situation, the local constabularies will be looking the other way where personal production is concerned. I personally—and the town counsel, I might add—take the idea of states' rights seriously and see the central government's encroachment in Maryland's affairs as a grave injustice." He flicked his cigarette onto the brick roadway. "No, Father, I don't think any of our citizens need worry about Nevis filling up its little jailhouse with well-meaning citizens who just want to have a drink or two. Do you follow me?"

"I believe so," the priest said, eyes searching Jackson's face.

"Yeah. So no need for you to go breaking any vows or anything by setting up production in the rectory basement. I think the Germans will be fine."

"Brewing in our basement? Oh, heavens no! I don't think Isaiah had that in mind. But in the spirit of what you've said, the church wouldn't be worrying overmuch if the woods in the acres surrounding the church were to become something of a safe haven for those who want to pursue their rights. If you follow me . . ."

"I do, Father. Rest assured, no one is going to pay you a bit of attention down there at the end of Parkers Wharf. Anybody who mattered probably couldn't make it past the first fork in the road without getting lost, and if they ask, we never had this conversation."

He clapped the old man on the back and sent him on his way, seemingly a little happier, as a group of revelers, singing loudly and off-key, stumbled out of Kelly's and proceeded in his direction.

No doubt Father McGee could handle what he seemed to be proposing, but where would the Germans market their contraband, and how would they get it there? McGee's church at Parkers Wharf had no direct railway connection, and the steamboats didn't stop there anymore. The land was mostly church owned, and underdeveloped. And the best way to move the fruits of their labor would be by boat—a time-consuming operation given the distance back to town. He didn't want to know. If Father McGee could keep the Germans off the con side of his list, he didn't need to know.

CHAPTER SIX

Speakeasy and Carry a Big Stick

The black Lizzie coupe swung onto the first notch road south of town and puttered and snorted up the hilly country lane, all the way to the dead end at the terminus of a rail spur. The area could only be described as a graveyard: hulky remains of boxcars, pumpers, and sundry hunks of metal scattered on and around deteriorating rails.

Prentis got out and headed up the track. Jackson popped out the other side and followed, eyes sweeping the area as he went. "Where was Chief McCall when we left town?" he asked.

"Didn't see him, which means he didn't see us, either."

"I don't need my picture splashed across the front page of the *Evening Star*," Jackson said, peering back down the lane.

Relax," Prentis said. "Nobody's going to track us way the hell out here. And the biddies are all in church."

"They ever do mission work out this way?" Jackson asked, eyes still darting about. He stepped around a blue steel door tossed near the tracks' right-of-way, its window still intact but too filthy to see through. He ran his finger through the grime. "What in God's good name is all this?"

"You never been out here?" Prentis headed for two rusty boxcars parked at the very end of the track. "This is where unloved pieces of the Chesapeake Railway Express come to die. From the blue color, I'd venture that there's a door from one of the old passenger carriages."

"Don't they know there's money in scrap?"

"You'd think," Prentis said with a shrug. "I am surprised some of this hasn't grown legs and meandered off. For the Chesapeake, I guess it's out of sight out of mind, lost in a shuffle of paperwork, or the company is so flush with cash that they're indifferent. Kind of makes you sick, no? But think of it this way: their loss, our gain—the perfect place to hide the stash from Kelly's saloon." He checked right and then left before rapping three times on the door of the boxcar. "See Kelly's dog out here anywhere?"

Jackson didn't hear or see anything, but not wanting a face-full of dog's teeth, he felt it prudent to stay back as the big metal door groaned open. Happily, all that greeted him was Nate Kelly's buck-toothed grin. Kelly gave them a hand up into the car, which had been joined to the second one by metal sheeting that formed a crude hallway between the two. The interior was deceptively large.

"'Bout time," Kelly said, propping his feet up on a wooden crate. Pops sat on an oak keg, nursing an amber bottle, with a plump white pig sleeping at his feet.

"A bit quaint for a speakeasy," Jackson said, peering through the dim light. He goosed the pig with the toe of his boot, but the pig didn't stir. "I thought you had a dog."

"Better than a dog when they get to squealing," Kelly said. "And have you ever had an angry one chase you down?"

"This is the best you can do to protect our stake? Maybe you should have got a live one."

"Ha. Nothing wrong with Bosco," Kelly said. "He's a keeper. He'll be back on duty when he sobers up." He reached down and scratched a floppy ear.

Prentis's mouth dropped open. "You've been serving our good stock to the pig?"

"Hell no. Well, hell yes and hell no. Not the good stuff, though." Kelly swung his legs down. "Come have a look." Stepping over to a table made of sawhorses and rough planks, he pulled over two mason jars full of clear liquid. "Here's the good stuff," he said, unscrewing the lid on one of the jars. "Care for a nip?"

"Not particularly," Prentis said, eying a nearby crate of Pabst. "If it's so good, why is it going to the porker?"

"Cause if it isn't good, I'd rather old Bosco buy the farm than one of us, and I can't tell unless somebody tastes it. So I watered it down and put it in his bowl. This one right here," he said, picking up the opened jar, "this is as fine a hooch as you'll ever taste. Flanagan's still. Don't even have to test it. But this one," he said, picking up the other, "is truly nasty stuff. Somebody else's still, and I've got no guarantees by looking. So that's where good ol' Bosco comes in. If it doesn't hurt him, we'll be fine, too. Lucky for Bosco here, we used Rusty's oinker for this one. God rest his soul."

Jackson picked up the jar of bad shine. It looked no different from Flanagan's high-grade. "So what I'm hearing is, there's a still out there somewhere in the woods that's going to poison some people tonight?"

"Nah. We bought the batch, then busted up the still. But next week's run, wherever they decide to drip it, I can't vouch for. Keep it," he said, gesturing to the second jar. "As a reminder of how evil Mr. Volstead is, and the extremes he'll push good men to."

"I'll serve it next time the temperance ladies come for tea."

"You do that," Kelly said, cackling.

"Temperature's not bad in here," Prentis said, sitting down on the crate next to the Pabst. "But how are you going to stay warm next week after the January thaw is over and the cold weather returns?"

"Grin and bear it, I guess," Kelly said with a shrug. "Come March, it will be okay."

Jackson took his hat off and dropped down onto an oversize oak-footed love seat amid an odd assortment of wooden benches, slat-backed chairs, and crates. He had found it in a vacant building in town, its bulky frame apparently too cumbersome to be moved by its original owners. He had arranged to have it dragged to Kelly's front porch for safekeeping, half expecting Mrs. Kelly to lay claim to it and move it inside.

"Didja know it did this?" Kelly pulled one of the rolled arms up and then out, extending the love seat another foot or so. "Chaise longue." He pronounced it *shay lon-zhay*. "The missus showed me right before I told her she couldn't keep it." He returned to the mandolin he had been strumming when they arrived, and settled back in his place. "Prentis, go ahead and help yourself to that Pabst you've been drooling over."

"If you hadn't laughed at me, the Club might also have procured several other fine upholstered pieces and two elegant mahogany side tables," Jackson said. He stretched out his six-foot frame and prepared to float away to the strains of some unidentifiable hillbilly ditty. Kelly would never be mistaken for a virtuoso, but his playing did lend some much-needed ambience.

The screech of metal against metal brought the playing to a halt, and Kelly to his feet. "Bring anybody else?" he whispered, looking toward the boxcar's rolling door.

Prentis shook his head while Pop froze like a jacklit rabbit. Jackson hid the mason jar behind the sofa, blew out the candle on a nearby crate, and withdrew to the deeper shadows of a corner. Kelly inventoried his surroundings, but before he could hide any incriminating bottles, a head peered into the room, nailing him in place. It was Chief McCall, with his pistol drawn, nightstick in his other hand, and a steely look on his mug.

"What's going on in here?" he asked, hoisting himself into up into the car. His eyes darted around the space until they fell upon the saloon keeper. "Why, if it isn't Kelly." He holstered the pistol and stepped closer. "Hi, Pops!" he said, patting the old man on the back. "Everything okay in here?"

Kelly offered a feeble smile. "Right as rain. What can we do for you, Chief?"

"Just walking the beat." His roving eyes continued their sweeping assessment of the situation before next settling on Flannigan's brew sitting on the table. "This is railway property. Do you have permission to be here?"

"Certainly."

"'Cause otherwise, I'd have to either ask you to leave, or arrest you for trespassing. He leaned forward and squinted through the dim light. "Nice to see you, Mayor."

Jackson nodded, a queasy feeling in his stomach as he envisioned his promising political career burning to ash in a conflagration of town scandal.

Kelly glanced toward the second boxcar, where he kept most of the liquor from the saloon. He moved farther away and back toward the door McCall had come through. "Nope, nothing like that. In fact, you just missed Stationmaster Curtis."

"You fellas wouldn't be selling any liquor out of here, now, would you?"

Kelly cleared his throat. "Of course, not, Chief. That'd be illegal."

"It's f-f-free," Pops warbled. "With a membership."

"Membership?" McCall roared with laughter. "I believe that's still an illegal enterprise, gentlemen." He pointed his stick at Pops and then Nate. "See you back in town, fellas."

As the two men bolted, Kelly looked at Jackson, and Jackson looked at Prentis, silently pleading with him to work his political magic. The silence was unnerving, and somebody had to make a move.

Prentis stood up. "Drink?" he offered.

McCall put down his nightstick on a nearby keg. "Thought you'd never ask. But I'm not paying," he quickly added, "and I ain't joining no club. Got it?"

They all agreed that such formalities would be unnecessary, and Kelly got right to pouring him a double Hannis rye whiskey from his personal reserve, hidden in the crate he had been using as a footstool. Jackson watched him overshoot the rim of the glass before he got his shaking hand to be still.

"Easy there," McCall said. "Worth its weight, you know?" He downed half the glass. "Shame we can't do this all the time."

"Maybe it doesn't have to end right here," Kelly said, topping off the drink.

McCall chuckled. "Oh, boys. You know Mr. Volstead doesn't like all this drinking."

Jackson walked out of the shadows and returned to the chaise longue. "I think we need to be clear about what's going on here. It's not about drinking *per se*. We all know that if there's a will, there's bound to be a still. Bootlegging is exploding across the country, even in areas that are vehemently dry. What we're trying to do," he said, gesturing at the others, "is provide a safe environment for people to do what they're going to do anyway. This is a local thing. No rumrunners flying up and down backroads in an attempt to make a fast buck off the poor souls who can't make it through the day without their booze. And no bad shine crippling, blinding, or killing anyone. We simply want to take care of our citizens."

Prentis drew a money clip from his pocket and eased three greenbacks across the table. "What Mr. Volstead doesn't know . . ."

McCall took a sip of his whiskey. "A man would be a fool to take that kind of money and risk going to jail, Mr. Gant."

Prentis drew out three more and added them to the pile.

"Now, you see, it becomes worth the risk. Nothing foolish about that." Smiling, McCall slid the money off the table and into his pants pocket. "Gentlemen, I think we have an arrangement."

Prentis gave him an uneasy smile. "Will that do some talking with your friends?"

"We'll see." McCall took a longer draught, tapping his finger on his glass as he scrutinized their surroundings. "You like this arrangement? I don't get out here much, except when I need to follow around suspiciously behaving individuals." He side-eyed Jackson. "Once we get through the thaw, it's gonna get cold in here. Someplace in the middle of town might be warmer, a little more upscale, and easier to keep an eye on." He grunted and took another drink.

"You have something better suited?" Prentis asked. "Something both convenient and discreet?"

"Matter of fact, I'm on close personal terms with the owner of a soon-to-be available place right next door to the Wesson building. Isn't that right, Mayor?"

"No idea. Prentis?"

"I haven't heard," Prentis said.

"We'd have to move all this stuff again," Kelly said, watching McCall closely.

"Done," McCall said. He put his glass down. "I'll be talking to you." He picked up his nightstick and sauntered out.

"I hope you got a lot more where that came from," Kelly said, waving a hand at Prentis. "I think you'll be giving until it hurts."

"Nah. McCall didn't make chief without being smart enough to know there's a limit," Prentis said. "And we can expense that through the mayor's petty-cash fund."

"No, we won't," Jackson said. He could see the headline now: *Mayor Bribes Local Constabulary.* "Come on, Prentis. We've got an hour before church lets out, right?"

CHAPTER SEVEN

Mumbling and Grumbling

Barnaby McCall was a workhorse, and a staunch enforcer of the law as he saw it. But Jackson soon discovered, praised be the Lord, that he was an even better protector of illegal liquor activities in Nevis. Not only was he fully behind the Nevis Gentlemen's Club, he had even found some prime space for it downtown, just off Main Street. They quickly dubbed it *Mumbles*.

True to his moral compass, Jackson insisted that no town money change hands, so Kelly paid McCall out of club membership funds. Jackson would have preferred that the payment come from an unnamed third party, but what was done was done. McCall seemed content with the monetary arrangement, so they had effectively neutralized any constabulary interference. In fact, all seemed well until one Wednesday afternoon when Jackson received an unsettling note from Kelly, requesting an urgent meeting.

At nine that evening, standing in the darkened alley between the Wesson building and Waldo Hudson's haberdashery, Jackson tried to meld into the brick wall of the men's store as he waited for someone to answer Mumbles's unmarked door.

"Classy, discreet—what more could you want?" Prentis asked, rapping on the entrance a second time.

"Room service. Although I do like the idea of leaving here and not having to stumble far to Oscar's." Jackson nodded in the direction of the seafood restaurant on Weem's pier, its lights shining like a beacon through the gloaming.

The wooden peephole cover in the door rattled open, and a man's face appeared, blocking out the light behind him. "What?"

Prentis passed his club card through the opening and said, "Mumbles redbird number eighty-seven and eighty-eight." The door creaked open, and they were swept into an ambience of shiny chrome and red leather that rivaled any of the speakeasies that Jackson and Prentis had seen in Baltimore or Annapolis. McCall had outdone himself. By tapping into a few cash-flush anonymous sources—Jackson would have called it *leaning,* though he didn't delve too deeply—McCall had created a clandestine drinking paradise. The club members sopped it up, and McCall made a tidy profit.

Tonight, though, mere weeks after they had relocated, the two politicos weren't here for the drinking. A fidgeting and dispirited Kelly pulled them into the back room and pointed to the row of wooden barrels lining the wall. "We need another source."

"What've you been doing with it all?" Jackson asked, rocking empty kegs as he walked down one wall of the storeroom. He didn't hit a full one until the end of the line.

Prentis ran his hand across the empty liquor bottles stacked in crates on the opposite wall. "Been doing a little business on your own?" he asked, throwing Kelly a burning look.

"If you don't know me any better'n that . . .They've been drinking like rockfish. We figured there'd be enough in here until they repealed this nonsense."

Prentis took a step back and rubbed the back of his neck. "Yes, yes, sorry. Ill-chosen words, long day. How long we got?"

"Well, if we cut in half what we've already been limiting them to . . . maybe another month. My *supply* can't keep up. Feds are snatching too many shipments coming south."

"Don't need to know," Jackson said, waving away the explanation. He flipped over a crate and sat down. "This could be troublesome. I feel a club revolt coming on."

Prentis joined him. "Solution's simple enough. We need an additional liquor source here. Don't look at it like it's a setback. Just think *step two*."

Kelly pulled up another crate. "The problem may be simple, but the solution ain't. What you're proposing is illegal, remember? Production of alcohol is illegal."

"And this speakeasy isn't?" Jackson laughed to cover the sick feeling rising in him.

"If you ignore some *gifts* from friends, which can never be traced back? Technically, no. We haven't sold any alcohol, just membership in our little exclusive club."

"Never hold up in court," Jackson said.

Well, no, I suppose not," Kelly replied, "but it lets us sleep at night."

"Jackson hasn't missed a night of sleep in his life," Prentis added.

"Not in the last thirty years, and I don't plan to start now," Jackson said. His eyes roved down the row of empty kegs. How had they drunk it up so fast?

"Hmm," Kelly said, half to himself. "Maybe there is something else," he said, turning to look at Jackson. "The law has an exemption for druggists. Wally Harper was bragging about getting liquor that way.

Not that backwoods stuff, neither, that tastes like your dog pissed in it—name brands. Old Grand-Dad, Early Times—stuff like that. Maybe Doc could write us all prescriptions."

Prentis shook his head. "Too complicated. If it were just you and me, that'd be a fine idea, but we'd never get enough to stock this place."

"Not what I'm hearing. It's as simple as three bucks for a prescription and another three with the druggist for a pint of whatever's your pleasure. Mac don't really care. He and the doc are making out like bandits. If we could lose a few members, we could conserve better."

"The new one? Doc Patterson?"

"No. The newer one, down on the docks."

Jackson grimaced and shook his head. "Not even for Old Grand-Dad, Kelly. That place reeks of syphilis."

Prentis laughed. "Pick your poison, Jackson."

"Well, the truth is, I don't want to pick any of the poisons. Been down that road before."

Kelly studied him with a thoughtful expression. "Jackson, after all these years, I think you can handle a drink if you want one. I've often wondered how you don't touch a drop and can sit there watching everyone around you get hammered."

Surrounded by the faint, mingled smell of cigarettes and spilled beer, the feel of a cold dewy bottle still fresh in his mind, Jackson considered it a moment. "All about consequences."

"Well, let each man pursue his own pleasures, but you should at least have a pint hidden someplace. What happens if the medicinal exemption disappears? Are you willing to trust your health—and everybody else's—to one of these fly-by-night stills? Just a thought."

I'll think about it," Jackson said. Kelly was a patient listener and generally had good advice. It was a bartender's skill, Jackson guessed. He didn't want to drink. Well, he didn't and he did. He never stopped wanting to knock one back, but could he stop at one? Still, a pint stashed somewhere for a sick day probably wasn't a bad idea.

"So we're back to dripping our own," Prentis said.

"There's always Flannigan's still," Kelly said. "He's stingy with what he makes, but I heard he's supplying some of the gentry—a few council members here, some Bayland bosses there. He's a small operation, but maybe we could convince him to punch it up. And there's a few other good'uns that might hop on board in exchange for protection."

Jackson studied his shoes. "Where is this all going to end? Because I sure don't like the direction we're headed. Turning a blind eye to a small local speakeasy is one thing; then you throw bribery on top of that . . . But now we're talking about liquor production, the chance of killing somebody with bad shine, and providing a little muscle to see that it runs smoothly? I think it might be time to step back and reevaluate. We can't ensure all this liquor is drinkable, and Nevis doesn't have enough swine to make sure all these backyard operations know what they're doing. Not to mention I won't look good in prison stripes."

Prentis and Kelly studied their own shoes.

"Is it true his hooch hasn't jaked anybody yet?" Jackson asked.

"Flanagan? Not that I know of," Kelly said. "He's the best around. Been dripping his own for years. We should at least talk to him."

"Him and who else?" Prentis asked. "Flanagan's would have to be one hell of a big operation to provide all the booze we'll need to keep this bunch happy."

Jackson stood up. "There's another option. Maybe we've just bit off more than we can chew. Close up the joint and let people fend for themselves."

Prentis stood up, too, glaring. "People gonna get jake-legged, blind, or dead that way, Jackson. There's bad hooch floating all over the place.

You've read the papers. It's everywhere. You really ready to do that to all those men you call *friends*? The ones that think you walk on water, that put you in office—and will do it again next election cycle?"

Jackson glared right back. "Who said I signed up for life?" Then his visage softened and he rubbed at the weariness and frustration there. "Kelly, any other operator besides Flanagan?"

"Maybe."

"Heaven help us," Jackson said. "Okay, but I'm not traipsing out in the woods to have a conversation or get shot full of holes by some bootlegger thinking I'm a prohibition agent. You go talk to 'em, but leave my name out of it. I've got lots of heat on me right now. I don't like the arrangement with McCall, but as long as our payments are prompt, he'd be insane to rock the boat. Some of the more vocal ladies in town have collared a few of the councilmen who don't drink, and are asking why Nevis is still awash in booze, and complaining about our, um, *lenient* enforcement. It seems a few of our club members have staggered home to their wives, singing ditties in questionable taste. I can dodge some issues, but if they can tie me to production, I'm in serious hot water."

"I'm sure Missus McClelland's in there somewhere, throwing coal oil on the flames," Kelly said. "What'd you ever do to set her off, anyways?"

Jackson had seen fire in Camilla's eyes many times, but not the way they looked the afternoon she bounced her promise ring off his besotted noggin. Jackson shook his head. "A falling-out, years ago. The woman is not known for her forgiving nature." And whatever was behind that cryptic wave in the cemetery? He kept those musings to himself.

"Woman's just crazy," Kelly said.

"How well do we know all these people coming into Mumbles?" Prentis asked. "Anybody new? Friends of friends, that sort? Borrowed memberships and passwords floating around? We might have been running a little loose lately. Anybody think to make a membership list?"

"There's never been a list," Kelly said. "I think we're tight, but I can have 'em start signing in at the door. Of course, some will balk at the idea of putting their name to paper in a place like this."

Jackson pulled out his pack of cigarettes and ran his index finger across the golden camel standing in the desert with palm trees and pyramids in the background. It had a certain *let's-run-off-and-join-th e-Foreign-Legion* appeal. He tapped out a smoke and scratched a match. "I'll bet there's more people than we think coming up that alley. It would explain the suds running out so soon. Best start that list tonight."

"Something's got to change," Prentis said, looking off into space. "Or we're out of the liquor business."

Jackson considered what his father would have done and silently rejected all the illegal activities that popped into his head. He'd reached his limit. "True, but you honcho it. My hands are tied."

— —

Dr. Patterson wiped his palms on his pant legs again. The good doctor looked out of his element. A request to visit the mayor's office wasn't your average house call.

"Have a seat," Jackson said, beckoning toward his sitting area. "Normally, I'd offer you something worthy of the word 'refreshment,' but, well, the federal government doesn't think that's a good idea. So, coffee?" he asked, picking up a pot from the silver tray on the table before him.

The doctor sat down on the sofa, perching on the edge with his rather large hands clutching his knees. "Thank you, nothing for me. But you go right ahead. There's something I can assist you with?"

Jackson returned the coffee pot to the table without pouring and sat in one of the armchairs. "Well, yes, and it's one I trust you can handle with the utmost discretion. That's why I invited you here rather than to my home."

The doc gave a thin smile. "Of course. The Hippocratic Oath is a sacred trust. I pride myself on my discretion."

"As you should," Jackson said. "Nevis is in the midst of growth not seen since the building of the amusement park, and as you might expect, the pressures of this office are enormous. I'm not sleeping at night, Doc. Mind's turning over again and again about everything that's befallen me during the preceding day, and the daunting prospects for the following one. Tossing and turning. It's all so depressing. And then in the day, I'm plagued by nausea and pain," he said, rubbing his stomach.

"So, anxiety at night and indigestion during the day? Not unusual for one to lead to the other. Without medical intervention, one can soon find oneself in a vicious cycle."

"Exactly." Jackson slid forward in his chair and clutched his knees, mimicking the doctor's posture. "It's not normal . . . not normal for *me* at all."

Patterson reached for the black leather medical bag sitting next to his feet. "Well, let's take a look."

Jackson pulled over the stack of papers sitting next to the coffee service. "Today's work, Doctor. It should have been completed yesterday. The truth is, I don't have time for a physical exam. I was hoping you might just write me a prescription—a quick trip to the druggist. A stimulant, perhaps?"

Doctor Patterson let go of his bag. "Oh. I think I see. . . . But just to make sure . . . what stimulant would that be, Mr. Mayor?"

Jackson felt the heat rising to his face. Was the man being willfully obtuse, or was there some sort of code associated with this transaction? How did thickheaded Prentis Harper manage it? He locked eyes with the doctor, hoping to convey his irritation. "Whiskey."

Patterson didn't blink, but he broke eye contact after several seconds. "I do have the authority to write that," he said, reaching for his bag again. "But don't think for a moment that this is the answer, unless you're obsessing about where your next drink is coming from. If that's the case, there's a bigger problem you should be dealing with."

"Oh, no, not at all," Jackson said, raising his hands in protest. "It's the job, you know? Just a difficult, demanding job." Jackson gave his best overworked-public-servant sigh.

Patterson was too busy writing to notice. He tore the top slip of paper free from his prescription pad and handed it to Jackson. "It says one tablespoonful three times a day. Nonrefillable."

"Oh, I have to come back?" Jackson asked, studying the slip.

"Yes, and I can't prescribe to you again for at least thirty days." Patterson zipped the bag shut.

"I see," Jackson said, shaking his head and frowning. "Would it be possible for you to fill out a few of these, maybe postdate them? I'm terribly busy right now."

"Not if I want to keep my license. If thirty days is a problem, you might want to consider a career change. Politics is a taxing business, Mr. Mayor. Not everybody's cut out for it."

"Don't I know it. I agonize over it all night long, flopping around on the mattress like a landed fish." Jackson looked at the PRESCRIPTION FOR MEDICINAL WHISKEY form again, and its caution at the bottom in red capital letters: DO NOT REFILL OR TRANSFER UNDER PENALTY OF LAW. He folded it in half and slid it into his jacket pocket. "This'll be fine, Doc.," he said, rising from his seat. "Thanks for your time and for making the trip. Might be seeing you in another month if this doesn't take care of the problem."

"More liquor is never the answer to anything, Mr. Mayor. All it does is buy a boatload of heartache."

On that much, they could agree.

CHAPTER EIGHT

A Fast Buck

Jackson could direct him to trudge through the deep forests of Nevis all he wanted. At the moment, Prentis had no intentions of getting his cap toes muddy. He was a civil servant, not a backwoodsman. He took the contact information for Nathan Tarkington, the persistent gentleman inquiring about "business opportunities." He knew the name and its quiet reputation for striking deals, and even had a notion about what the man might be pandering. Jackson wouldn't like it, but he set up a meeting immediately—he could justify it to Jackson later. Prentis found it mildly amusing that while he had spent most of his time trying to keep Boss Dwyer on the legal side of things, his first end run around Jackson would be to head straight for the potentially illicit.

Mr. Tarkington jumped at the invitation. They agreed to meet on the boardwalk where it swept away from the shore, toward the grand carousel in the center of the park. Prentis arrived early and leaned back against the boardwalk rail, scoping out his surroundings as the park's Wurlitzer plinked and thumped out a fair version of Joplin's "Ragtime

Dance", and the Great Derby rollercoaster clackety-clacked along its wooden rails. As he had hoped for this early hour, foot traffic was light. Tarkington was directly across the walkway in the arcades building, talking to Eugene, the manager. The man was as Prentis remembered him: tall and athletic, well dressed without being flashy. Prentis watched the hushed conversation with Eugene. He knew the body language of cutting a deal, and these two were deep into it. Few words were exchanged, and only the keenest observer would have seen the palmed money changing hands.

Apparently unaware that his little operation was being observed, Tarkington concluded his deal, looked up to find Prentis looking at him, and gave him a bright, unimpeachable smile, as if they were long-separated brothers. Prentis touched his hat brim in acknowledgment. For all his finely cut suits and magnetic smile, Tarkington was only one cut above the con men to be found on any town street corner where dreams were big and cash was short. Today's meeting would be all about the hustle, and until Prentis understood the angle, his answer would be no to whatever Tarkington proposed. Still, it was a song and dance that both men expected. After all, one had to start somewhere.

"Mr. Deputy Mayor, I'm so glad you could see me," Tarkington said, pumping Prentis's hand. "You haven't changed a bit."

Prentis politely withdrew his hand. "Just a councilman. Mayor Jackson's booked solid, but given your persistence over the last few days, he thought it easiest just to squeeze you in. What brings you back to Nevis?"

"I'm here as a goodwill gesture, nothing more. I think we may have gotten off on the wrong foot the first time we met. No festering ill feelings, I hope?" Tarkington offered a contrite smile.

"Can't say I've given it a second thought. Still working with the group in Philadelphia?"

Tarkington settled in next to him against the railing. "Yes, and others. Good people, Philadelphia. Some of my business comes out of there, but I have clients from Boston to Miami."

"So, you've expanded your enterprises?" Prentis said, tipping his hat to a pair of older, well-dressed women strolling by.

Focusing intently on Prentis, Tarkington ignored the passersby. "You might say, but no need to say it like that. My business is to bring together people who have mutual interests, to create a pooling of resources. Private citizens, elected officials—whoever, whenever, whatever. I'm a middle man of sorts."

Prentis gave him an incredulous look. "And you traveled all the way from Philadelphia to Nevis just to say hello?"

Tarkington chuckled. "Passing through, actually. And if what you're really asking me is whether I'm here on behalf of John J. McClure, the answer is no. I'm based in Delaware."

Prentis nodded toward the arcade building—the flashing red and blue lights on the façade creating an eerie glow across its arched portals. He wondered how many of the patrons inside were there to cut deals. "You and Eugene seem to have hit it off."

"Mutual interests," Tarkington said, breaking out in a broad smile as he gazed up the boardwalk. "I like Nevis—lots of potential." He pulled out a slim leather case of cigarettes and offered one.

Prentis declined. "And we're not in a particular rush to explore all that potential. We prefer the 'nothing's on fire' approach. Intelligent planning goes a long way." He studied Tarkington a moment—the cigarette held just so between his elegant fingers, the casual indifference he projected. All posturing, and phony as a wooden duck. "I don't want to appear rude, but to be perfectly honest, Mr. Tarkington—"

"Oh, call me Nathan."

"Well, *Nathan,* I can't help but feel that there is an invitation in here somewhere, but I don't want to waste anyone's time. I'm not sure Nevis and any of your associates have any *mutual* interests."

Again the smile. "Then why are we meeting? You're not just a wee bit intrigued?"

"Not especially. You were so persistent, I realized you weren't going away until you got your meeting."

Tarkington nodded. "I understand. Very professional of you." He flicked the cigarette into the bay and watched as the water swept it under the boardwalk. "You don't care much for middle men like me, do you? You do realize what a blunder you made, showing me the door that first time we met? You'd be sitting pretty in the state house by now."

Prentis smiled politely and studied the rollercoaster in the distance. "I'm happy right where I am, thanks. I don't like to be beholden to other people."

"Of course. It's an admirable, if rare, trait. Now, Mr. Eugene Mitcham over there," he said, nodding toward the stout, mustachioed man pretending to polish the glass on a Lonestar poker game. "*He's* the one going places. Another year, and he'll be his own man, calling his own shots, living with his family in a house twice the size of yours."

"Being an honest councilman has its own rewards."

"That's what I've been telling Eugene. With the right backing . . ."

Prentis looked from Eugene to Tarkington. "The day that man sits on the city council is the day I move to Mississippi. Have a safe trip home, Mr. Tarkington." He tipped his hat again and started away.

"Wait," Tarkington said, touching his sleeve. The smile and casual posturing had vanished. "People like Eugene are a dime a dozen. Now, your Mayor Dwyer—his ethics intrigue me. Diogenes obviously never made it to Nevis. Everybody loves a genuinely honest man. But there's nothing wrong with a little back-scratching, as long as there is mutual respect and a common goal."

"And what might such a common goal look like?"

Tarkington didn't respond, instead pointing across the bay. "What kind of ships come up this way?"

"Steamers out of Baltimore. They run down as far as Solomons Island on the tip of the peninsula. Deep water down there, and sea access. They take on passengers and freight and then double back."

Tarkington arched an eyebrow. "Deep water, you say?"

Prentis's eyes narrowed. "Direct sea access. Why? Plan on taking an ocean cruise?"

This got him another ten-dollar smile. "Might be an interesting excursion. Maybe I'll pick up a map while I'm here. I suppose there are any number of inlets and coves to poke around in between here and there?"

"Oh, yeah, definitely. You could get good and lost out there."

"Interesting."

"You'll pardon my saying so, but you don't strike me as the boating type."

Tarkington chuckled. "Me? Heavens no, but I'm always open for new business opportunities for clients. Got my eye on one right now over there near the pier—Millman's Glass and Varnish?"

"If that's your goal, forget Daniel Millman's. He doesn't have two pennies to rub together. Shuttering the liquor business has had an effect on everything down here. Run that nice little Millman business right into the ground. Idle German brewers don't need bottles. Six months ago, he couldn't keep up with the demand."

"A motivated seller, then?" Tarkington said, eyebrows raised. "May have to float an offer to Mr. Millman on my return trip. I have a client in need of a bottling facility. See?" he said, tapping the rail with his knuckles. "This is where people in my line of business become invaluable. Happy buyer, relieved seller flush with cash and the ability to start fresh. Rectifying Nevis's liquor situation would no doubt solve a lot of people's problems."

"Is that one of your current business goals?"

Tarkington ignored the question and pointed in the direction of the steamboat pier. "What about Nichols's boathouse over there next to it? Maybe you could get me in touch with Mr. Nichols. With a little minor refurbishing, someone could turn a tidy profit there rather quickly."

"Mr. Nichols has passed."

"And the current owner?" Tarkington asked, a new glint in his eye.

"Mayor Jackson."

Tarkington chuckled. "Could make him lots of money there."

"No. He has plans for that property." Prentis checked his watch. Jackson would soon be hunting him down. "If I may give you a word of advice before I go, Mr. Tarkington, we're very protective of our little town. You'll have to work very closely with the town council if you're considering the expansion of your business here. If you're serious about *legitimate* investment in Nevis, I can give you the names of half a dozen other places within striking distance that will give you better return on your dollar. I can draw up a list now and save you that return trip. The mayor's office is always open to sound business investments. Send your clients around."

"Said like a truly dedicated civil servant. Rest assured that my business never goes anywhere it isn't wanted."

"So, back to my question. What business opportunities are you really looking at in Nevis?"

"Mr. Gant, to be good in any business, you have to pay attention. Then, when an opportunity comes along, you can hop on it early. That's why I'm here. Buy you a drink to discuss it?"

"Not in a dry town like this, I'm afraid. But then, I suspect you already knew that."

Tarkington drew a small silver flask from an inside coat pocket. "I could change that. Where there's a will . . ."

"Not today," Prentis said, putting his hands in his coat pockets. "But you're right, I am intrigued. For future reference, what would you be prepared to put on the table?"

"Enough medium- and high-quality product to make everybody happy."

"And the cost?"

"Negotiable. Standard business terms and fair cuts for all. It's just business."

"Like Chicago?"

Tarkington laughed. "Heavens, no." Delaware Valley people are old stock—levelheaded people. Everybody operates in good faith, and there are few problems."

Prentis ran his knuckle along his lower lip. It sounded good. But then, he wouldn't have expected less from a veteran pettifogger.

"You could do worse than us," Tarkington added, looking at him keenly. "And trust me, there will be others What do you say we head over to Bayland? I think we can find a drink or two there."

"Another time, maybe. Have a nice visit to Solomons, and a speedy trip back to Delaware."

Tarkington put out his hand. "Well, I do appreciate you fitting me into your schedule. I have a few other errands in town and then I'll be off to Solomons. No hard feelings?"

"None," Prentis said, shaking his hand.

Tarkington took a swig and put the flask away, pulling out a card from the same pocket. "If you should change your mind about that drink, don't hesitate to contact me. I know all the right people, and from what I've seen, we're a good fit for Nevis. I can't say the same for others that will come a-knocking."

"Thanks, but I already have your card."

"Then perhaps you have a friend. Someday, I'd really like to meet that mayor of yours." Tarkington slipped the card into Prentis's breast pocket.

"Don't worry, I'll make sure he's filled in."

Tarkington flashed his charismatic smile, tipped his hat, and walked off toward the amusement park. Stopping, he turned and said, "Oh, one more thing. It might not be too shabby an idea to check out Hickory Dickory to win in the fourth this afternoon at the Blue Grass prelim. Same pedigree as Exterminator. I hear that horse can run."

If the tip had been passed along by anyone else, Prentis might have jumped at it. But coming from this cocky shyster, it felt tainted—an insider's tip rooted in the reality of race fixing. His dislike for the man doubled, but he held his tongue and nodded. When Tarkington was out of sight, he turned and flicked the second business card into the water, being careful to save the folded banknote that Tarkington had wrapped around it. The channels of communications and negotiation were officially open, but it would take much more than this to buy Prentis's affection.

So Tarkington was all about liquor. And any deals would be with someone in Delaware and not John J. McClure's group. He didn't trust Nathan any farther than he could toss him, but if Delaware could ease Nevis through its liquor crisis, so be it. And if Tarkington was on the level about brokering fair, two-sided deals, Jackson might be forced to live with that.

Prentis glanced at Eugene again. Who were the other players sidling into Nevis unnoticed while Jackson obsessed over buildings and Camilla? Maybe he needed to find someone to take a closer look into the Bayland Park arcades and root out anything questionable, including the manager, if need be. And while they were at it, they needed to keep a closer eye on Millman's and the rest of the waterfront. Tarkington's interest there was unsettling. Did he really intend to bottle liquor right in the middle of town?

CHAPTER NINE

No Options

It started with Lyle, the janitor. At half past nine, he confided to Jackson that the local women's organization planned to picket the courthouse over his failure to enforce Volstead. Jackson cringed to think of their protest placards splashed across the front page of the newspaper. But as long as he had the support of the men in town, he rationalized, he could survive bad press. By ten thirty, he began to doubt his supporters. Several short errands around town convinced him that members of the Gentlemen's Club were either outright avoiding him in public or talking behind his back in private. Apparently, rationing Kelly's booze was not going over well. His constituent base—solidly pro-alcohol and in dire need of a swig—was crumbling. With solid backing, political heat could always be ameliorated, but Jackson suspected he would die of heat stroke before he found any.

He looked up at his office ceiling, searching its smooth white surface for a chink he could escape through, unnoticed and untraceable. Even this young newshound Shoemaker was doing him no favors. Hell, the

Tanner familyrun *Evening Star* hadn't given him any support of late. Mr. Shoemaker here needed to listen more and think less.

Jackson leaned across the desk and pointed at the last few lines on the reporter's tablet. He said, "You're giving me heartburn when you start talking about local options. It might be better if the paper just stated the facts. You know, what the Eighteenth Amendment actually says: no making, transporting, or selling alcohol. Maybe a comment or two about the Volstead Act—that it defines what an intoxicating beverage is, and just what enforcement of the Amendment will entail. Make it simple so folks are clear about what's going on. You're confusing them with all these options and opinions."

Jackson studied Shoemaker, gauging how much of what he said was sinking through the young man's thick skull. He was an energetic upstart of a journalist raring to go—attributes that most seasoned politicians hated. So, friend or foe to Jackson's political career? The jury was still out on that one, and Jackson would proceed with great caution. "Strictly off the record—"

Tate Shoemaker put down his pen and pushed back from the table. "Of course."

"As mayor, I intend to follow the state's lead in all this. Governor Ritchie and others consider the amendment and the act to infringe on states' rights. Maryland must be able to make its own way where liquor is concerned. The populace has already made it abundantly clear that they want the federal government to keep its nose out of their homes, businesses, and leisure time. So we don't need to go stirring people up talking about local options and what laws Nevis can pass to regulate consumption of alcohol by the good folks around here. If the feds want to harass people, let 'em come out here and enforce the laws they've enacted. Our resources are better used elsewhere—" He paused as his office door swung open and Prentis walked in. "The last thing I need is the local biddies—"

Prentis exploded in a spasm of coughing. "He means *ladies.*"

Jackson nodded. "Right. *Ladies.* What did I say?"

"You said 'ladies,'" Prentis insisted, walking over to the newspaperman. "Don't believe we've met. Name's Prentis Gant, the mayor's assistant. Is Riley Tanner tied up somewhere?"

"Tatum Bartholomew Shoemaker Junior," the reporter said as he stood and shook hands. "but *Shoe* will do. Perhaps you knew my father? He worked at the *Evening Star.* And yes, Mr. Tanner's tied up, but we'll hash over everything before it hits the press."

"Well, Shoe, welcome aboard, and good to hear. The mayor's office and the paper have had a great working relationship over the years, and if the *Star* will follow the mayor's lead on this, it would be most helpful. What do you think, Shoe?" He handed him his tablet from the table and started guiding him toward the door of the office suite.

Tate rotated his shoulder out from under Prentis's hand. "Well, what about the local ladies, the ones who want their spouses out of the drinking establishments and at home being responsible, contributing members of society? Can you give me a quote on that, Mr. Mayor?"

Prentis opened the main office door, draped an arm around the young man's broad shoulders, and eased him out into the hallway. "The mayor hopes that the Eighteenth Amendment works well for all the good citizens of Nevis. We'll get back to you with a nice quote you can print. At the moment, however, Mayor Jackson is late for a briefing. We'll talk soon. Have a good day, sir." He stepped back inside and closed the door.

Jackson sighed and resumed his inspection of the ceiling. "Don't know about that Tanner family—sending a cub reporter to cover the mayor's office. Is there something Dad did for them that I should know about, or is it just the sting of having the post office moved out of their store? God Almighty, I need to find something to appease those people. I don't need a daily scourging in the press."

"I think we'll be okay," Prentis said. "Chance Dwyer had so many irons in the fire, it'd be a waste of energy to try to piece together all that he was up to. Treat Tanner like a confidant and he'll print the world according to Jackson Dwyer. Just watch your language about the biddies."

"And the last thing in the world I need is for those crazy suffragettes to find out about local options. I'll never hear the end of it."

"Women do talk—certainly, better than we menfolk do. But I don't think we need worry too much. By the time they get to vote—and it does look as though the country is headed that way—the autumn election will be well under way and their opinions won't have any weight at all. Let them have their little tempest in their afternoon cup of tea."

"You think?" Jackson asked. His chief of staff reminded him of a banty rooster—strutting and crowing as if it held some sway in the henhouse. Truth be told, the man was as inept as Jackson at deciphering the mind of the fairer sex. "Those little tempests could suck you down and hold you under for a long time."

"I'm not worried."

"Well, I am. I haven't heard anything about replenishing our liquor supplies, or the Bayland financial assessment. Where have you been all morning? Wait," he said, sitting up in his chair. "You bought the house? No . . . Millman's. You bought Millman's."

Prentis sat down next to him. "You'll get your house, but nothing yet on Millman's. It's something else, but don't get alarmed. I've come to give you a heads-up. You'll thank me in a minute—just like you already should have for saving you from that disparaging remark about Camilla McClelland and all the fine ladies of her movement." He reached into his jacket and withdrew a white calling card. "Remember that fast-talker that swung through here a few years back peddling some sort of quiet arrangement with the political machine in Philly? He approached a few of us behind your father's back?"

"The good-looking one we sent back empty-handed."

"The very same. Nathan Tarkington. I was over at Bayland getting the lowdown on their financials when suddenly I catch sight of this guy hanging around the boardwalk arcades. Not *playing*, mind you, but conducting business with the arcades' manager. Not much of a surprise there. Those games consistently rake in too much dough not to invite outside interest, but considering we didn't want to be friends the first time around, it seemed a little strange he'd be back in town. Anyway, they got real sly when they caught me watching, so I pushed off and waited outside to see where he'd go. Surprisingly, he comes right over, intent on renewing acquaintances. And what's the first thing he says?"

Jackson massaged his temples. "No mood, Prentis. What?"

"He says to me, '*Where can a guy get a drink around here?*'"

"For real?"

"Would I lie? Said it *just* like that. No '*Nice weather we're having, do you remember me?*' or any of the other polite formalities. It caught me so off guard, I had to check and see whether I had an Anheuser-Busch sandwich board hanging from my shoulders."

"He remembered you?"

"Called me by name. Asked how you were, too." He offered Jackson the card. "Said to call if you felt like it. Be in town till next Tuesday."

Jackson pointed to the wastebasket. "So, liquor's the issue. Is he buying or peddling?"

"Didn't say outright. Danced all around it, but the message was clear. He has access to liquor, and if we want it, he can make arrangements. This could be the answer to all of Kelly's problems."

"It's a con," Jackson said.

"Uh-uh. Man was serious. I think if I had okayed it, he would have pulled a truck up and started unloading kegs right then and there. Maybe you should meet—"

"No. The list, man, the list," Jackson said, pulling out the sheet they had drawn up earlier. "Another one for the *con* column. I'll bet Philly would love to set up an illicit booze operation here. Nevis is a plumb location— within pissing distance of thousands of thirsty patrons in the District of Columbia, and easy access to deep water down at Solomons. Solomons, by the way—big topic of conversation at the mayors' meeting. Lot of ships already anchored offshore that are running rum from Cuba up and down the coast. What's not to like about Nevis? If that big Philly machine moves an operation in here, we'll lose control. I'll lose control of everything."

Prentis took the list from him. "So we tell him no a second time. But I think you're looking at this all wrong. Kelly's already hurting for liquor. This man is a godsend. And he made it perfectly clear he's not a middle man for McClure anymore. He's running out of Delaware now. Maybe, just maybe, we should let the illegal-liquor bigwigs come in and set up shop. It solves Kelly's problems. We accept some help from people that know what they're doing, ride this thing out, and walk away rich men. The town could comfortably stay wet without a lot of effort on our part."

"Dad-*bean* it, Prentis!" Jackson snatched the list back. "We're not talking small-town hooch with these people. This is serious jail time if they nail us." He changed the column heading from "Con" to "Convict."

Prentis leaned over and scratched through the added letters. "Stop thinking like a victim and work this to your advantage. As mayor, you're more powerful than you realize. With the right partners, the feds won't nail us. Tarkington and company will protect us if they have a vested interest. Might even be more secure than just turning a blind eye to the locals' white lightning. And it might even get the biddies off your back."

"How so?"

"Because you'd no longer be directly involved. You can swear up and down that you'll root out the Volstead violators, all the while giving them free rein. Camilla McClelland will eat it up."

Jackson brightened. "You think so?"

"I'm almost certain. She'll believe it—respect you even more. She'll call off her biddy militia and there'll be no more marching up and down Main Street."

"Oh, how I wish." Jackson strummed his lip with his fingers. "Delaware, Philly—those are some nasty characters. Once they get a foot in the door, I doubt we'll be able to get rid of them. Nevis's interests will take a backseat—no, they'll be thumbing at the side of the road. You're beginning to sound like the old Mayor Dwyer, who could justify anything."

The sudden revving of a motor outside drew them both to the window. Down below, seemingly without a care in the world, two men sat side-by-side on red motorcycles, laughing and talking above the roar of their machines. Jackson wondered how fast one of those modern wonders would go and how much it would set you back. He said, "I have property up in the mountains. Someday, I might hop on one of those darlings and zoom off into obscurity."

"Which mountains?"

Jackson shrugged. "Aren't they all about the same?"

"I have no idea," Prentis said. "I much prefer the beach. Whatever happened to those two Indian bikes your daddy had? Beautiful blue. I didn't see any in the inventory of his estate."

"Oh, yeah, *that*. Promised me one of them, but then we had words one day down at Parkers Wharf, and next thing I knew, he was giving them away to some crony. Guess he thought he'd get more goodwill that way. My father never was a smart man. A C-note and a fifth of whiskey was all it took to get his attention. I loved those bikes." He sighed and shook his head. "We'd take off early in the morning, swipe whatever cold meat and bread we could out of the icebox while Mother's back was turned, and off we'd go. We visited every church, wharf, and ferry within ten miles of Nevis—every notch road we could find. What I wouldn't give to have one of those bikes back."

"Your father loved cultivating power and prestige, Jackson, and was no different than some other people we know in politics. I'm sure there were many times when he did put you first."

Jackson didn't think so. He cleared his throat and looked back at Prentis. "We're not *some* people. Seriously, do we really want these people in Nevis—the cronies, the bosses, the deal makers . . . the corruptors?"

"I think we need to be pragmatic. They're already here."

Jackson nodded. "But who cares if they skim off some winnings at the arcades? Small potatoes, and they're doing it without us being involved. Other than their overtures to put me on the fast track to the State House, they've been content to stay out of the political game here."

"You got that one, too, huh?"

"But to run a liquor operation . . ."

"I agree," Prentis said. "Bootlegging whiskey is a hell of a lot bigger operation than skimming proceeds off the arcades, but it's naive to think bootlegging won't happen. It's merely a question of scale. And it's making men rich beyond belief. Philosophically speaking, is it so bad to want to help people get what they want, and make some money in the process? A C-note would be pocket change. You could finish out your term, buy one of those bikes and a hell of a lot more."

Jackson was beginning to hate every day he spent in elected office. Didn't anyone stand by their principles anymore? He looked at the two motorcyclists again, coveting the sense of freedom he saw. Were his convictions even something to be admired? Or were they just proof of his own inflexibility and his cluelessness to what his constituents needed? He slowly shook his head. "No. It's a con to add to the list, even if it is a late addition. If we let them set up shop, they aren't going to leave here willingly. We have no idea whether we can trust them. And next thing you know, I get the heave-ho out of office, their cronies are running everything, Nevis suffers, and I die penniless and disrespected."

"As your closest friend, I need to say it once more: Camilla will never know. Don't throw your life away on some pipe dream of winning her back. When you accepted public service, you took off your Jackson Dwyer hat and put on the constituency's. An alliance is the right thing to do."

Jackson closed his eyes and massaged the bridge of his nose. "And you don't think that struggling over doing the right thing isn't eating me up night and day? This isn't about Camilla. When I said I wasn't going to let corruption continue in Nevis, I meant every word. I entered the office with a good reputation, and I intend to leave with one. We're not giving Nathan Tarkington the time of day. Don't engage him."

"All right, then," Prentis said with a sigh that was not altogether theatrical. "You're the boss, and I'm sorry if it appears I'm leaning on you. I realize you have a lot at stake. If it's all right with you, I'm going to hire someone to snoop around Bayland. We need a better handle on all the parties who are skimming, funneling, and controlling the various activities there. I'm not sure how much control the Bayland Partnership actually has anymore."

"Yes, the impact of wet or dry on the finances of Bayland—you were going to get back to me on that. Do we need to get someone to handle that, too?"

"No. I'm practically finished."

"Today. Specifically, how has the park fared since the feds squeezed out liquor? Or are they still serving the hard stuff on the sly? I'd imagine the town's brewers would have a hard time walking away from the profits. And the Germans—how are they fitting into all this?"

"I'll get back to you on that," Prentis said. "By the way, you look a little beat-up this morning. How about taking a break? I heard there's a few barnstormers hanging out at Miller's field. Planes just like your son flew. I can ask about flying lessons if you'd like. A few loop-the-loops might do you a world of good."

"I would be ever so grateful," Jackson said retreating to his desk. He loosened his necktie and pulled it off.

He watched Prentis go. His old chum was particularly keen on liquor today, but it still didn't feel right. Being mayor was wearing Jackson down. Despite his best intentions, he felt his integrity being assailed with every problem he faced, every decision he made.

He looked over and fished the calling card out of the garbage. He would make sure that his last shred of dignity never went to a man of Nathan Tarkington's ilk.

CHAPTER TEN

Both Feet and No Shovel

Tate Shoemaker straightened his jacket and bounced down the court-house steps as if he had just inherited an oil field. It wasn't often one got the bum's rush out of the mayor's office. His dad would be proud. The eighteen-month timetable Tate had set for himself was looking less and less likely. He knew he was too hard on himself, but he had big shoes to fill. He brushed off the sudden doubt. In six months' time, everyone in Nevis would know his name. In five years, he could be publishing the *Evening Star*. Or, better yet, running a competitor at the other end of Main Street, consistently scooping the tiresome *Star*.

He entered the newspaper office through the rear door and walked past the printing press churning out the latest edition. With only a head-high divider between his desk and the machine, he would be deaf before he landed his first big scoop. He tossed his hat onto a hall tree and ran his finger across the picture of his best girl, Mary Pickford, pinned in the middle of his wall, then plunked himself into a chair that rattled with every turn of the printer. Where was Tanner? His closed office door at the end of the hall suggested the editor was having a come-to-Jesus meeting with some unlucky soul.

Tate flipped through his meeting notes, hoping something would jump off the page at him. But he found only mindless blah-blah-blah from a midlevel bureaucrat with limited power and few things to do. He flicked the papers across the desk. Who was he kidding? Nevis was a town of little news, and there would be no glory, no honing of skills, with nonstories from the mayor's office. A return trip to Philadelphia looked more appealing by the day. He picked his feet up as the janitor ran a broom past him, and stared out the window to Main Street. Nevis looked like any other Small Town, USA: quaint, tidy, and boring.

"Wayne," he said to the fresh-faced broom pusher, "Nevis has got to be the deadest place on earth. Do you count the days until you can escape?"

Wayne chuckled but kept the broom moving. "Nope. Love it here. Roof over my head, clothes on my back, and Mr. Grover's promised me a job down on the docks come fall. Sky's the limit."

"You talk like an old man. What are you, fifteen?"

The broom stopped. "I . . . I have my wild moments."

"Like what?" *This would be good,* Tate thought, doubting the kid had yet managed to cut his mother's apron strings.

"I've had my share of the ladies and drinking."

Tate almost choked. "Impressive. Guess you'll have to substitute more of one now that the other's illegal."

"Nah. Half a dozen stills within a mile of town. Ain't nothing going to change."

"Son, got to watch that illegal hooch. Some of it will kill you."

Wayne leaned on the broom, apparently warming to the subject. "Just got to watch where the bigwigs go. Drink from the same well, so to speak."

"Bigwigs?"

"Yeah, you know, people like . . ." Wayne's eyes suddenly widened and his mouth snapped shut. The broom continued on its way. "I'll get by," he muttered, intent on his task.

Illegal stills and drinking bigwigs, huh? Tate's eyes drifted toward the courthouse. Was the mayor a drinker? That same mayor who had just given him a polite little lecture on upholding the Eighteenth Amendment? Now, that was the kind of story that could get your name on the masthead. And so much more captivating than a third-page yawner about constitutional amendments. He glanced at his notes, then glanced at Tanner's door again. He had no other assignment, so he was getting paid for sitting. He could afford to wait.

Several minutes later, the door popped open and he watched a dispirited fellow reporter shuffle out. "Mr. Tanner, if I may, sir?" Tate called out. He scooped up his notes and bounded for the office.

"Mayor's notes?" Riley asked as he pulled off his spectacles and massaged the bridge of his nose. It was late morning, and his wastebasket was already overflowing, his desk covered in galley proofs.

Tate sat down and launched into recounting his meeting with the mayor. He still wasn't sure where the boss's ambitions and political affiliations lay, so he didn't offer any opinions.

"No surprises, Tanner mumbled. "Write up what you've got by noon and put it on my chair if I'm not here. But make sure I see it. And don't ruffle any feathers. Then head over to the pier. The *Chessie Belle*'s due at noon."

"Right on it," Tate said, grinning. "What's the story angle?"

"Just find out who and what's coming in on the boat. No angle, just gossip. Human interest. Women in town love it, so we give it to 'em—*every* Wednesday."

Tate's shoulders drooped, and he glanced over Tanner's shoulder and out the window again. Wayne had hung up his broom and found something else to lean on—the bed of a small farm buckboard as he engaged in jovial conversation with the wagoner. Tate wondered whether they were boasting about ladies or about drinking. Probably a little of both. Then the tone of the conversation seemed to grow serious as the driver got down and walked around to the covered load in the wagon bed, Wayne close on his heels. Their furtive looks and closed body language reminded Tate of little boys plotting to shoplift their first bag of peanuts from the circus. The driver flipped up the edge of the tarp, and Tate caught the fleeting gleam of new copper tubing beneath the covering.

A throat clearing brought his attention back inside. "Problem?" Tanner asked.

Tate returned Tanner's gaze for a moment, then shook his head. "Nope, got it. I do have an idea for an article, though. It has a human-interest angle and maybe a bit of controversy." Tanner continued to stare, but Tate thought he saw a flicker of interest. He barreled on. "What if I told you I had a lead on illegal booze-making in town, and the involvement of some very important people? Wouldn't take a whole lotta . . ."

Tanner pointed toward the door. "No. If there's any controversy to be had, it'll come from me. There's an important concept you need to grasp. Nevis is a small town, but with an intricate weave of personalities, histories, and affiliations. If you don't understand all those and how they relate to each other, you're gonna end up in a deep pile o' manure without a shovel. Right now, you stick to Bayside Park's most popular flavor of taffy, and the latest gentleman on the boardwalk to have his pocket picked. After you've earned your stripes, then, and not before, we'll talk about something interesting for you to do. Now, go do what I told you needed done."

"But, think of the readership interest—"

"That's just it, son. I don't pay you enough to think. Just write up the meeting facts nice and neat and have them in my office by lunchtime.

My little red pen and the typesetter will handle the rest. Then hoof it down to the pier and catalogue what's going on there. Too hard for you?"

Tate shook his head and walked back to his desk, where he sat down and scrolled paper into his battered Corona. Neither Wayne nor the wagon had moved. It was an adventure begging to be told, but Tanner was going to keep him on too short a leash to dig deep. Hooch, sanctimonious politicians, and Prohibition—he knew a good story when he sniffed one. He checked the clock on the wall and considered his newest assignment. Just the facts? Piece of cake. He grabbed his notebook and his bowler and went out for a little stroll down Main Street. It would take more than a dressing down to pull him off this case.

— • —

Tate Shoemaker watched the wagon rumble up over the hill and out of town, with Wayne wedged in next to the still in the bed. He looked around, desperate for a horse to borrow or another wagon to thumb a ride on. *Trust the instincts sooner, Shoe. Sharpen your game.* No one was about except two schoolmarms chatting at the door of the post office, and a youngster kicking a can around. He whistled the boy over.

"What's your name, son?" he asked him. "Shouldn't you be in school?"

"Jack Byrne. Too sick to stay in school. I'm heading straight home, sir."

The kid was the picture of health. "Tell me," Tate said, pointing down the road after the wagon. "Who does that wagon belong to?"

Without so much as a glance, Jack shook his head.

Tate sighed and counted three Indian-head pennies out onto his palm. "Recognize it now?"

Jack scooped up the pennies. "Possibly." He took off at a run.

"Hey! Shoemaker at the *Evening Star*!" Tate yelled after him. He turned his attention to the two women, who were working their way down the post office steps. If memory served, the roly-poly one on the right was Mrs. McClelland, widow of Archibald, and self-appointed field general of the local suffragette movement.

"Mrs. McClelland," he called as he scurried her way, catching her at the bottom of the steps. "Tatum Shoemaker, *Evening Star*." He offered his hand, which she ignored. "Could I get a comment from you about the local options?"

"Local options?" she repeated, frowning.

"Mayor Dwyer informed me that the State of Maryland won't pass any legislation to enforce Prohibition. The governor is leaving it up to the individual jurisdictions. Should Nevis enact legislation enforcing Prohibition? What's your position?"

The two women exchanged glances. Mrs. McClelland dispatched her companion with a whisper and turned to Tate, her bright smile bringing a blush to his face. "How nice of you to ask. How about you tell me where the mayor's office stands on options, and I'll respond to that. Fair enough?"

He didn't want to say that it was the only thing working for him, but there didn't appear to be any immediate return on his Indian heads, and he had no idea where Wayne might be. "Of course." Tate offered her his arm, and they headed for her wagon. He could put the treatment on Wayne the next time they met. The kid would never even know how easily he had been worked.

CHAPTER ELEVEN

Bigger Concerns

"Don't say I don't give my all for you," Prentis said to Jackson as he swept back into the mayor's office just before dusk. He carried a small paper bag, a stack of papers, and something wrapped in brown butcher paper. "Lunch," he said, peeling back the brown paper to reveal a stacked ham sandwich. He wolfed down half of it in three huge bites and took a seat at Jackson's elbow.

"Well, you're one meal ahead of me," Jackson said, looking wistfully at the sandwich. "Nate's?"

"Mmm," Prentis said, swallowing. He motioned for Jackson to pick up his pen. "Here's the lowdown on liquor at Bayside; then I've got to go home and check in with the little woman."

"I would assume that's the wife and not Alice?"

"Of course. I've already seen Alice today. We spent our lunchtime together." He pushed the rest of the sandwich aside and said, "All sources suggest that prohibiting alcohol in the Bayland Amusement Park is going to kill them, and they won't go down without a fight. Smart money is speculating that they will be violating the Volstead Act to stay in the black. Probably a speakeasy squirreled away in the complex somewhere. The rides and bay breezes aren't the only drawing card for the park—not by a long shot. Sixty percent of its profits come from the smooth notes of the German beer, and another twenty percent from the soft gambling enterprises."

Jackson stopped writing. "Did you write all this down so I can study it?"

Prentis tipped his chin toward Jackson's notes. "Keep jotting. As I said, I've been very busy. I won't have a full written report for you until tomorrow morning, unless you want my notes." He pulled a creased sheet of paper from a pocket and consulted it. "People anticipated that the feds could successfully crack down on production, and they were stockpiling their own supply before buying became illegal. The Germans in town didn't want to get hauled off to the poky, so they stopped production just like the major breweries. But just like we thought, there are rumblings of illegal operations springing up all over the place. Farm revenue isn't going to fill in the void from lost beer profits. My little bird says people in Washington are singing the blues over the lack of beer. Bathtub gin and rotgut shine aren't going to cut it. Ridership these last few weeks has been up slightly. Seems people are hitting the trains and coming down here, where it's still relatively wet. They may hate the Germans in Versailles, but they'll overlook that for a pint of Nevis lager. Also, I've no doubt that Bayland has some back rooms supplying pretty fine liquor for those who can pay. And I wouldn't be surprised if the Chesapeake Railway Express is transporting hooch for Bayland. But, it won't be enough volume to save our amusement park."

"Whew, boy," Jackson said, scratching the back of his neck. "Who's your source?"

"Just consider my paycheck a good investment in your political career and the well-being of Nevis."

Jackson grunted. "If only I could be sure those two things went hand in hand. Well, at any rate, that would jibe with the chat Father McGee and I had the last night Kelly's was open. He left me with the direct impression that he had no problem brewing up a batch or twenty if it helped the Germans in his parish make ends meet. It was the damnedest conversation, Prentis. That's a man of the cloth who stands up for what he believes—even if it lands him in the clink." He stopped talking as Prentis pulled three sugar-coated kolaches out of his bag. "Betty's?"

"That woman can bake," Prentis said. He handed one over. "A priest offering sanctuary to a bunch of scofflaws who happen to attend mass every Sunday? Sounds very churchy to me. And they might just get away with it. Right on the water but well off the beaten track, and swampy enough to raise gators. Feds would have a difficult time down there. If you didn't know those woods, you could set out hunting for a still and not find your way back out—maybe ever."

Jackson scribbled an asterisk next to each of the major points he had jotted down and set aside his pen. "Yeah, and they're thick as thieves in the foggy bottom. You wouldn't make it past the first house without some Irish Paul Revere sounding the alarm. Father McGee has a great business sense. If they put their heart and soul into it, I suspect they'll do all right."

Prentis returned his notes to his pocket and said, "It's doable in the short term. The park beer makers could maintain their income, a dozen men in town I can think of would avoid the DTs, and we don't risk people's lives on a bad batch from some still. Everybody wins."

"Except the suffragettes." Jackson licked the powdered sugar off his fingers. "So what I'm hearing from you is that as an elected official, to keep the good people of Nevis safe and prosperous through this trying period, I should turn a blind eye to the illegal liquor trade?"

"Only if you're not going to quote me on it," Prentis said with a laugh. "But think about it. The more money people have, the more they spend—most of it right here in town. What else does Nevis have going for it?"

Jackson reviewed the notes before him and slowly shook his head. "So we've moved from personal drinking to saving the economy of Nevis?"

"It would seem so."

"Here's what I think," Jackson said. "I still don't like it, but in this instance, what I want and what's good for the town seem to be in accord. Our decision to let the town continue to run wet is a sound one. But—and it's a sizable *but*—we continue to keep this all a tight circle. No outsiders, and most definitely not Tarkington or Philly. Under those conditions, I think we can control the situation and keep ourselves from becoming guests of the state. Agreed?"

"I do think we have another alternative, but if that's how you see it . . ." Prentis got up to leave.

Jackson waved at the stack of papers Prentis had deposited on his desk. "Sure you don't want to leave what you've done so far?"

"Oh, that's not the report, but you can thank me anyway. You need to put someone in Missus Hasson's empty chair. Those are inquiries about employment, résumés, letters of recommendation—everything you need to pick a good office manager. Find someone compatible. *Soon.*"

Jackson riffled through the stack. "Half of these are Tanners! Riley Tanner's tittle-tattling sister-in-law; Mary Tanner, the undertaker's nephew's silly young wife. Tanner, Tanner, Tanner, and all of them no doubt woefully undertrained." He pushed the stack toward the wastebasket at the end of his desk.

Prentis chuckled. "Get with it, Mr. Mayor. It's customary to reward supporters with government positions."

"You don't have to verse me in political patronage. Dad's middle name, remember?" Jackson looked at the various piles of paperwork stacked around the room. "I need someone who can hit the ground running. Cronyism would be suicide."

"I'm sure there's someone in there that will do quite nicely. We need better treatment from the fourth estate." Prentis winked at him and walked out.

CHAPTER TWELVE

Considering Romantic Partners

Jackson ushered the job applicant into his personal office and sat down at his desk, across from her. She was young, lovely, and a little nervous, it seemed, as she once again put a hand to the loose bun at the nape of her neck. If she was intimidated by his position, nervous was okay. But if she didn't know which end was up . . . He picked up her résumé.

"Francis Byrne. Are you Patrick and Anna Byrne's daughter?"

She nodded, a guarded look in her eyes. "People call me Fannie."

"Well, Fannie, I didn't know him well, but I understand your father was a good man. I was sorry to hear about his untimely passing. And goodness knows, Miz Betty's is practically a town institution. Maybe you knew my son, Reynolds?"

She shook her head, and Jackson watched her hand return to check her hair. He continued perusing the immaculately typed résumé. "You've been attending Drexel Business School." He put the résumé back down on the desk. "Impressive. Aren't you going to finish?"

"Money's tight right now."

"I see. My previous secretary, Missus Hasson, recommends you wholeheartedly. 'Meticulous, observant, and discreet'—I believe those were her words." He nodded at the thin gold band gracing the ring finger of her left hand. "Married?"

She blushed and hid her left hand under her right. "Not yet."

"Oh, dear," he said, feeling the heat rush to his face. "My only purpose in asking is to determine whether you intend to stay in Nevis, so that I can count on your services for a while."

"Yes, sir. Mr. Millman and I have not set a date yet."

"Daniel Millman? Paints and glass?" He scooped the application back up. Her credentials were impeccable. And Danny Millman's fiancée! He looked back up, beaming. "When can you start, Miss Byrne?"

Fanny stopped fidgeting and returned his smile. "Right away, Mr. Dwyer. I've already moved back to town. I'll be living with my mother."

It was all too good to be true. And with Prentis elsewhere, there would be no sparring over the selection. He slapped the table as if his hand were a judge's gavel. "Settled, then, Miss Byrne. I'm sure this will work out just fine." He saw her to the door. "Monday morning. Eight thirty sharp."

"Thank you for the opportunity, Mayor Dwyer. You won't regret it." Fannie shook his hand and left, on the way out crossing paths with Prentis, who stepped aside at the doorway.

"Constituent problem?" Prentis asked when he had closed the door behind her.

"Not at all," Jackson said, heading back to his desk with Prentis close behind. "That's Frances Byrne, constituent and new hire. She starts Monday."

Prentis stood and stared. "You're joshing me, right? What happened to the stack of résumés I gave you—you know, from your *well-connected* constituents? Do you *set out* to offend your supporters, or has your brain gone on vacation?"

"She comes highly recommended. Attended Drexel Business, dresses professionally, and Missus Hasson says she's discreet. Perfect fit." He handed Prentis the stack of résumés. "For next time," he said. He placed her application under his telephone and began to hum.

Prentis dropped the stack in the wastebasket. "If she's that good, she dies at her desk. And considering how young she looks, that should be many administrations from now."

"There's a lot to be said for being young. Oh, and did I mention that she's Danny Millman's fiancée?"

"I'm sure that'll get you somewhere, but not as far as keeping up your father's patronage," Prentis muttered, pouring his customary mid-morning coffee. He blew across the steaming surface, eyeing Jackson. "You're also obviously pleased with sticking it to the Tanners—and me."

"Not at all. I just don't want them getting a foothold in this office."

"Well, if you're going to be vindictive, you've got to make it subtler. And let *me* do your dirty work. People adore your affable, squeaky-clean image."

Jackson grunted and pulled his schedule book closer. "I don't know," he murmured, staring at the week's appointments.

"Like that. Something I can take care of for you?"

"No, all under control. Why, do I look vindictive?"

"No, not really. You suddenly look like your dog just died."

"I should be so lucky," Jackson kneaded the back of his neck. "*That* woman will be the death of me." He began thumbing through the mail.

"What does Camilla want now?"

"She's invited me to tea."

"On neutral ground, I hope? Don't let them surround you—you'll have no more chance than a gobbler at Thanksgiving."

"Her house."

"You're not thinking of going?" Prentis put his cup down too hard, sloshing coffee on the rug. "Dear God, you are!"

"No," Jackson said, slicing open an envelope with enough force to knock over the horse figurine on the end of his desk. "Well, uh . . ."

"Really, now, Jackson. Tea, indeed. Don't let this woman get into your head. She hasn't broken bread with you in thirty years, and now she invites you over for *tea*? I was drunk when I suggested you give it another go with her. It will *not* be better the second time around. She wants something."

Jackson gave him a hangdog look. "Her husband just died. It's a courtesy call from the mayor. All on the up-and-up, and liquor will not be a topic of conversation. If she weren't capable of being civil, she wouldn't have invited me."

Prentis threw his hands up in the air. "You're a romantic old fart, Jackson. Don't say I didn't warn you. These women will pluck and truss you."

CHAPTER THIRTEEN

Tea, No Sugar

Jackson checked his tie in the hall tree mirror, smoothed out what was left of his hair, then closed his eyes and lingered a moment. A man's heart could be broken but once, it was said, and they had already crossed that bridge. He scooped up the bouquet of yellow daisies he had bought fresh off the *Chessie Belle,* and locked his front door behind him.

In all the years he had known the McClelland farmstead—forty-some and counting—it hadn't changed much. It was like a lot of the other farms around Nevis: two-story clapboard house, tin-roofed barns with vertical slats missing every so many feet for drying the baccy leaves, a decent-size corncrib, and a big old dairy barn. Throw a new coat of whitewash on the main house, and any Nevisite would have felt right at home.

He parked his car under a leafy maple tree next to the hitching post. He paused momentarily and removed his hat to run a sweaty palm once more over the top of his head. Then he climbed the porch steps and rapped three times.

Camilla McClelland opened the door, a slight scowl on her face. "Mayor Dwyer."

He shoved the bouquet at her. "Good morning. I'd like to offer deepest condolences on behalf of the town of Nevis, ma'am . . . er . . . Mrs. McClelland." He winced inwardly. It had sounded more polished at his house. He tipped his hat and waited.

And waited.

Finally, she stopped scowling and said, "Would you like to come in, Mayor?"

He nodded, and she ushered him into her parlor, where he took off his hat and sat down on the maroon velvet settee. The room was sparsely furnished and about as uninviting as his greeting at the door.

She put his flowers in a vase and sat down across from him, straight backed and prim with her hands clasped tightly in her lap. She seemed poised to do battle—the same fiery woman he had known, not the one he had hoped to see this morning after her unexpected invitation. He approached her with the same caution he used when he found a copperhead in his path out in the foggy bottom: keep a bit of distance and refrain from sudden moves.

"Good morning," he said again. "I'm very sorry about Archibald."

"Well, God decided he had suffered enough," she said, and her face softened somewhat. "Not quite like your Patricia, I suppose. Influenza took her fast."

"Yes, it did. Good woman, my Patricia."

One part of him wanted to hug her, bond in their bereavement. The other half wanted to flee before she could lash out at him. He cleared his throat. "If there's anything you need, just give a holler. Farm's a lot of responsibility. We all talked, and we'll do what we can to help keep up with things."

"Because a woman couldn't possibly handle all this? And all the *good* men in town want to assist the helpless widow. Just like Archibald." She shook her head. "Won't be making that mistake again."

"No," he said, shaking his head. "I mean, yes. Oh, you know what I mean, Camilla. I never could keep up with you anyway." He looked into the most mesmerizing brown eyes he had ever known, and sighed.

"Tea?" She asked, rising slightly to pick up the pot in its violet chintz cozy, on the table between them.

He nodded.

"You've done well for yourself these last few years," she said, pouring him a cup. "That's a fine business you have at the wharf, and who would have guessed you'd be mayor someday? I sure did—"

He laughed uncomfortably. "On that we can agree. I had a rough start. But thirty years offers lots of opportunities for change. I've tried to take advantage of every day the good Lord has let me see."

A fleeting smile crossed her lips; then she seemed to catch herself, and her expression hardened. "I thank the Lord every day for the Eighteenth Amendment and all the good work it will do to stop the evil that has caused so many to suffer."

Jackson feigned interested in the contents of his teacup and took too big a sip of Earl Gray, scalding his lip and tongue. "Hoo, that's good."

"And the Maryland legislature, hard at work on a state law to support it?" she asked, not responding to his distress.

He picked the cup back up to give his hands something to do. "No, they don't seem keen on doing that, Camilla."

"So, it will be a local option for Nevis?" she asked sweetly.

Jackson's cup rattled in the saucer, but he managed to put it down again without spilling any. He looked squarely into eyes that could change in an instant from deep and kind to cold and hawkish. "No.

We're going to leave it up to the feds. It's their law, and to be honest, we don't really have the resources to enforce it for them."

"Mr. Shoemaker at the *Evening Star* doesn't seem to think your supporters would like that."

"Quite the contrary. The electorate is firmly behind the position. Perhaps Mr. Shoemaker hasn't been in town long enough to recognize that."

"Many women in town don't support it."

"But, uh . . ."

"Women don't vote? *Yet*," she said, a defiant spark now in her eyes. "So your only concern is what voters want. Wouldn't it be better to be inclusive? What about the rest of us?"

Oh, boy. "I hope to represent *all* the good citizens of Nevis. I consider a man's vote to be representational, reflecting the desires of the entire household."

"And what about single women like me?"

Jackson started to speak, then considered it wiser to shut his mouth. She seemed content to let the statement hang in the air for a bit.

"Well, Jackson, I suppose women can contribute money to candidates' campaigns, can they not?"

"Yes, ma'am." My, the woman could needle, though he knew she didn't have extra money to throw around. "Or they can find a decent partner to help them through life and be their voice. There are good men . . ." He seized his cup as a shield and sipped, peeking at her over the rim. The expression in her eyes was like an open invitation to pour his heart out.

Camilla poured herself tea. A thrill ran through Jackson as he watched her hand tremble. She dropped a sugar cube on the table. He pretended not to notice.

He never could outthink or outtalk this barracuda when she was on the hunt, but this? Maybe, just maybe . . . Jackson rose and picked up his hat. They could part on a good note. "This has been lovely, Camilla. After all these years . . . Rest assured that I will do the best I can for all of Nevis. My office door is always open. Perhaps you'd like to come to town one day and we can discuss things?"

Camilla put down her cup and rose stiffly, eyes burning again. The invitation had been rescinded. "Oh, you'll be hearing from me again. The Woman's League will be marching in town next week. I don't need any man to speak for me. Have a quick trip back to town."

And that was it. There was no separating the venom from the honey. With a tip of his hat, Jackson returned to his car.

He drove until he was beyond her plentiful fields and had crossed over the little plank bridge to Lower Marlboro Road. There he sat under a somber gray sky threatening rain and tried to rid himself of all the hate he had just inhaled. He pulled out Prentis's list and scribbled "Camilla" in the con column before balling the paper up and tossing it onto the backseat.

Camilla was an enigma, and Volstead the root of all evil. The hand wave at Saint Peter's, the softness in her eyes just now. If not for the liquor, would they be fighting at all? Reaching behind him, he retrieved the list and smoothed it out. He had to figure out how to move her from con to pro. She would always be antiliquor, but how could he make her believe he was, too? She was keen on local options. Maybe he could introduce a referendum on which way Nevis should lean. All for show, of course. He wouldn't push it, the council would shoot it down, and she would respect him. That was it! He would invite her out to discuss it. She'd love it.

— —

Camilla touched the daisy petals and wondered if he had paid for them with ill-gotten gains. Why did he spoil everything? She plucked the flowers out of the vase and tossed them out the front door toward William's—and Archibald's, in his turn—planted fields. Even though they were lush from good spring rain, they were never as lovely as they were that summer day so long ago.

She could still see the sunflowers with their bright yellow faces staring back at her, past the hay bales with heat rising in wavy lines around them, to the ribbon of dirt road that wound its circuitous way toward young William McClelland's farm. He was late. Again.

"He's coming?" William had asked as he hopped off the stack of cinder blocks and tossed the sunflower—its beautiful spirals picked clean—onto the compost heap with the others.

"Or drinking?" Archibald said.

She shrugged. They sounded like her father. Conversation would open the door to a place she didn't want to go, a direction William would relish. She picked up the last sunflower and began to pluck the petals. *He loves me, he loves me not . . .*

Camilla shook her head, banishing the memory. She closed the door. Jackson Dwyer would remain the only man she ever loved, but how he failed her when it came to liquor.

CHAPTER FOURTEEN

War

Prentis left the Model T parked in the middle of the road—if a double track in the dirt could be called such—and ventured into the woods. Ducking and thrashing his way through dense thicket, he kept a sharp eye out for the little swatches of red cloth Kelly had tied on branch tips to guide him. His trek into the wilds today had him seriously questioning his dedication to public service. The Club had wasted no time in setting up a network of stills to alleviate its liquor-supply crisis. In the Irish area in the foggy bottom, down dirt roads forgotten by all but the few closemouthed locals who lived here, and in woods so deep that even a map and compass were useless, Prentis had reluctantly assumed oversight of a major bootlegging operation. But the enthusiasm and hope of the Nevis Gentlemen's Club were being systematically reduced to piles of smashed metal and shattered glass, one demolished still at a time. Hell had broken loose and was spreading faster than the Spanish influenza ever did.

In the middle of Archer's Woods on the north side of town, Prentis joined the grieving Pitney Benson at the shambles of his most productive still. The bootlegger's shoulders drooped as he surveyed the shards of glass mason jars, the squashed copper kettle, the kinked and flattened copper tubing. With the arthritis slowing him down, and a nagging cough pulling him up short, Pitney had no doubt seen his share of bad days, but this had to be one of the worst. Maybe the old moonshiner would just hang it up and never run another batch of sour mash.

"I'll be damned if that McClelland banshee didn't destroy the best still we ever had," Pitney said without looking up. "Mayor's got to do something about those meddling harpies." He kicked at the debris. "Maybe we should give her tit for tat. Go set fire to a few of her cows. See how she likes that." He gazed out across the woods as if there might be a rabid, hatchet-wielding temperance woman skulking behind a hickory tree.

"Well, now, hold on, Pitney," Prentis said. There's no proof, and we don't condone mob justice in this town. If you ask me, all these stills going down is much too efficient for a gaggle of women who wouldn't dream of getting their button shoes muddy. You seen anybody sneaking around these woods? Anything unusual? Nosy questions of late?"

Benson threw his hands up in the air. "That's just it. I've been keeping a pretty good eye out here and I didn't see nothing. If it's the feds, they're some we haven't seen before, 'cause I got eyes all over town. I got to ask you, what good is all this protection money we're funneling to McCall if we can't keep a still up long enough to run the first batch?" He turned around and gazed out toward the road, a quarter mile off. "Where's the mayor, anyway?"

Prentis raised his hands in mock surrender. "Whoa, I don't know anything about paying off the police. The mayor's not involved here. He's off taking care of town business."

"*Shee-it*," Benson said. He spat a six-foot stripe of black juice across the rubble pile. "Ain't no secret. Ever'body knows the ropes."

"So now?" Prentis asked. "Build another, maybe move it outta here?"

"Oh, hell yeah," Pitney said. "I'm gonna build another one, and twelve more after that if I need to. And I got half a mind to locate the next one up on the edge o' that battle-axe's property and then call the feds on *her*. She's a pain in my backside. Nothing to do but clean up this mess and find another place. You important people need to figure it out before I move to Leonardtown, where they leave you be." His head snapped around to the sound of rustling and crackling behind them. He relaxed again as Kelly's head appeared around the perimeter of cut evergreen boughs that Benson had piled up to hide the still. Benson, still fuming but apparently talked out, gave him a nod, then turned and took off with a splash through the stream and headed for his two pack mules tied nearby.

"Didn't mean to run him off," Kelly said, looking at the devastation. "Dozen good ones down in the last two weeks. I don't know who's running this little deal, but nothing's safe out here—except Flanagan, of course."

Prentis's eyebrows shot up. "You don't think—"

"Flanagan? Nah, he's a sneaky old cuss, and no mistake. Been doing this for years and can hide a still like nobody else. But I suspect even he won't last too much longer. I'm not here to mourn the still, but to let you know that all kind of commotion broke out late last night at Parkers Wharf. Didn't touch the church, but busted up half the stills. If it hadn't been for their watchman doing his nightly rounds, they might have torn down the lot of 'em."

"Shit." Prentis paced off a few feet and came right back. "Got a good look at 'em, though?"

"Nope. They slipped away by skiff."

Prentis started back in the direction of his car—at least, he hoped he was headed right. Kelly fell into stride next to him. "Benson's pretty hot. He wants to go after Camilla McClelland, but the biddies aren't capable of this—not without some help."

"Nope," Kelly said. "They'd need to know too much, and McCall would be pretty quick to put an end to their troublemaking. He's also eager to make a dollar, and too tightfisted to let a good thing end. Why would he let them endanger the sweet little operation he's overseeing? On the other hand, he's not exactly doing a bang-up job for us here, is he?"

Prentis rubbed the neck stubble that he had missed with his morning shave. "Been giving him some thought. I suspect he knows people who know people. No feds are going to make the trip clear out to Nevis, bust up multiple stills over a two-week period, and sneak back out again without him knowing. Maybe *he's* our problem."

"Someone else's money is more motivating than ours?"

"That'd be my guess. McCall doesn't give a damn about politics." Prentis paused and looked around for a red marker, shifted left, and took off again.

"Road's not far," Kelly said, pointing straight ahead of them. "Has to be someone with deep pockets, Prentis. We're already paying him a hefty sum. I can't imagine the Feds paying him off, going to all the trouble of shutting illegal operations down, and then not dragging off a paddy wagon full of moonshiners."

Prentis didn't reply but increased his walking speed. The black hulk of the Lizzie was now visible through the pines.

Kelly stopped, unable or unwilling to keep up. "You have a pretty good idea, though, don't you?" he called after him, an edge of annoyance creeping into his voice.

Prentis kept walking.

"You and McCall aren't the only ones who knows things, you know. We've all got connections to Baltimore and Philly. It's bootlegging heaven up there—illegal interests running wild, building empires, killing off the competition. New York, Chicago, Cleveland—all the big cities. It's not a giant leap from small-time rackets running the arcades, to the same people wanting a share of illegal liquor. Drinking, gambling, and extortion kind of go hand in hand."

At this, Prentis stopped. "That's a mighty big leap," he said, wondering just how confidential his and Jackson's meetings were. "Get me some proof and we can act on it. Until then, we're stumbling around in the dark. Gotta go," he said, moving again.

Kelly was right up on him. "It's not that you and Jackson haven't been discreet, but, damn, I'm watching Jackson's hair go grayer by the hour, and you look like you haven't slept in weeks. The pressure's coming from Philadelphia, right?" Kelly whispered. "That's where I'm placing my chips."

"Got it all figured out, huh?" Prentis said, forcing a chuckle. "There's no Philadelphia." *Delaware,* perhaps, but not the Philly crew."

"Figured enough to question why you're fighting the people that could solve our problem."

"Enlighten me, Kelly. What am I missing?" he called over his shoulder as he opened the car door.

"That we can't run a big booze operation by ourselves. There's plenty people willing to get involved if you'd let them. Partner with *somebody.* Then we'd have plenty to go around. You, me, Delaware, Philly—enough for everybody. Nobody goes home unhappy under that system. Ol' Chance Dwyer certainly would have embraced it."

Prentis got in and started the engine. "Chance Dwyer, God rest his soul, embraced anything that lined his pockets. As long as he kept it local, nobody cared. As I'm sure you noticed, there's not much in common between him and his son. Jackson's set on cleaning this place up, and rightly so."

"You know what I mean."

"Running a big-time bootlegging operation doesn't make any sense with us being next-door to Washington. It'd draw too much attention."

Kelly draped himself over the door on the passenger side. "And how's that going for you with Camilla McClelland, Carrie Nation's less-homely stepsister, watching everything you do? We bring in some big boys and they'll see we get the protection we need from those harpies. Guarantee you, we'll be running a booze surplus in two months. Then we turn around and send the extra to Solomons and ship it elsewhere for a tidy profit. I'll wager the Chesapeake Railway Express will want in for a cut too. I'm telling you, it's an enormous, oozing apple pie and we can cut it anyway we want. Plain as a pikestaff."

Prentis sighed. "What we do in politics isn't necessarily logical, Kelly. Just see what you can do out here. We'll get it all right sooner or later." He scanned the woods one last time and released the hand brake.

"Whoa." Kelly tossed papers onto the passenger seat. "Here's your Mumbles sign-in sheets. Nothing odd that I can see. Take a peek. Meanwhile, I'll do what I can, but I have a livelihood to protect. If you can't help me ensure a liquor supply, I'll have to look elsewhere for support."

"We're all in a protective mode, Kelly. Try not to panic. Just find the leak. That'll be the key to fixing everything."

CHAPTER FIFTEEN

The Bad News

Jackson gave up. Camilla, God bless her complicated heart, wasn't coming. She had graciously accepted his invitation to discuss her concerns about liquor, only to stand him up. If dinner at Oscar's and a discussion of local liquor enforcement options couldn't bring her out, nothing would. He looked at the flickering candles on his table, the romantic view of the bay, and wanted to melt into his chair.

He broke down and ordered oyster stew and the fried oyster special. Then, mulling over his inadequacies, he poked at the oyster crackers floating like little buoys, until he finally succeeded in pinning one to the bottom of the bowl with the back of his spoon. If he owned Millman's, these would be little Ollies staring back at him, not some stale imports from New Jersey. He shoved the bowl aside. When Prentis suddenly appeared, he almost welcomed it.

"Sorry to intrude," Prentis said, glancing around. "Where's your date?"

"Obviously, not here," Jackson grumbled. "We were going to discuss local options. Keeping tabs?"

"Nah. I just came for a bite and saw you sitting here. Care for some company?"

Jackson nodded to the opposite chair. "There's a bottle stashed in the bottom drawer of my office file cabinet. Let's go have a shot and I'll be fine."

Prentis took the seat. "Yeah, with all that's going on, that's what Nevis needs: another drunk mayor."

"Oh, for all his many faults, dear Dad seemed to operate an efficient enough government. Things got done."

Prentis gave him a searching look. "Why are you hiding liquor? Imbibing again?"

"I wish," Jackson said. "What's new since last we met?"

"You don't need to resort to that. If only for my sake, stay sober—I hate cleaning up after binges."

Jackson poked at another cracker. "I need you to draft something. A bill on the liquor issue. I realize it doesn't have a hope in hell of passing the council, so no lecturing. Just shut up and draft it. Don't bother pushing it. In fact, bury it, but not so deep I can't point to it and look like I'm trying to support Volstead."

"Is this another of your lame attempts to win Camilla's heart, because I have to tell you, the woman doesn't have one. Rest assured, I have no problem in burying it, and if that'll keep you from moping around like a lovesick puppy, so be it." He pulled his chair in closer and lowered his voice. "I have bad news and worse news. Which first?"

Jackson sighed. "Let's start with the bleak and utterly demoralizing."

Prentis tossed a black folder down next to Jackson's plate. "Here's your Bayland report. I'm finished."

Jackson fanned through it. "You know, it shouldn't be too hard to find someone who can provide me with more timely information," he said, happy to unload his displeasure on any available target. "Anything we didn't discuss yesterday?"

"Nothing, if you don't include the police report at the back, concerning the two bodies they found down at the wharf earlier tonight. And under that, a copy of the police report covering the break-in at Mac's pharmacy downtown. The *second* break-in, mind you."

Jackson arched an eyebrow and slowed his flipping of pages. "Busy night. How much money did they get from Mac's?"

"Cleaned out all the medicinal whiskey he had just restocked after the first robbery. Plus his cough syrup."

"Oh, dear. Tear the place up, or just a grab and go?"

"Quick and quiet. They pried open the rear entrance, loaded up, and scooted. Neighbors on either side never heard a peep. Mr. Silas says he's going to sleep with his double-barrel from now on. It's all in the report there," Prentis said with a wave. "Except the part about him paying you a visit early tomorrow to complain about the security of the town going to hell."

"Highlight of my day," Jackson muttered as he continued perusing. "The other—they kill each other?"

"It doesn't appear so. No sign of a struggle. A couple of well-known alkies that have been hanging around that area recently. They had a stash of mason jars squirreled away up in the support beams at the end of the wharf. I wouldn't make Kelly's pig drink that stuff."

Jackson closed up the folder. "So, it's booze and booze."

"And *booze,* if you add in that Bayland report. I'll summarize for you. The park needs to serve it up. It keeps the German brewers in the black and ensures a steady flow of patrons from DC, especially through bad weather. Bayland pays for most of our police force and subsidizes the rail line. Without their help, Nevis loses money, and the infrastructure begins to crumble."

"Hallelujah, sweet Jesus," Jackson said, scratching his head. "If crime's on the rise right now, can you imagine what it'll be like without an adequate police force?"

"Why, we'll follow the good Mr. Silas's lead until we can regroup. Everybody owns a firearm. We'll police our own."

Jackson glowered at him. "You do realize there are some who would like that idea? So, don't even go there in jest. You're right, anybody in this town who can fog a mirror owns a gun. That's why we had a police force in the first place."

"Noted." Prentis pulled a carefully folded document from his jacket pocket. "Now for the bad news. Here's Kelly's attendance sheet from Mumbles."

Jackson almost dropped it in his soup. *"Nathan Tarkington?"* You're kidding! I thought we got rid of that carpetbagger. Obviously, he didn't take to heart anything you two discussed."

"I ceased kidding a long time ago," Prentis said, shaking his head at the approaching waiter. "He visited Mumbles three times, and his name immediately follows McCall's on every visit."

Jackson looked at the list again. "McCall's aligned himself—"

"With booze runners," Prentis said. "And the all-out war on our stills? I reckon it's not the feds or Camilla and her gang of bully-pulpitists. It's Tarkington. These visits are part of his message."

"To make us want him and his gang." Jackson crumpled the paper in his fist.

"Make us *need* them, more like. We either invite them to the table or we dine alone—without beverage. They may never find Flanagan's hooch operations, but they know he can't supply *all* our liquor." Prentis flipped up the red cloth covering the bread basket and took a Parker House roll.

Jackson stabbed an oyster with his fork and swallowed it without chewing. He had oyster dredgers and trawlers battling for territory off the coast, and a budget shortfall threatening to chase off the best accountant the town ever employed. *Those* should be his pressing issues.

Getting overinvested with the wets might prove to be the biggest mistake of his tenure. "I don't know. We should have left everyone to fend for themselves."

"Stop saying you don't know," Prentis said. "Because you do. Tarkington's people just may turn out to be the only game in town."

"Over my dead body."

Prentis put a hand on Jackson's elbow. "Please don't say that again. These are serious people."

Jackson shook his fork at Prentis. "So am I, and I'm not turning this town over to a bunch of hoodlums!"

Prentis closed his eyes, took a deep breath, and let it out. "Our attempt to run a civilized liquor program in Nevis is a failed experiment. *Prohibition* is a failed experiment, and your administration will fail if you don't adapt to the reality of the situation. God help us," he said. His raised voice was drawing stares, and he lowered the volume. "Right now, you're so hamstrung by some personal honor code that you're incapable of making decisions for the greater good! Call Tarkington in and discuss terms with him. This may be his last invitation to dance. Cooperating would make all our lives so much easier. *Negotiate,* damn it. You can't keep burying your head in the sand. Nobility went out the window when they decided to set up shop in Nevis. Didn't you say the key to success is diversification? It works in business, and it works in politics. This will only get worse, and they'll steamroll right over you. Surely you see that. You'll be a lame duck if they don't shoot you first and toss your carcass in a ditch somewhere."

"A lame duck can have quite a bit of political clout, you know—free to make decisions with no fear of the consequences. That's very appealing at the moment." Jackson wiped his mouth and threw the napkin down on the rest of his oysters. "All I see at the moment is my closest friend offering no support and doing his damnedest to let Nevis be swallowed up by lowlifes. You feeding at the same trough as McCall?"

"Really now, Jackson."

"Then how about a little support? You know we're not just talking about Tarkington's bunch. It's also people like John J. McClure and his whole Pennsylvania Irish machine, ready to wash over us like a tidal wave." Jackson flipped the Mumbles list over. "Pen?"

Prentis leaned across the table. "Please tell me you're not making another pro-and-con list. For pity's sake. Pull out the old list if you must. And then go right to the one that says "*keep locals safe.*" Damn it, Jackson, the decision is obvious. We need to protect and promote booze, booze, and more booze! Get some backbone."

Jackson swallowed hard. "Have a pleasant evening—somewhere else," he growled, nodding toward the door.

Prentis's napkin dropped like a gauntlet. "Face it!" he said. "We're running out of options. What's left? Casting our lot with Father McGee's little German project down at Parkers Wharf, or cooking up white lightning in the basement."

"Not in my courthouse! And apparently, you've forgotten one of the first tenets of political life: never negotiate from a position of weakness."

"Our weakness," Prentis said, "is in stepping aside and letting them take everything."

Jackson pulled out his money clip. "Well, then. We'll just up the ante and control it. That means talking to the right Reverend Father McGee. Didn't he suggest he might be willing to help his flock through this difficult time? I think it's about time we paid him a visit to see how his brewers are doing. Maybe we can expand their business for them."

"We don't want Father McG—"

"Hell we don't! In times of crisis, one should always feel comfortable turning to the church." Jackson rose and slid three dollar bills under the edge of his plate.

Prentis picked up the report and shoved it at him. "Obviously, you're determined to go your own way on this, but mark my words, Jackson. Things are only going to get worse. What will it take for you to accept the inevitable? More deaths?"

— —

Prentis watched Jackson go left at the end of the pier, likely heading for the sofa in his office. Prentis headed out the opposite way, a few blocks down. There was no way he would swing Jackson around to entertain a proposal from Tarkington. And he told that to the man standing in the shadows of the first alley off Third Street. The only relief in it was that the man didn't demand he return any of Tarkington's good-faith money.

CHAPTER SIXTEEN

Relying on Rascals

Tate Shoemaker pressed his hands to his ears. Between the tapping at the Chandler and Price press, the profanity-laced mumbling of Perkins, the Linotype operator, and the editor's earlier tantrum, he was down to his last nerve. The latest scuttlebutt about Baltimore was tugging at his journalistic soul. According to his newspaper buddies, booze was alive and thriving in the city, with the governor's tacit approval. The feds were the only stumbling block, and with a city as big as Baltimore—and scores of police on the take—it was a free-for-all. Nevis, on the other hand, was one long-drawn-out yawn. That he had to report on who visited their aunt Myrtle for the christening, the price per yard of crepe La Molladora at Tanner's mercantile, and the headliner at the Palace Theatre just added to his misery.

"If you knew the difference between *your* and *you're,* you wouldn't have to do that twice," he shouted at Perkins.

Perkins's grumbling grew louder. "How the hell do I know how an extra few lines ended up in Tanner's page-three ad? Damn thing only ran in the first dozen copies or so. I couldn't care less about illegal stills and optional whatever the hell they're talking about. Nothing wrong with a little nip now and then. Somebody gunning for me to get fired, that's all. Ain't nobody been back here but me and you." The tapping at the linotype stopped. He advanced toward Tate and peered at him through his thick glasses. "Did you see anybody here messing with my machine?"

Tate kept writing. "No sir. Haven't see anybody back here but me and you." Which was true. After Perkins left for the day, he didn't need anyone's okay to switch out the mercantile advertisement for his little nugget about local options and bootlegging. After all, he had started his career as a Linotyper back in Philly. It wouldn't be the last time, either. The truth would out. But next time, he would avoid cutting into the powerful Tanner family's ads—maybe spread the info around a bit. And next time, Tanner might be shaking his hand instead of going apoplectic on an innocent Linotyper.

"Perk, maybe it's time for you to retire."

Of course, Perkins's six kids and frail wife made retiring out of the question, but it was Tate's favorite incitement when he wanted to wind the old man up. This time, he got no rise; the Linotyper had disappeared.

A different sort of tapping began, this time coming from the window, where a flat-capped boy stared in at him. And if he wasn't mistaken, it was the same little hoodlum who had run off with his three cents. Tate bolted out the back door. He would shake his coins out of the scrawny little ruffian's pockets.

"You—Jack Byrne," he said, pointing at the youngster. "Give me back my three Indians."

To his surprise, the youngster didn't flee, but stood his ground, hands on hips, eyes flashing.

"No sir. Deal's a deal. That's why I'm here. You want the info or not?" He took a quick look around. "I have a reputation to keep up."

Tate pointed toward the rear of the building and gave him a nudge. "Get around here so we can talk. I'm glad you had some guilt about running off with my money."

"Oh, no sir," Jack said, striding along with him. "I take my responsibilities very seriously. And I have your information about the wagon and all. After you hear what I've got for you, who knows? We might even form a partnership."

Tate managed not to laugh. "How old are you, Jack?"

"Almost fourteen."

"Sorry, I can't legally form a partnership until you're *at least thirteen*. Now, give me a reason to want to—and see if you can be truthful this time."

Jack's head drooped, and with eyes downcast, he said, "That was parts to Pitney Benson's new still in the wagon. They built it in Wilson's woods, up near Maidstone where the mayor lives. Right before the Willow Wisp flows into the Mattapokipsee." He peered up at the reporter with narrowed eyes. "Do you know where I'm talking about, or am I wasting my breath?"

Tate drew back and stared at the young rogue. "I've half a mind to talk to your parents. Have you no manners?"

"Are we gonna talk about you frequenting Mumbles, too, Mr. Shoemaker?" He had a taunting gleam in his eye.

"That all you've got for all that money?"

"For *that* money, yeah, 'cause that's what you asked me to find out. If you want more, it's gonna cost ya more Indians."

"Balls of fire!" Tate fumbled in his pockets a moment and pulled out a jitney. "All I've got. If you can't handle that, I'll have to find someone else. Now what more do you have?"

Jack shoved the nickel in his back pocket. "If I knew what you were writing about, I could help you better. 'Cause there's stills all over the woods. There's a good one down near King's Landing. And Mr. Flanagan . . . They say he makes the best brew, but I ain't never tasted it. He's got one hid near Brownies beach, but it's so backwoods you'd need a bloodhound to get to it. But the biggest show by far is down at Parkers Wharf. Oh, my lands!" he said, holding his head. "You wouldn't believe how much liquor comes outta that place! I've watched 'em roll that stuff by the barrelsful down to the old wharf and out onto boats. A source tells me they're selling off white dog mighty cheap."

Tate gaped at him. The kid was a bona fide source. "Wait, Jack, slow down. I'm not familiar with Parkers Wharf. We still talking Nevis?"

"Yeah. Saint Raphael church down in the foggy bottom. *Chessie Belle* doesn't stop, but the wharf's still there."

Tate gave him a hard look. "Come on, Jack. This is serious stuff. You've actually seen bootlegging in the church?"

"Not *in* the church. In the woods around it."

"Give me a name, and if it starts with *Father,* I'm done with you."

Jack hesitated half a beat. "Danny Millman. Yeah, I heard it's him, and I've seen barrels come off the *Chessie Belle* that have his name all over them. I think they come in empty and go out full. Leastways, that's what Robb . . . That's the story going 'round."

Tate smiled. The kid had information *and* connections. "You're amazing, Jack. If you were a bit older, we might be talking partnership. Two great leads in one outing. Now, I don't suppose you know a way to see the operation at Parker's Wharf without being seen."

Jack grinned.

"Jack!" A woman's voice and the crunch of gravel whirled them both around. "Come home right now, Jack," a comely brunette yelled as she stomped toward them. "I've been looking all over for you." She grabbed him by the arm and gave him a jerk while fending off a slap at her head.

Tate grabbed Jack's other arm. "Hey, hey, never hit a woman."

"Fannie's my sister." Jack twisted free and darted toward the street.

"Diner!" Fannie yelled. She turned to Tate. "So sorry, Mr.—"

"You! From the *Chessie Belle!*" he blurted out. "Shoemaker. Tate Shoemaker, remember?"

"From the *big* city," she said, nodding.

Tate tried to smile, but only one corner of his mouth would cooperate. "Your brother, I assume, Miss . . .?"

"Fannie Byrne. Yes, Mr. Shoemaker, there goes the wickedest boy in Nevis. Did he, um, take something of yours?" She opened her purse. "I might not be able to retrieve it, but I'll compensate you as best I can."

Tate stayed her arm. "No, we were just chatting. Your brother's been helpful. I'm reporting for the *Evening Star,* and if I'm not mistaken, you're my new point of contact in the mayor's office. A nice change from Missus Hasson, I might add." *Byrne.* He finally had a name for this angel.

She blushed, and her hand went to the wisps of hair escaping her bun. "Well, um, thank you for your help, Mr. Shoemaker. And if I were you, I wouldn't put great stock in everything my brother says. He lives in a world of his own." She started back down the alley.

"Miss Byrne," he called, following a few steps behind. "Would you by any chance be interested in lunch sometime? You know, in compensation for the activities of your rascally little brother?"

She shook her head and kept walking, but that was okay. He had time. She was cute as could be, but more importantly, he'd bet the farm she was a fount of knowledge about some of Mayor Dwyer's personal habits.

CHAPTER SEVENTEEN

Measured Whispers on Foggy Streets

While Tanner scolded a copyboy who had wandered too close to the press, Tate eased out the back door and set off at a furious pace toward Trotts Produce Market, for a rendezvous with Jack. When he caught sight of the lad, he slowed just long enough to say, "When we get down here, don't say a word till I say you can."

"Yes sir," Jack said, scrambling to keep up with the long-legged reporter. "Are you sure Mr. Tanner okayed me tagging along with you?"

"You're fine, son. And you got your sister's permission to miss school this morning to learn about how the newspaper works?"

"Uh, yep."

"Good," Tate said, not entirely buying his answer. "This will be quiet investigative work this morning. Mr. Tanner thought I'd need another set of eyes, and someone to watch my back. You are sure that Mr. Millman is getting regular shipments of barrels?"

"Yes sir. Seen it with my own eyes."

"Terrific." Tate stopped and looked Jack dead in the eyes. "This is hush-hush work, son. You understand? Not a word to anyone—not even Tanner. He wants to maintain an impartial newsman's role. Otherwise, I'll have to go back and rescue Lloyd and have him help me. If you prove yourself on this assignment, I'll have you take me down to Parkers Wharf. Consider it a trial partnership sort of thing. You okay with that?"

"May God strike me dead," Jack said, raising his right hand.

Tate hated to trust anyone else, but it just felt like more than a one-man operation. His meeting with Mrs. McClelland hadn't gone as planned; he had given more information than he got. The most valuable tidbit he had gleaned was that she was clearly a force to be reckoned with in the town. And as he had learned in Philly, that was just the sort of contact all ace newshounds cultivated.

The pier teemed with humanity: longshoremen, leisure travelers, hawkers, and tradesmen, all waiting for the morning arrival of the *Chessie Belle,* due within the half hour. Tate lost himself in the crowd and found a position with a good view of Millman's Glass and Varnish. He didn't know a Millman from a milliner, but by the end of the day he hoped to understand everything about the business and how it fit into the burgeoning world of bootlegging. When he felt comfortable with the traffic moving in and out of the store, he said to Jack, "I want you to count the number of barrels that roll in or out of that place." Then he left a disappointed Jack to stand watch outside.

A familiar face greeted him several paces inside Millman's. It was the very same man who had spirited Fannie Byrne away from him that first day in Nevis. He stifled his lingering tinge of resentment and veered off to look at merchandise on the right side of the store, although the term "store" might be something of an overstatement. The interior space was nothing more than a warehouse of weathered rough-hewn planks and a metal roof. With the still air and the spring humidity, there was little to disperse the noxious odor inside. He browsed the shelves and stacked cans of paints, varnishes, and thinners. Then, after he had made a loop around the perimeter and was certain there were no other customers, he returned to the store entrance.

"Are you Mr. Millman, proprietor?" he asked the smiling aproned man who had initially greeted him.

"That I am," Millman said. "How may I help you? If you don't see it, I can make or mix it while you wait, or run it out to you later."

Overly earnest, Tate decided. And by the look of his polished but run-down shoes and the tight collar he kept tugging on, not a man given to spending cash. Probably not thrifty, but cash strapped—a poor fellow not remotely worthy of Fannie Byrne.

"Name's Tate Shoemaker," he said. "I'm working on a story for the *Evening Star,* and I need your expertise. May I have a moment of your time?"

"Seeing as how there's no one else here . . ." He shrugged. "What's your question?"

"How much alcohol can you sell me?"

"Why, n-none," Millman said, growing red in the face. "I think you have the wrong place. Did I get your name?" he asked, eyes roving as if he anticipated government men to burst in and arrest him for a Volstead infraction.

"Shoemaker, but you can call me Shoe. I work for the *Star,*" he said, pointing toward Main Street. "You don't use alcohol to make your varnish?"

"Yes, but it's all denatured—you can't drink it. Well, you could, but that would be a fatal mistake. Are you serious?"

"No, not really," Tate said with a chuckle. "Just wanted to see your reaction. Congratulations, Mr. Millman. I can see you're an honest man, and that's who reporters like me want to interview." Settling himself on the edge of the oak sales counter next to the cash register, he said, "Tell me about this denatured stuff and how you get it. All off the record, of course. I just need background."

"We-e-ell, I don't know. Don't like politics, and that's a pretty hot topic right now. You say you're doing a story?"

"You could say that." Tate pushed his hat farther back on his head as he had seen Tanner do, and pulled his fountain pen out. "Rest assured, Mr. Millman, we journalists rely heavily on our anonymous sources, and I never reveal mine. And you know, there's a bit of truth in those old detective stories where important information is passed along in measured whispers on foggy street corners at midnight. We investigative reporters don't want yappy sources who'll blow our stories before they're published. See what I'm saying?"

Millman nodded warily. "Yes, okay, long as we're off the record, but if a customer comes in, we're done." He moved to the other side of the cash register. "I get barrels shipped by steamship from Philadelphia to Nevis, and like I said, all the alcohol is denatured when it gets here."

"All legal?"

"All legal. Everybody's a bit confused about the liquor laws. It's not illegal to make alcohol. It's made legally every day. Just try making a felt hat, a pencil, or photographic film without it. Volstead has exemptions for businesses that rely on alcohol for production. You can trust me on this; I studied what's going on. I'm not interested in going to jail, Mr. Shoe. The area around Philly supplies the whole industrial complex in the Delaware Valley. Like I said, all legal. It just has to be denatured before it can leave the manufacturing plant."

"And how is that done?" Tate asked, his head down as he scribbled.

"They poison it. Formaldehyde, sulfuric acid, tannic acid—something noxious like that is mixed in before it leaves the plant. I can't let that hit the street, now, can I? I'm not interested in killing the entire male population of Nevis—and a few of the womenfolk, too, I might add. You should see the mountain of forms I have to fill out just to get the stuff," he said, holding his thumb and forefinger apart. "I would imagine Doc Patterson has writer's cramp filling out forms for the medicinal stuff, too."

"Probably so." Tate glanced out the window to check on Jack. His protégé was right where Tate had left him, leaning against a green lamp-post and watching both ends of the street. The kid had definite potential. He returned his gaze to Millman. "If you can put the denaturing agent in there, can you can take it out, too?"

"Any chemist worth his salt can. Wouldn't be me, though, and no one in Nevis that I know of has the skill, thank God. Hey, sorry if I came across as rude earlier. I've owned this place for five years and, until Volstead, made a decent living. Since Prohibition lowered the boom on drinking, my glassworks has taken a real hit, and I'm barely scraping by. Now, all of a sudden, people are coming at me from all directions. They want some alcohol; they want me to sell; the newspaper wants information. It's all a bit much, you know? It'll be sweet relief when the sale goes through."

The bell on the top of the door clattered.

"You got enough?" Millman said, turning away.

Tate was right behind him. "Someone's buying the place? Who? Local sort?"

Millman gave him a sheepish look. "Sorry, Mr. Shoe. "You have a good day."

"Likewise." Tate tipped his hat and headed outside to collect Jack, who hadn't moved an inch. "Jack, are you free tomorrow?"

"Whatcha need?"

"Mr. Millman seems to be on the up-and-up, so we have to figure out who else might be running the show down at Saint Raphael. I need you to take me to Parkers Wharf. And if you can, I want you to work on finding out who's in charge there. A very important part of my job is cultivating sources, and I'd hate to screw up and spill my guts to someone who doesn't want me snooping around. But you have to be subtle. I'd never forgive myself if someone caught you and packed you off in one of those barrels."

"I might be free," Jack said, rubbing his forefinger and thumb together.

Tate shoved a dollar at him. They were onto something good. Alcohol could make a man do strange things: throw away a good job, mistreat his family, and, quite possibly, buy a business that had nothing going for it but poisoned alcohol. Now, why would anyone do a thing like that? And why go to all that trouble to buy if you already had a big production going on down at Parkers? There were more players here, and to be in on this game, he had to figure out who they all were.

CHAPTER EIGHTEEN

An Equilibrium

The Ford headed south toward St. Raphael the Archangel Catholic Church. Jackson had been there a few times before finding more comfort in the bottle. Liquor—it did seem to follow him like a plague of locusts.

The secluded old church was a treasure nestled deep in the bosom of the foggy bottom—one of a string of colonial missions set up along the coast by Jesuits as they ministered to the growing numbers of Catholic settlers who arrived on Maryland's shores seeking religious freedom. So, as Jackson drew near, his heart skipped a beat at the sight of rising smoke. But when he drew closer and the woods fell away to open fields that rolled down to the bay, he realized there was no fire. The smoke was rising from the bellows of a can-shaped smoker pumped by a figure dressed head to toe in white. Close by, another figure busied himself pulling wooden frames out of half a dozen rectangular beehives. Jackson parked, and a smiling Father McGee came to greet him, pulling off his netted broad-brimmed hat as he walked.

"Didn't know you were an apiarist," Jackson said, studying the priest's buckets. "Honey for the table, or straight to mead?"

"Depends on who's asking," the priest said with a laugh. He tipped one of his buckets to reveal several large honeycombs. "You ask that in jest, but the church has a long tradition of making mead. I've considered it, but where does the time seem to go? No, today's adventure is all about *wax*. The bees start the candles, and I finish them."

"We can go inside," he said, and headed for the church, depositing his hat and gloves on a bench outside the broad oak double doors, which had been propped open. Jackson could hardly take his eyes off the bright red Indian motorcycle parked in the bushes nearby—apparently the churchmen's main mode of transportation.

The church was cool and hushed inside, illuminated only by the soft light filtering through the blue stained-glass windows that ran the length of the nave on both sides. A sense of holiness and its companion, guilt, washed over Jackson. He reached out and patted the cold, smooth whitewashed brick wall. "Thick old wall," he said, his eyes following it up to the dark sawn beams overhead.

"Yes sir. Jesuits made them to last. Twenty inches thick—almost as thick as Saint Ignatius. Sometimes you need a thick skin to last in this old world." The old cleric rubbed a bushy white eyebrow and shifted his weight. "Might we be heading toward the confessional?" he asked, his tone neither accusing nor optimistic.

Jackson cleared his throat. "Not today, Father. I'll come back another time, when I'm less hurried. And I'll make sure you get first crack at me when I'm dead. You're my favorite."

Father McGee snorted. "My son, I'll settle for a little less praise and a smidgen more devotion. Now, what is it I can do for you today?"

"Maybe a bit more privacy, Father. In here?" he asked, tilting his head toward the confessional.

"Not unless you begin our conversation with 'Bless me, Father, for I have sinned. It's been forty-odd years since my last confession.' Come. I think my office would be more appropriate."

They walked past three dark-haired children in overalls shouting and running circles in the green patch between the buildings, to the white framed rectory next door. It was a modest space with simple wooden furniture, a beaten dark tweed rocking chair, and pillars of books rising from every horizontal surface.

"Here," Father McGee said, removing a pile of papers to clear a chair. He settled into the rocker. "Now, what are we discussing?"

"The last conversation we had, you, uh . . ."

"Yes, the liquor problem," McGee said.

Jackson shifted in his seat. "If I may be so bold, Father, is it still what you might term a *problem*?"

McGee threw his head back and roared with laughter. "How do you get anything done at City Hall with all your beating around the bush? Of course we're bootlegging. I have a flock to care for."

"And you do it well." Jackson chuckled. Then he grew serious and said, "Blunt, then. I have a flock of my own to shepherd, and they need liquor—*your* liquor. Or, if that isn't possible, I would like permission to piggyback your operation—move Nevis's most reliable bootleggers down here into the woods surrounding the church and let them produce enough safe hooch to get us through this trying period. I don't want to read any more reports of men dying on our waterfront because they got a bad batch or decided that 'just one sip' of denatured alcohol wouldn't hurt them." He looked deep into the old priest's bright blue eyes. They were still full of patience and understanding.

"And what about you, Jackson?" McGee got up and walked over to the window. "Youth is wasted on the young. To have such energy again," he said, pointing at the children outside. "I believe it is the duty of the church to provide sanctuary, and so I break the law and encourage others to do the same. But bootlegging—such a precarious thing," he said as if to himself. "One has to weigh the benefits against the risk. And for me," he said, turning back around, "I need to decide which way the scale will tip. Too heavy on the right, and I put the very livelihood of good people in jeopardy. Too heavily the other side, and I have a hand in leading well-intended, decent individuals into excess and a life of inebriation. People such as you, Jackson. It troubles me deeply to see you associated with this."

"I have no intention of falling off the wagon, Father. Rest easy. I know I can't handle the stuff. And you know what's strange? I'm not even tempted."

"Good to hear. But what happens when you *are* tempted? Can you handle it then?"

"As God is my witness," Jackson said, crossing himself, "I'm done with it. I almost lost everything the first time around, and I swear there won't be a second."

"Political office is a demanding job," McGee said. "I'll continue to keep you and your burdens in my prayers." He returned to the rocking chair but didn't sit. "I hope you can appreciate that I can't make a unilateral decision. Too many other interests are involved. May I get back to you?"

Jackson stood up and offered his hand. "Of course. I'm the one asking the favor. Soon?"

"Of course."

"Excellent. Because if the answer is no, I need to consider other choices. And honestly, Father, none of them are good ones."

Jackson left him in the rectory and walked back to the car—past the robins who didn't sow or reap, and an ancient stone church that had miraculously survived a British bombardment in 1812. He made the sign of the cross, then pulled a pack of Camels out of his shirt pocket.

CHAPTER NINETEEN

Sick Uncles and Big Heathens

Tate had a new spring in his step. News sources seemed to be popping up all over the place. The first promising sign was on his desk upon his return from Millman's—an eloquently crafted note on crisp white stationary from Mrs. McClelland, inquiring as to his availability for tea. And later that night, a slip of paper shoved under his door at the boarding house. It was light on details, sloppily written, but titillating all the same: *Come at eleven, bring your notebook, and do it alone.* Of course, it was unsigned. He put Mrs. McClelland on the back burner. She was good at winkling out information but gave little in return.

And that was how Tate Shoemaker found himself in a Nevis alley in the deep of night. Eyes flicking back and forth between the two ends of the lane, he walked over and leaned against a downspout that drained the rear roof of the haberdashery. Was this a hazing by the old-timers at the *Star*? He prayed not. He didn't realize he had moved back down the narrow passageway, paced as far as the door to

Mumbles, until it jerked open and he was yanked inside and shoved facefirst against a wall.

"Lay off," he yelled, flailing. "Tate Shoemaker Junior. *Evening Star.*" A second, harder shove cut his breath short. He stopped struggling, and a pair of hands frisked him.

"You're the reporter?"

He nodded. A request to turn around got his face reacquainted with the wall. The overpowering stench of liquored breath made his stomach roil.

"You the one snooping around down at the varnish shop?"

"Maybe." His face rebounded off the wall once more. "Yes."

"Stay out of other people's business."

"Okay. But a legitimate question coming, so don't shove me again until you've heard it all. Okay? Whose business am I staying out of? Just so I know what to avoid."

"Don't be a wise guy."

His forehead hit the wall again, and he was alone. He stayed there for several minutes—no need to antagonize anyone. At last satisfied that he was alone, he located his shredded notebook in the alley and went home to put something on his face. He was stepping on toes. Fat chance he was letting this story go.

— —

Tate showed up for work with a scraped cheek, a deep bruise on his forehead, and a dozen questions flung at him by his coworkers. A series of outlandish answers put these to rest and, by the reactions he got, convinced him that no one in the office was in cahoots with his assailant. When the meeting broke up and Tanner was ensconced behind closed doors with the assistant editor, Tate scooted out.

The newspaper's flivver sat unattended near the front door of the building, the key conveniently in the switch on the coil box. Tate studied the Ford's hand crank. He was not particularly mechanical, and he could break his arm in a backfire. On the other hand, considering the distance to the schoolhouse, being away from his desk for an extended time was also asking for trouble. He casually circled the car, checking whether he had an audience. Satisfied no one was around, he flipped, pulled, and adjusted the various knobs and switches to choke, prime, and gear up the Tin Lizzie. Then he walked back up front and gave it a half crank. Miraculously, the machine sputtered to life.

The school stood at the corner of Sixth and Chestnut. The one-room white batten-board building stood like a sentinel gatekeeper between the spacious houses of the affluent Nevis merchants, and the smaller downtown abodes of its workers. Tate didn't enter, but grabbed the green-painted milk box from the porch and stood on it to peer through a side window.

The classroom had about a dozen children watching the teacher write on the chalkboard. Jack wasn't one of them. Driven by a hunch, perhaps informed by his own less-than-fond educational experiences, Tate walked around to the back entrance. There was Jack, bristle brush in hand and a metal bucket at his elbow as he scrubbed the rear steps of the building. Tate found a dry spot and sat down. "Things not working out?" he asked.

Jack mumbled something and kept scrubbing.

"Could use your help this morning on Parkers Wharf. Want me to see if I can set you free?"

Jack kept his head down but nodded.

Tate disappeared around the side of the building and reappeared several minutes later with a smug look. "Come on, Jack. If anyone asks, your uncle from Pittsburgh is still very sick. Come on. I need your brain."

Jack laid the brush across the top of the bucket and hurried off after Tate. They rode in silence until they reached First and Chestnut, where Tate pulled out of the roadway and idled under one of the sprawling chestnuts lining the street.

"Okay, here's the deal, Jack. I need to know if you've found out anything else about the Parkers Wharf setup."

"Gonna cost you," Jack said, running his hand along the Ford's smooth black door frame.

"Come on, Jack. We negotiated this yesterday." Tate made a U-turn and began retracing their route. "If you're going to be greedy, I'm taking you back to school. Tell your teacher that your uncle made a sudden, miraculous recovery."

"No, he hasn't," Jack said with a sigh. "It's Father McGee running the show down there. I think the beer they used to make for the park is now being brewed at the church."

The car stopped with a jerk. "The Germans are brewing right in Saint Raphael?"

Jack looked at him as if he had two heads. "Not *inside*. Out in the woods. Nobody goes down that way unless they have to. It's a *church*, for God's sake."

No, son. It's a church with a bootlegging operation. Front-page news. "Get us in and out without being seen, and I can assure you, Jack Byrne, there'll be a bonus in there for you. But there is one more thing. Did you, by chance, talk to anyone about our little trip down to the waterfront?"

"No."

"Because last night I got my face rearranged by someone who didn't approve. Now, *I* didn't tell anyone, and as jittery as Mr. Millman was, I'm pretty sure he didn't blab. That would leave only you."

Jack looked at him with big eyes and closed lips.

"Okay, if that's the way you want it. I thought we were partners. You do realize I'm going to get roughed up again if I don't understand what's going on?"

"Officer McCall. He wanted to know why I wasn't in school. I told him I was helping you with a very important story about illegal liquor. I'm sorry, but I had to tell him something. He threatened to throw me in the pokey. Isn't honesty the best policy?"

"Son, I seriously doubt you'd know honest if it bit . . . never mind. Did he say anything else?"

Jack pursed his lips and then slowly pulled a wadded dollar bill from his pocket. "He wants me to keep him informed . . . so he can help."

"Tell me you didn't buy that."

Jack shook his head, but Tate could see the confusion in the boy's eyes. "Put that away and don't spend it in all in the same place. You see, Jack, there are good people and bad people in this world. Right now there seem to be more of the latter hanging around, and some of them can do you a world of hurt. I don't want that. You take me down to the wharf and then lie low, stop skipping school, and steer clear of Chief McCall. I'm going to keep you in the dark for a while so you don't have to worry about lying."

He turned the car south on Main Street and headed for Parkers Wharf, relying on the boy to get him down a series of backwoods lanes that crossed rickety bridges and twisted like the copperheads that frequented the area in warmer weather. Then, abruptly, they broke out into open space and fields that rolled down to a small white church sitting by the sparkling waters of the Chesapeake Bay. Tate paused at the top of the hill as another car climbed the hill toward them. "Fine work, Jack, but I didn't want to advertise I was here."

Jack pointed right, to a dirt track that veered off through the uppermost field. "Relax, we're going this way."

Tate stopped and backed off the road. But he didn't go far. His dad had taught him to embrace his hunches. He hunkered down in his seat and waved at Jack to do likewise. The other car passed by moments later.

"I'll be damned," Tate said as the car sped away. "The mayor—he's Catholic?"

Jack gave the usual shrug. "Miz McClelland says he's the biggest heathen this side of Solomons."

"Well, apparently, he's found religion." Tate shoved another dime at Jack. "Now, get me down where I can see the stills. Looks like it's payday for both of us."

CHAPTER TWENTY

Entertaining Offers

The trip to Parkers Wharf had been a brilliant move, and yet Jackson fumed. Prentis was a no-show this Monday morning. In fact, they hadn't spoken since their little tiff Friday night. Prentis was naturally pigheaded, and Jackson blamed his own poor behavior on the Camilla effect. He would apologize the first chance he got, because as much as he hated to admit it, Jackson couldn't operate without his chief of staff managing the town council. They were a fractious lot—half of them invested in the good of the town's people, and the others devoted entirely to the interests of Nevis's business elite—but to a man, cronies of his father, and he wished them gone.

To take his mind off his wayward friend, stymied business aspirations, and the woman he seemed forever doomed to worship from afar, Jackson sat at his desk watching Fanny Byrne in the reception area as she refilled her fountain pen. She was an efficient secretary, but he missed the rapport he had developed with crotchety Mrs. Hasson. She was blunt and kept him honest on those rare days when he was tempted to be otherwise. Fanny Byrne was still an unknown.

He got up and walked to the window near her desk. The weather was dismal, and the blue Bayland flag at the end of the street drooped lifelessly around its pole. "Good weekend, Miss Byrne?"

She screwed the lid back on the inkwell, pressed the pen's nib against a blotter, and looked up, eyes sparkling. "We spent most of Saturday at Saint Peter's bull roast. Saturday night, Danny took me to Bayland—a sky full of stars, dancing to "A Pretty Girl Is Like a Melody." It was wonderful."

"Irving Berlin?"

"Yes, but not him. The singer was nobody famous. It all ended much too soon. Sometimes Danny is a little . . ." She shrugged and offered a forced smile.

"If you don't mind my saying so, you and Daniel are the perfect couple. Why, in no time at all, I can see the two of you settling down and running that store of his. Just give a heads-up because it will be hard to replace a dedicated worker like you."

Fannie blushed and put her pen down. "I don't know, Mr. Dwyer. And Danny's store hasn't been doing as well as he'd hoped."

"Don't worry too much over it. All businesses have their good and bad times. Maybe someone will come along someday and buy him out— give him a crack at something new. And when they do, I hope you let me know right away. I'll take you both to dinner at the Bayside Hotel." He drummed his fingers happily on her desk and headed back to his.

"So, Danny told you about the deal?"

Jackson froze mid step. "What deal might that be?" he asked.

"To sell the shop. Someone made him an offer that's almost too good to be true—an outrageous amount of money."

"Would that be . . . someone from Nevis?"

"Oh, dear," Fannie said, her eyes growing large. "I should probably stop talking or Danny will be upset. Mr. Dwyer, please don't mention it to anyone."

Jackson tried to keep his eyes focused on her, but all he could see were little Ollies jumping off the end of the pier, where they were promptly snatched up by ravenous blue crabs. "Oh, no, dear. Your secret is safe with me. But you know the old saw about things sounding too good to be true? Tell him to think it through a while before he gives an answer."

"I have, Mr. Dwyer, and he did," she said. "A whole day before he agreed to sell the whole kit and caboodle. They're drawing up papers today."

The front door opened, and to Jackson's relief, Prentis came in. He gave Jackson a guarded look as he hung his hat by the door.

"Prentis, just the man I need to see. A word?" Jackson asked, cocking his head toward his office."

"Yes. Be right in as soon as I get a cuppa joe."

"Now. Bring the hat."

Jackson followed him to the office and closed the door. Prentis took his customary chair by the window, but Jackson didn't let him get too comfortable. "We need to talk."

Prentis held up a hand. "I should apologize. It was rude of me to interrupt your personal time Friday night. It was neither the time nor place. I do hope you patched up your misunderstanding with Camilla."

"Under the bridge," Jackson said. "We're all doing our best during this difficult time. And no, she's still mad as a snake. Something about local options in the newspaper. That fool of a young reporter, I'll bet. But more pressing at the moment," he said, shaking his head, "I need you to check on something. Immediately."

"Sure. Father McGee said no and you've reconsidered Tarkington?"

"Hardly. McGee said he'd get right back to me, and I'm positive that Parker's Wharf will pan out. No, this is something more pressing. I thought you said Millman wasn't entertaining offers to sell his place. It seems someone just offered him a boatload of cash to sell his business. Did you know?"

Prentis shook his head and picked up the latest edition of the *Evening Star*. "Anything in this one about our efforts to curb liquor?"

"Put your paper down, damn it. I thought Robert, the star accountant, was staying on this. If I didn't need him to calculate the budget shortfall for next year, he'd be looking for another paycheck. You need to find out if it's Tarkington, or somebody from Philly."

Prentis lowered the paper. "Coffee, a quick look at the world, and I'll get right on it."

Jackson shoved his own freshly poured mug at him. "Time, essence, skedaddle."

Prentis looked at the wall clock. "What about our meeting on the trawlers and dredgers? I don't have time to go anywhere and get back in time. Ollie's isn't going anywhere without a decent oyster business," he said with a wink.

"There is no Ollie's without that property. Never back away from a sudden opportunity, Prentis."

Prentis studied him intently for a moment. "And I'm doing my best to follow that, Jackson." He accepted the coffee and headed out.

As he approached the front door, it flew open, knocked the cup from his hand, and sent him staggering back toward Fanny's desk. "Ow! Hot, hot!" Prentis yelped, shaking his scalded fingers and sticking them in his mouth.

Lloyd, copyboy at the *Evening Star,* barreled in, out of breath and flush-faced. Ignoring Prentis, he turned to Jackson.

"Your packing house, sir," he panted. "It's engulfed in flames!"

CHAPTER TWENTY-ONE

Railing

Black and yellowcoated firefighters swarmed like wasps around the remains of Dwyer's Oyster Cannery, now reduced to a heap of glowing embers and half a back wall. Billowing clouds of smoke pushed their way up through the beginnings of a soft late spring rain as a damp, acrid smell filled the air and hung there. Jackson pushed the end of a charred oak door around with the toe of his shoe. The town's bright red pumper fire truck, a days-old American LaFrance beauty worth more than Jackson's house and everything in it, stood idly by, its forty gallons of water long since expended uselessly against the conflagration. From floor to roof peak, the building had been constructed entirely of wood. It was a catastrophic loss as soon as the fire began.

Jackson felt a sudden kinship with Pitney Benson and the rest of the deep-woods moonshiners. Their sense of overwhelming loss and impotent rage was no doubt much like his. It rose like bile in his throat. He turned away as the brigade hooked their pike poles onto the top of the remaining wall and brought it down. Prentis stood behind him, pacing back and forth between Jackson and the pier, his hands shoved deep into his coat pockets.

Jackson looked at the knot of gawkers gathered on the steamboat pier. Arsonists loved to watch their work. Whoever had started the fire was likely right there, observing the whole affair. He recognized the faces. It hurt to think the culprit could be someone he knew.

"Think," Jackson said. "Did you use any ill-chosen turns of phrase with Tarkington? 'Over my dead body,' for instance?"

"Of course not, though I might've said that we prefer the 'nothing's on fire' approach. Whatever I might have said, *'Play ball or else'* is the answer."

"Doesn't make sense. There's some half a dozen other properties along here they could purchase. They wouldn't have had to torch anything."

"Sure, it does—makes all kinds of sense. We said they can't play here. They'll only accept *yes*. Did you run into anyone on your trip to see McGee? Anybody else got a beef with you?"

Jackson threw him an incredulous look. "I'm mayor. Is there anyone who *doesn't* have a beef? It was just Father McGee and me."

"Well," Prentis said, "perhaps we'd better reassess the *no* answer, don't you think?"

"There will be no reassessing." Jackson stepped away from the rubble and walked back toward the courthouse. Prentis went, too, but kept his mouth shut, which Jackson thought a wise decision. Jackson wouldn't give them the satisfaction of watching him react. Politics and personal issues could wait till he was behind closed doors.

"Mr. Mayor! Mayor Dwyer." It was Shoemaker, cutting catty-corner across Main Street to intercept them. "Can I get a quote, sir? Any possible connection to the pharmacy break-in the other night? You have a take on the recent uptick of violence in Nevis?"

Jackson just walked faster, and Prentis gave the reporter a cold stare as they passed. "No comment. Does Tanner know you're out here badgering the mayor?" He trotted until he drew abreast of Jackson. "I gotta have a word with Riley Tanner about that one."

"Let's deal with Tarkington first," Jackson whispered as they walked. "I have three other properties in town. Hire some dicks to keep an eye on them. I'll have Fannie contact the Chesapeake Insurance Company. I guess I should thank them for clearing my lot for me. As soon as it's cool, I'm rebuilding. While you're at it, go over to Nevis First National and find out where the money offer for Danny Millman's property is coming from, before half the waterfront is razed. If it's Tarkington, I'm going to hunt him down and have him arrested for loitering, spitting on sidewalks, or anything else that could possibly stick."

— —

Prentis was back within the hour. "Mr. Dunnard at First National says the money for the deal was wired from the Regional Bank of Delaware, and the buyer's proxy will be Jack Kettering, its president."

"Delaware," Jackson repeated as he motioned for him to close the door. "Dunnard and Kettering—they acquainted?"

"Dunnard ceased being chatty when I pushed on Kettering, so I'd venture he knows him—maybe not personally, but enough to be wary of talking freely about him."

"Hmm."

"If you want to send me back out again, let's be quick about it," Prentis said, tugging at his jacket. "This suit needs to go. I reek of smoke."

"I need a minute to think," Jackson said. "Tarkington?"

"Dunnard claims not to know him. But I was able to touch base with someone who knows things."

"Another of your *confidential* sources?"

"Of course. Aren't they always the best?"

Jackson looked outside. The rain had lifted, and the sky was bluing up in places, though obscured by smoky haze. *His* haze. "Depends on what we owe them in return. Tarkington's people in Delaware—do they want Millman's operation for bottling bootleg beer, or they going to use the dockside location to ferry it out to boats waiting off the coast? Or maybe both?"

Prentis pulled a small silver flask from his jacket and took a swig. "The source thinks the interest in Millman's is not really about the location or the profit to be made by pumping a little money into a cash-strapped business. It's related to the alcohol used in the production of varnish."

"They want to produce liquor right out on the wharf?"

Prentis took a second nip and tucked the flask away. "The industrial complex in the Delaware Valley has ready access to alcohol, but the feds aren't giving it a blind eye. The place is crawling with agents trying to make a case on Volstead violations. Millman's place provides direct water access, it has a bottling facility attached, and he ships in alcohol to make his varnish—although it's the undrinkable kind. If someone from the Valley denatured the alcohol and increased production, they could create a profitable hooch operation and none would be the wiser."

"So, the corruption is moving south."

"*Has* moved south. We need to negotiate the best terms while we can, Jackson."

Jackson gave Prentis a smug look. "So, you're telling me there's a common purpose: pursuing my Ollie's oyster crackers and protecting the town from these miscreants." He chuckled. "Has the Millman sale been completed, or can we outmaneuver that eel Tarkington?"

"No signatures yet. Depends on whether Millman will break a gentleman's agreement. He's a principled young man. But you're missing the point here, boss," Prentis said. "Millman is a side issue. If it's not his place, it'll be somewhere else. This isn't the time to stick it to anyone."

Jackson sniffed at his own shirt and said, "We both smell like a forest fire. I'm going home to change, and you do the same. But hightail it right back and get an offer to Millman as fast as can. If he's afraid his own place will go up in smoke, he'll be eager to get out of there. He needs to know someone else can bail him out. Triple whatever Nathan has promised him."

"I'm not some damn lackey. What's the matter with Miss Impressive Résumé?" Prentis asked, giving an eye roll toward the reception area. Why can't *she* call? Get her all excited and she'll seal the deal with her honey right over the phone. On the other hand, if you think she's gonna blab business, get rid of her. I happen to know an excellent replacement."

"Her services have been more than adequate—certainly, better than any with the surname Tanner. I don't trust anyone right now. Go make the offer. If he agrees, don't leave without getting it in writing. Gentlemen's agreements aren't worth the paper they're written on."

"Not last time I checked," Prentis said, donning his hat. "I'll go take care of this stuff, but I'm only going because nobody in their right mind wants a large-scale bootlegger right out on Main Street. When I get back, we'll discuss calling Tarkington in and arranging a truce. If you're not okay with that, I'm tendering my resignation. I spent the entire weekend coming to terms with this mess, Jackson. Nobody needs an adviser they never listen to."

"Oh, we're going to call him in and have a very serious discussion. But a truce? That's not going to happen."

Prentis heaved a long-suffering sigh. "And while I'm gone, you sit put, don't do anything rash, and keep your mouth shut. No fighting fire with fire. Understood?"

"Perfectly, Prentis. Now, go take care of business, and make it quick. We're going to run that son of a bitch out on a rail, and I will relish it."

CHAPTER TWENTY-TWO

The Shill

Prentis flew out the rear entrance of the courthouse. With Jackson's hardnosed thinking, his administration was teetering on the edge of the abyss. Voters in Nevis drank, and all the feds in Maryland wouldn't keep them from their liquor. Whoever provided it was golden, and those golden boys were not to be toyed with. Meanwhile, Prentis was in no mood to find a new meal ticket, and he certainly wasn't going to fall on his sword for his friend. He started for the slip of paper he had been carrying around for weeks in his breast pocket, then remembered he had tossed it on a whim after deciding that he couldn't use the contact information. But he had been tempted many times and knew its contents by heart.

He doubted Jackson would be watching him, but heeded his instincts all the same, heading downtown a few blocks before doubling back on Second Street to Bayland. The ticket taker waved him through the park entrance without a ticket—positions of political influence did have their perks. If he were king, the pretentious, horse-topped masonry passageway would be one of the first things to go. If he were king, many things would change. . . .

Bayland's speakeasy was located behind Rose's saltwater taffy shop at the far end of the park. Prentis followed the graceful sweep of the grand promenade, past half a dozen candy-striped awnings: funnel cakes, pink cotton candy, sticky popcorn. He ducked into Rose's.

"Do you have any watermelon taffy made fresh?" he asked the plump woman filling a display case with tan and green striped confections.

She nodded and whisked him into the saloon, through a private entrance behind a curtain in the kitchen. The place was no match for Mumbles. Its dark wood tables, dim lighting, and few quiet patrons lost in their thoughts and suds created a dreary atmosphere. At ten in the morning, these were the serious drinkers, who had beer for breakfast, then dragged their life's woes from joint to joint until they staggered home at suppertime to slap the wife and kids around. The Prohibitionists had a legitimate beef with them.

A waiter in a crisp white shirt, with hair slicked down so tightly that looked like three coats of lacquer, scurried up to greet him. Before Prentis had a chance to speak, the young man whisked him down a short hallway to a snug but private room with a small round table and four chairs, two of which were already occupied.

Nathan Tarkington looked up from his menu and blinked twice. "So nice to see you again, Mr. Gant. Care to join us?"

Prentis sat down across from him and nodded to the other man. "Chief McCall. Doing triple duty, I see." The policeman studied him a moment over the top of his beer stein but said nothing. "Take a hike," Prentis said.

McCall's gaze shifted to Tarkington, who nodded. McCall grunted and left, carrying his beer with him.

The waiter reappeared briefly. "Our special menu, sir." He handed Prentis a small red folder.

"Start us off with highballs," Tarkington said, raising two fingers. The waiter nodded and left again.

Prentis flipped open the menu. While Mumbles was charging a few cents for libations just a cut above rotgut, this high-rolling establishment appeared to be awash in the finest Kentucky bourbon, French champagne, and highballs that would soak you for as much as a dollar a pop.

"Bubbles may not be as fancy as Mumbles," Tarkington said, nodding at the menu, "but you have to admit, the selection can't be beat. Glad you decided to drop by. After your message to my associate the other evening, I was beginning to worry that there would never be a chance to sort things out."

Prentis put down the menu and looked around. "There is a case to be made for ambience. The Chesapeake Railway Express another quiet partner in the ever-widening world of Nevis bootlegging?"

Tarkington shrugged. "It would be a little naive to think any railroad would sit this one out. That would be a poor business decision."

"And how *is* business?"

"Which one?" Tarkington said with a Cheshire smile. He pushed a bowl of peanuts across the table.

"The one that has you burning down half the waterfront?"

Tarkington shook his head. "Sad state of affairs, isn't it? Why would anyone want to destroy other people's things?"

"Because they're greedy sons of bitches who will do whatever it takes?"

"I'm sure the two bodies discovered on the pier over the weekend wouldn't share that sentiment. Too bad they didn't have a place like this. Not members of Mumbles, I take it?"

"As long as someone's busting up the local stills, Mumbles doesn't have enough booze to stay open."

"A speakeasy without liquor doesn't say much. With a consistent supplier like the one Bubbles has, Mumbles could be doing quite well. The liquor here is safe, varied, reliable. Just think of all the lives we could save."

"Yeah, the altruistic motivation smacked me in the face the moment I cleared the taffy counter." Prentis leaned forward. "Listen. How about we cut to the chase? We can't afford to have you incinerate the waterfront. How do we tap into the safe, varied, and reliable supply?"

Tarkington's lighthearted banter and effervescence vanished. "Where's the mayor?"

"Tied up, but I have his full confidence." A half-truth, but in this negotiation, Prentis needed whatever clout he could pretend to have.

"I need a face-to-face."

"I can get you an audience, but first you need to stop with the torching and the break-ins. Then I'll get your audience, and potentially a lot more."

"You made it very clear at our last meeting that I could take a hike. Which is what I did, no questions asked. But let's be frank. Without liquor to sell, this park will be all but shuttered by Labor Day. The German beer craftsmen will be out of business, and the railroad will choke off the flow of visitors by directing its trains and schedules elsewhere. Sandy Point, maybe."

It seemed that Tarkington had been expecting him. Prentis hated being predicted. "Where are you getting this from?"

"Procuring information is what I do. Then I put people together to maximize their profit from said information . . . create business arrangements."

"*Those people*—that's the information I need right now. Who would be the business associates?"

"It's too early in the process for me to tell you that. Let me just say that these associates can keep the park and Nevis afloat through these difficult times."

"Afloat in illegal liquor."

"Well, yes, of course. That goes without saying. All buying and selling of liquor is illegal. Prohibition is the single biggest economic mistake of the twentieth century, after Communism. It doesn't take a genius to see corruption rolling in to make a profit. One need only look at what's going on in Chicago. Money always talks, sir. It's just a question of how many businesses go under, and how many politicians get tarred and feathered, before the feds acknowledge their folly and repeal all this nonsense."

Prentis watched the middleman shell another peanut and toss the shell onto the table. He talked of breaking the law the way he might discuss where to pop in for a bite to eat. He lived free from the impediment of any moral compass whatever.

"You look shocked. What were you expecting?"

"I've seen people skirt and break the law, but never with such relish. The prospect of getting thrown in the clink doesn't dampen your enthusiasm the least little bit?"

Tarkington's smile returned. "It's a cat-and-mouse game. We hide and carry on business; they try to root us out. They think of new ways to put poison in alcohol, and I accept the challenge of removing whatever evil potion they're throwing in there. You know, if they would stop denaturing the stuff, fewer decent, otherwise law-abiding citizens would be crippled or killed drinking that stuff. They have no regard for Billy down the street who just wants to end the day with a nightcap."

Prentis watched him dexterously shell a peanut with one hand. He gave up trying to resist and took one, too. "We need a guarantee that you won't hang us out to dry when the heat turns up and the vice squad is camped out on the courthouse steps. You're going to keep us out of trouble. Understood?"

"Quite. I'd love to take credit for the pharmacy burglary, by the way, but alas . . ." Tarkington shrugged. "As for the rest? Absolutely. As you have already surmised, there are participants, and there are bystanders. Why look on from the sidelines when you can take part? Opportunity doesn't often knock twice." He pulled a white business envelope from his breast pocket and slid it across the table. "The agreement is solely about liquor."

"Right," Prentis said, leaving the bulging envelope untouched but wondering what denominations made up its thickness. "No gambling, no peep shows, pornography, or painted floozies. And no power grab of Nevis political offices."

"None, I assure you, although I can't guarantee what nonassociates might envision."

"And one final thing, Mr. Tarkington. Danny Millman's place is off-limits. Cancel your sale."

"*Nathan,* please, if we're going to be business partners. Cancel the Millman deal? I'm afraid I can't accommodate you there. It's a fait accompli."

Prentis shook his head. "Not acceptable. A deal with him or a deal with us—which is it?"

"Why the interest? It's a failing business. The kid will walk away with enough to start fresh. You'd deprive him of a great opportunity?"

"The reason is none of your concern. I'm sure another chance will come along for Mr. Millman. Cancel or no deal."

Tarkington picked up his empty highball glass and lightly rattled the ice. "I'll consider it, but it may be too late, and other partners' plans would have to be unmade. What you have to consider is what a deal is worth to *you.* There are other parties interested in relocating to

Nevis, and it won't be long before you're having this same conversation with someone else—someone you have no rapport with, someone who doesn't even know the word. They're coming, and I can guarantee you they won't be nearly as accommodating." He stood up. "Don't make a decision based on Millman. Get back to me soon. We're all running out of time."

Prentis eyed the envelope and then Tarkington's retreating back. The man looked cocksure even while walking away. Prentis had to admire his skills, though not his causes. The two of them were not so different—two puppet masters vying for control. He understood what made Nathan tick. Make an offer to Millman at triple the money, and Nathan could just up the ante. Control and good faith in negotiation were the issues here. He would leave Millman alone and hope Nathan made a gracious concession to step away from the property. Meanwhile, he needed to steer Jackson in the right direction.

Prentis looked at the empty highball glasses and his nearly empty stein. He recognized the ale. It was a local German one, and the brewer clearly knew his trade. He pulled the envelope over. The stack of bills inside would spend just like honestly made money—and potentially ruin a lifelong friendship. He drained his stein, tucked the money in his inside jacket pocket, and headed back to City Hall.

■ ━

Jackson peered down Main Street again. Still no Prentis. Obviously, Millman had refused to stoop to everyone else's level and break his verbal agreement to sell to Tarkington. *Triple the money.* How could that not be attractive to the impoverished young man? If Millman only knew the trouble his business scruples would cause.

As he pondered these things, he saw a man with a familiar stride come out of the park and head back into town. What did Prentis need in the park when Millman was down at the wharf? Jackson returned to his desk, put his feet up, and waited.

"How do we deal with Millman now?" Jackson asked, pouncing on Prentis before he even cleared the doorway.

Prentis closed the door quietly behind him and sat down. "Let me tell you, sir, where money is concerned, there is little honor—except where Daniel Millman is concerned. We're at an impasse. He's refused to budge from his understanding with Tarkington."

"So why were you wasting time at the park when you could have been finessing him? Are you sure you tried hard enough? Or maybe your skills are slipping."

Prentis gave him a withering look. "My skills are just fine, and I gave it my all, as I always do. How did you know I was at the park?"

Jackson pointed to his window.

"Uh . . . Alice wanted to talk to me."

"What'd you do, take her for a ride through the tunnel of love?"

"What?"

"Don't you have *any* morality? It's a little public for courting a mistress, don't you think?"

"No, no. I met with Millman near there, and she said it was urgent, so I asked her to meet me inside." Prentis felt the tips of his ears burning. He cleared his throat. "What could I say? Rest assured, we were discreet. I have a lovely wife to protect, remember? But I can't keep anything from you, now, can I?"

Jackson's feet hit the floor with a thud. "Enough about Alice. Exactly what did the man say?"

Prentis slapped the arms of his chair with both hands. "Cheese and crust, Jackson! Don't try to read between the lines, especially with someone as forthright as Daniel Millman. Face it, the kid is not remotely interested. Call in Nathan and give him what for! And while you're at it, try to find some common ground we all can survive on."

"*Nathan,* is it?"

"We can call him anything you want. Stop nitpicking and call. Conduct yourself like a mayor, or get the hell out so someone else can."

Jackson sprang to his feet.

Prentis stood up, glaring. "Y'know? I'm done with this mess. You'll have my formal resignation in the morning."

Jackson pulled Tarkington's calling card from under his desk blotter and shoved it at him. "The three of us, after hours, off the books."

CHAPTER TWENTY-THREE

Bum's Rush

Her stylish black shift, accentuated by several strands of lustrous pearls at the neck and a cummerbund at the waist, set her well apart from the locals. At first glance, he took her for just one more, moneyed do-gooder from out of town. But when Honora Lally made herself comfortable in Jackson Dwyer's office that late afternoon, lit up a Havana corona gorda, and looked him square in the eye, he decided there was probably nothing good about her. So he dismissed the idea of pleasantries over coffee and got right to it.

"Good afternoon, Miss Lally. Your message said you want to discuss business activities, but I'm confused about whether this is official business or something related to my personal holdings."

"Good afternoon, Mayor Dwyer," she said, eyes narrowing as she blew smoke from her heavily rouged lips. "Let's call it unofficially official."

"Um, okay," Jackson said, frowning. "Unofficially official" sounded like a term his father would have enjoyed.

"I'm here as an intermediary for a consortium of investors who are interested in creating a revenue stream from this area," she said. "They've conducted a lengthy and most thorough analysis and have concluded that such a venture would be of mutual benefit to them *and* the Nevis community."

Jackson studied her through an ever-thickening miasma of smoke. "Could you be more specific?"

"To be blunt, Mr. Mayor . . ."

He hated blunt women.

". . . Nevis seems to need liquor, and I'm in a position to supply it."

Yes, Miss Lally was a woman right out of Dad's playbook. "Well, that's certainly not mincing words. Let me ask my secretary to hold all calls."

He found Fanny sitting at her desk, filing her nails—ready to work, but with apparently nothing to do. "Fanny," he whispered, leaning in close, "I don't believe she's in a hurry to be ushered out. It's of the utmost urgency that you find Prentis and have him convey my regrets that I will be unable to attend our meeting, and have it rescheduled. He's down at Miller's field."

"On it, sir," she said with a smile, grabbing her purse. "Prentis, Miller's field, reschedule."

He returned to his office, praying that Prentis and Tarkington wouldn't come here for him. "Coffee?" Not waiting for an answer, he poured a single cup. Black. With half a dozen heaping spoonfuls of sugar. This was one tough broad to survive in a man's world of bootlegging. Or maybe she was a federal enforcement agent. He splashed the spoon around in the cup several times and sat back down. He could do hard-nosed, too. "What you're proposing would, of course, be illegal."

"Not really," she said, smiling at his cup. "Volstead isn't foolproof. You just have to know how the exemptions work. We have lawyers you can speak with if you're uncomfortable."

"I don't believe we'd be interested in trying to second-guess the Volstead Act, Miss Lally."

She discarded her cigar in a nearby ashtray and ran her fingers down a row of pearls. "Luckily for you, it isn't a question of second-guessing anything. There's a system already in place that's working quite nicely: producers, buyers, sellers, and a cadre of top-notch lawyers to keep everyone out of trouble. All you have to do is appreciate what we're about, let us take care of the details, and sit back and reap a wisely earned profit."

Jackson sipped his coffee. Yes, his father always had a few such lawyers, and their ability to keep the old crook out of jail had awed him. Jackson had shown them the door right after the mayoral election ballots were tallied. And this woman—she spoke so openly about what was obviously a massive bootlegging operation. He really didn't want to hear specifics. "While I can take it under consideration, I'm afraid, Miss Lally, at the moment, Nevis has its hands full with other priorities. Perhaps Friendship, to the north, or Solomons, to the south, could offer better business opportunities." He checked his wristwatch.

"You were an aviator?" she asked, admiring the watch.

"Unfortunately, I did not have the honor. It belonged to my son, Reynolds. Sent back from France with the rest of his things."

For the first time, her expression softened. "My brother, also. The ultimate sacrifice. You have my most sincere condolence and thanks."

He nodded and rose from his desk. "Would there be anything else I can do for you today?"

"Here. If you'd like to reconsider," she said, producing yet another calling card. "But before I go, there is some helpful information you could provide me. The late Mayor Dwyer—where is he buried? I promised someone I'd pay respects to our dear old friend before leaving town."

"Saint Peter's," he said. "Did you know him well?"

"Oh, very."

He found her smile unsettling. "Well, it was a pleasure meeting you, Miss Lally. When you get out on the road, ask for directions." Jackson opened the hallway door and stepped out with her.

She nodded and headed for the stairs. "Yes, I will. And thank you for your time. I'll let my client know that we met and you were not remotely interested."

"For future reference, who would that be?" he called after her.

"John McClure, Philadelphia," she said, and was gone.

Heaven help him. There was no future. He had just given the bum's rush to the boss of the biggest political machine Pennsylvania had ever produced.

CHAPTER TWENTY-FOUR

A Little Competition

Jackson drilled the red ball across the thick, manicured lawn and sent Milton, his fox terrier, sprinting after it. "You're never here when I need you, Prentis. Where is all this cleaning up, smoothing over, and making nice that you promised me? Get me out of this." He waited for some lifesaving words to issue from Prentis's open, drooping mouth.

"For Chrissakes, I'm not a miracle worker! And may I remind you, I was off setting up a meeting for you." Prentis pulled the ball out of the dog's mouth and hurled it into the azalea bed. "Why didn't you feel her out before you opened your big yap and shut her down? Your concerns should have been obvious: entrapment by a federal agent or someone engaged in illegitimate activity! And *nobody* walks into a public office with that much bravado unless they have the muscle to back it up. Do I have to hold your hand all the time?" He dropped into the closest teak lawn chair and put his head in his hands.

"Don't deflect," Jackson said. "Dear old Dad was no doubt on a first-name basis with this crowd. You were up to your elbows in the muck, weren't you? You should have anticipated their arrival and advised the appropriate evasive action. Who, exactly, is this woman?"

"Well, to be fair, I was so busy cleaning up behind Chance, I never saw where his messes started." Prentis ran a hand through his coppery hair. "Who is Honora Lally? John J. McClure's right-hand girl, is who. As I understand it, if you want to talk to him, you've gotta go through her. Not one to be trifled with."

Jackson kicked the ball at his feet, and Milton dashed after it. "We're in a hard place. I'm afraid to leave my house."

Prentis looked up and laughed. "Like they don't know where you live. It's too late, Jackson. Buck up and pick the side that causes the least damage to the good people of Nevis. In this case, it's Tarkington. McClure is notorious. Maryland isn't exactly in his backyard, but who knows how far his influence extends?"

"Maybe I should take your advice. I'll resign first and just run my businesses. It's all I ever wanted to do, anyway. Camilla wouldn't like this. No matter what Dad thought, it never pays to skirt the law."

Prentis waved him off. "Wimp! I really thought there was more to you. Go run your little businesses, then. Keep trying to woo your unwooable maneater and leave the rest of us in the lurch. Maybe we'll figure it out."

"Name-calling solves nothing, you fool." Jackson sat down and pulled the terrier up into his lap. "There's nothing ignoble or cowardly about being a businessman. With their own money on the line, they quickly solve their own problems."

"There's nothing that says we can't run this town like a business—one that benefits all the people, not just the mayor and a few close chums. Use the skills God gave you."

"Right. And how do we turn this villains' joust to our healthy advantage?" Jackson ran his hand over the dark pattern in Milton's fur. The hand stopped. "*Unofficially official.* What if we make 'em *compete* for the concession to supply Nevis? Pit one group against the other?"

Prentis cocked an eyebrow. "We take bids and keep it all off the books? Now, that's the Jackson Dwyer I've come to respect. Unconventional, but I like it. With the right safeguards, we could step back from this mess and let others deal with any brouhaha."

"Do you think Tarkington will bolt as soon as he finds out who the competition is?"

"Uh-uh. I suspect old Nathan knows the score. He probably thought he could slide in here and sew things up long before McClure arrived."

"And the potential for a bloody turf war?"

"Which would start with us?" Prentis shook his head. "Don't see it. We're on the coast, good water access, but we're not the only one. The losing party will seek locations north or south of us. It'll all shake out."

Jackson put the dog down and brushed a leaf off his lap. "Question is, how do we get both parties to play off against each other? Do we trust them in the same room together?"

"They don't come any more confident than these two. Neither one's going to walk away. Call Miss Lally and invite her back in. Make her think you're ready to strike a deal. I'll relay the same to Tarkington. Same time, same location."

"Agreed, but let's not get cocky on this end, either. Are we really the best people to be negotiating on our own behalf? Who would you say is the most successful businessman in town?"

"Besides you?" Prentis asked, a twinkle of hope returning to his eyes. "Well, he's not really a townie, but Hubert Carr, Lawrence's son. "Rich, well known, a bit pompous but he's our man. Make him feel important, put a decent cut in his pocket, and he'll make sure we're protected. Give him a title, too, and we'll be running hooch operations from Maryland to Delaware. Think he'd like 'liquor czar'?

"Pompous doesn't begin to cut it, but yeah, he'd probably love it if he's not a dry. Do we know?"

"I've seen him drink."

Jackson smiled. "Perfect. Get busy on your end with Tarkington. I'll contact the other two so we can get them all in here and strike a deal."

"Jackson?" Prentis asked, putting on his hat and adjusting the brim.

"Yeah?"

"I haven't seen you smile in weeks. You look like you just found out you're the long-lost son of John D. Rockefeller. If I'm not mistaken, I think you've hopped off the straight and narrow and are beginning to enjoy walking on the dark side."

"Hardly," Jackson said. "I'm merely being pragmatic. Only one group walks out of our meeting looking good. Want to know who?"

"You have no idea."

"*Us.* The townspeople are happy, I keep my reputation, and Camilla doesn't hate me. Why, the feeling is almost as freeing as choosing a point on the compass and heading off into the twilight on a motorbike."

CHAPTER TWENTY-FIVE

All Bets on Washington

Nathan Tarkington winked at Fannie Byrne, took a step into the mayor's office, and pulled up short. "Did I get my time wrong?" he asked, looking around at the roomful of people. His eyes finally settled on Prentis.

"No, you're aces," Jackson said, waving him in. "Miss Lally, this is Nathan Tarkington. He'll be joining the discussion today."

"Nice to see you again." Her brow furrowed, and her countenance darkened. She turned back to Jackson and said, "Anyone else?"

At that moment, the door opened again, and in swept a tall, elegant man who moved as if he had a train to catch.

"Just Mr. Carr here. How are you, sir?" Jackson asked, extending his hand and then directing the new arrival to the chair next to Prentis's, at the end of Jackson's desk. He nodded at Honora sitting on the loveseat and Tarkington to her right. "Now we can begin. Seeing as how we're all busy people, I'm going to let Mr. Carr launch right into things. Sir?"

The man put on his spectacles and peered over them, smiling affably. Then he took control of the room, just as Jackson had hoped he would. Jackson leaned back in his chair and relaxed a bit.

"Miss Lally, Mr. Tarkington, gentlemen," Carr said. "A little introduction might be in order. I'm Hubert Carr. Among other business interests, I am the executive vice president of the Bayland Partnership, and managing partner of the Bayland amusement park here in Nevis."

He paused to tidy the sheaf of papers he had brought with him. "In light of recent overtures made to the town, I've been put under retainer to study the provisions of the Eighteenth Amendment and the Volstead Act—that is, prohibition, production, sale, and transportation of intoxicating liquors—as it relates to the alcohol situation in Nevis. Specifically, what is the best course of action for the town to follow in consideration of said act, enforcement as determined by the state, and what is occurring in the neighboring jurisdictions, including the overall state of affairs on the Eastern Seaboard. That would, of course, include the overtures made by the various groups you represent. Before I go any further, any discussions here today will be in the strictest of confidence. Do we have the affidavits, Mr. Gant?"

Prentis popped up and distributed one to each participant.

"I'm not signing this," Miss Lally said, thrusting it back at Prentis

"You're joking," Tarkington said, laughing. "You expect this to stand up in court?"

"If you can't sign the confidentiality agreement, I'm afraid I must bid you good day," Hubert Carr said. "While we all can agree that the approach we are about to take is unorthodox to say the least, I think that we can also agree that our goal simply comes down to good business—cooperative working relationships, adequate and fair margins of profit, and consumer satisfaction."

Jackson studied the three faces: self-assurance coming and going across Tarkington's chiseled features as he tried to appear calm; the sphinxlike expression on the heavily rouged Miss Lally; and the natural confidence exuded by Hubert Carr. Jackson found the suspense exhilarating.

"Ah, what the hell, no skin off my back," Tarkington said. He signed in the signature block and turned to his rival. "Have a nice day, Miss Lally. Lovely to see you again."

"When fish talk and pigs fly," she muttered, and she, too, scribbled across her paper.

"Now, then," Carr said, "let's put this as succinctly as possible. Maryland has refused to enact legislation supporting Prohibition—the only such state in the union, I'm proud to say. Nevis needs liquor. Each of you has come here of your own accord and offered to provide it—for a profit, naturally. To seriously consider either of your offers, additional information is needed. First, will the product be made on-site, or transported in? Second, what assurances can you provide that the operation will run smoothly and without any, shall we say, outside interference? Third and last, what's in it for the town financially? A monthly projection rounded to the nearest dollar is appreciated."

He put down his notes. "We'd like to make clear that Nevis will assume no liability for any approved activities and will deny any involvement if pushed to defend said activities. If you're still interested, we'd like a written prospectus no later than noon two days hence. That would make it Friday, the tenth. Depending on how many proposals we get, expect to hear back from me by Wednesday, the fifteenth."

Miss Lally glanced at Tarkington, who was staring intently at Carr. "There are others?" she asked, her face still emotionless but her voice rising in volume and pitch.

"Open to any and all legitimate bidders," Carr replied. "Any other concerns?"

"You may be hearing from me," she said. She shoved the affidavit at Prentis, nodded curtly at Jackson, and slammed the door behind her.

"I'd best get busy, too, then," Tarkington said. "It's been a pleasure, gentlemen, and a most interesting morning. Well played, I might add." He left snickering.

"I think that went rather well," Prentis said, reviewing the signed documents. "Not that I trust either of them."

"Well, they're both too dirty to involve the authorities, so I think we're okay," Jackson said. "Mr. Carr, you're a brilliant man. Thank you for your talents and your time."

"We try to stay the righteous path, gentlemen, but I have to admit, this little adventure is invigorating, and I suspect we will soon know how it all plays out."

From the stories he had heard, Jackson questioned how closely the Carr family stayed on any path, but this was not the occasion to mention it to Hubert.

"Hang on to your hats, gentlemen," Prentis said, chuckling. "This is going to be a whirlwind." He held up the affidavits, one in each hand. "Sworn to by none other than *George Washington* and *Andrew Volstead*. Are we really going to be able to stay ahead of these two?"

—·—

Tate Shoemaker peered over the top of yesterday's newspaper as he sat on a stone bench on the courthouse lawn. His weekly face-to-face meeting with the mayor had been postponed to some date in the nebulous future. He needed to know why. What had ended his string of four straight weeks of propagandized information dumps by the office? Was it his questions down at the wharf? It hadn't escaped his attention that Mayor Jackson's office had been burning the midnight oil for several evenings—an uncommon occurrence for any of the government offices.

He felt something hit his sleeve and eyed the gray squirrel scampering along a bough overhead. His choice to sit under an oak tree came with its risks, he supposed. He resumed watching the door as a fetching woman in a long duster coat and matching brown hat left in a hurry. She sped off in one of the Tin Lizzies parked in the gravel lot. He jotted down the gold numbers on the Pennsylvania license plate: 213685.

"*Psst, psst, psst.*" His paper rattled as something small and hard bounced off it and landed in his lap. Young Jack Byrne plunked down on the bench. "Whatcha looking at, Shoe?"

"Fish in a barrel," Tate growled, smoothing out his newspaper. "We'll talk later, okay?"

Jack burst out laughing. "I don't see no fish. Whatcha *really* looking at?"

"*Shh.* I'm on a secret mission. You go on, now. Beat it. I'll get you involved later."

"So, you're watching who's coming and going from the mayor's office? For another nickel, that's an easy one."

Tate's eyes darted between the boy and the building. Others had yet to walk out that door and drive off in all those remaining flivvers. "What do you know? And be quick."

Jack put his hand out.

"Information first. That's how the working world turns."

"You drive a hard bargain, Mr. Shoe. But seeing as how you're my best source of income right now, I'll give it to you on faith." He pointed up to the building's second story. "My sister, Fannie, works there. She's the mayor's secretary, and she brings his appointment book home every evening. She works hard, but she doesn't know how to play. If you want to know who he's meeting with, all ya gotta do is sneak the book out of her purse and take a peek."

Tate lowered the paper and smiled at his young henchman. "You get me a list of who met with Mayor Jackson today, son, and you've earned yourself a dime. In fact, if you can get me a list for all his guests this week, I'll give you two bits. Is that a piece of business you can handle?"

"What will you give me for the whole book?" Jack asked, eyes sparkling.

Jack's scope of thought was a little frightening in a kid of such tender years. With proper guidance, he would be capable of great things. Under the wrong sort of tutelage, though . . . Tate shuddered to think. He fished three quarters out of his pocket. "You know where to find me. But not a word to anyone, Jack Byrne, or we're both headed to the hoosegow."

He watched as two men left the building—not together, but in quick enough succession to have been in the same meeting. Like the woman, they were impeccably dressed. The first man drove off in a car with a Delaware license plate. The second, who walked out several minutes later, he knew. His face was plastered in several places around town—the eldest son of Lawrence Carr, the grand designer and financier of the Bayland amusement park. Finally, a lead Tate could follow, and a question to cogitate on. What mutual interest did Pennsylvania, Delaware, and the amusement park have that would be of interest to the mayor?

He folded up his paper and hightailed it back to the *Star,* where the archives overflowed with information, and tongues wagged freely.

CHAPTER TWENTY-SIX

Stoning Crows and Pickling Lizards

Tate found the newsroom uncharacteristically tranquil, as in *tomblike*. He took up a chair at Joe Richards's desk. "Where is everybody? Something I should know about?"

The senior reporter acknowledged his existence with a grunt and kept writing. "Nope. Cat's away . . ."

Tate's gaze trailed to Tanner's open door. "Influenza?"

Joe stopped writing. "What do you want, Shoemaker?"

"I need a favor."

"You always need a favor." The pen began scratching again.

"Today I can make it worth your while," he said, reaching for his money clip.

"Ha. Forget it. I'm worth more than you've got. Make it quick. I've got better things to do."

"If I were interested in running down some license plate numbers, one Pennsylvania and the other Delaware, who would I call?"

"Tanner ask you to run them down?"

"Yeah, he's breathing down my neck, too. Hush-hush, though."

"Tell me about it." Joe ripped a piece of paper loose and jotted down some telephone numbers. "These don't go anywhere else," he said, handing over the paper. "Eat 'em when you're done. Got it?"

Joe was a good guy as long as you didn't annoy him *too* much. Tate thanked him and walked back to his desk. The press was silent, and he could actually collect his thoughts.

Tate hung up the phone and stared at the license plate information: Nathan Tarkington, in New Castle, Delaware; and Honora Lally, near Philly in Delaware County, Pennsylvania. Somehow, he had expected to get an instant connection, a prize-winning, have-'em-shaking-in-their-boots story unfolding right before him, but no bells were ringing in his head. Precocious Jack Byrne was probably better at putting two and two together than he was. He looked up at the picture pinned next to his oblivious sweetheart, Ms. Pickford. *What am I missing, Dad?*

The only person feeling happy and fulfilled seemed to be Wayne. Tate marveled at his good mood as he hummed to himself in his thankless, mindless job—hitting all the corners with his broom, flicking away at the detritus of the newsroom. Even Wayne might do better legwork than Tate. He was a capable enough soul to cart around a copper still for Flanagan, the top local moonshiner. At least, that was the information Tate's nickel had procured from young Byrne. Moonshining. Yeah, another blockbuster story that Tate hadn't been able to crack, and with Wayne going on to bigger and better career opportunities, that story could be thrown in the crapper. He wondered how much money it would take to make Wayne sing like a canary and save his tanking journalism career.

"Wayne. Haven't seen you in a while. I thought you were off to work with Mr. Grover."

"No sir, but it'll be sooner than expected. Next week."

"I'll miss our little chats. Sure you want to do that? Can't beat a newspaper office for being in the know."

"Got connections."

"And that's just what I need right now. Connections. I've got some buddies coming into town, and I'd like to treat 'em right. Know what I'm saying? Nothing at the park, right?"

Wayne didn't reply.

"Aw, come on, Wayne, help me out here," Tate said, tapping his pencil on his phone. "We both know you know who's got the booze, and you're my only good source of information around here. You'll be gone in a few days, and who's to know you told me anything? I'm a newsman—I keep my sources anonymous."

Wayne walked over. "Nothing at the park," he whispered. "They're really hurting. Might be a speakeasy in there for the high and mighty, but you and your friends aren't getting in—unless they know someone from out of town. Mumbles is all but closed—no supply."

Shoe bobbed his head. "Yeah, Prohibition's funny like that. If you're somebody, you get to keep drinking. If you're a nobody like us, you've got to quit or take your chances." He doodled on his notepad. "How about Flanagan's still? I hear the odds of getting decent shine with him are good."

"Don't know nothing 'bout that."

"Well, how's the park getting booze when Mumbles can't? Seems like Mumbles would be getting the locals' best. Germans selling on the sly?"

Wayne took a quick look around and sat down at Shoe's desk. "Don't think they're producing. Too many Germans and too little beer floating around for that to be so. They stick together."

"Come on, Wayne," Shoe said, leaning towards him. "I saw your friend with the copper kettle and coil still in his cart. All that stuff not going to the park? They have payments due."

"Let me put it this way. If you were a muckety-muck, would you come all the way down here just to pay for rotgut?" He was interrupted by the linotyper, who walked by with a box and began wiping down the magazine of the Mergenthaler linotype machine. "I got to finish sweeping up," Wayne said, and moved away.

Tate doubted he would get him to open up again, but Wayne had already given him something valuable. Good liquor was flowing in Nevis, it was better quality than Flanagan's, and there was evidently enough to attract outside folks.

He glanced again at his license plate information. New Castle, and Delaware County, Pennsylvania—outsiders from the Delaware Valley coming clear to Nevis to drink? Didn't make a great deal of sense. His bud, Pete Dowd, and the rest of his gang at the *Philadelphia Tribune* crowed constantly about the free-flowing liquor throughout the Valley. Why, they were making names for themselves with all their exposés about Dupont losing industrial alcohol to organized crime bosses who had much to gain and little to fear as they turned it into illicit liquor.

Well, stone the crows and pickle the lizards! Of course!

Industrial alcohol.

Like Danny Millman used.

Now, that would be a reason to buy a failing business.

CHAPTER TWENTY-SEVEN

Selling Unmentionables

Two days after all vying parties were informed of the rules for the Nevis liquor proposal, two bids arrived at the courthouse, by separate couriers. Jackson and Prentis were somewhat surprised, and relieved, that neither party felt it worthwhile to present their case in person.

The first courier arrived at half past ten: one of the clerks from the train depot, dressed head to toe in their familiar nickel-gray postal uniform. The second followed soon after: a gentleman in an ill-fitting brown suit, who took the outside steps two at a time, and did the same coming down when he left.

The envelopes were plain and brown and closed with a button and string. The carefully composed contents mentioned nothing about liquor, but both had enough particulars to be clear about intent.

Jackson read each with relish. "Very similar offers," he said, handing Hubert Carr the one signed by George Washington, and the one from Andrew Volstead to Prentis. "Do we know who's who?"

"Tarkington is old George who-never-told-a-lie, though I'll bet everybody in his family was a Tory."

Jackson laughed. "As much as I detest Tarkington, I'm almost hoping we go with him. She's an ice maiden. I seriously doubt there's a heart behind that lovely bosom, and we all know the baggage that's bound to come with McClure."

Prentis handed his letter to Hubert and grinned at Jackson. "In the end, we can do anything we want. Tarkington's our man. He has a heart—black as anthracite, no doubt, but there's a certain roguish charm about him. Once we pin him down on particulars, I can work with that. But, be damned, Jackson. You're getting a kick out of this, aren't you?"

"I so want this to be someone else's problem," Jackson said, watching for Hubert's reaction. "I'm not cut out for this sneaking-around nonsense. Once my term is up, I'm going far, far, away."

Prentis's gaze darted to Hubert, and then he shook his head at Jackson. "Funny one. How do they look, Hubert?"

"Like we're selling unmentionables to someone's grandmother," he said, circling something on one of the documents with his fountain pen. He made another notation on the other before looking up. "The production of the *product,* as it's referred to in each offer, is similar. Both parties reserve the right to produce in Nevis as well as transport in. And each expects to handle its own logistics, including acquiring operational space as necessary for production and sales, and the protection and security of said product as affected by federal laws and regulations. I assume that means the town turns the other cheek and they'll keep the feds at bay."

Hubert pushed his glasses up on his nose and jotted another entry in a margin. "As for what the financial incentive would be for the town, now, that's where the two parties differ significantly. John J. McClure's proposes two percent off the top of profits from sales, while Mr. Tarkington's group offers three percent for direct sales, and another percent for product shipped from local ports."

Prentis chuckled. "We should make them read that part aloud and do it with a straight face. I'm pretty sure we won't see any sudden influx into our coffers."

"This isn't about our share," Jackson snapped.

"I get it, Jackson. I'm not about to fret over lost revenue. I'm just saying that if you think these people will ever show you a profit on their books, much less share it with you, well, then I've got a bridge in New York you can have for cheap."

Jackson turned to Hubert. "Why would McClure's group want to come way down here, maybe open a speakeasy, and just sell beer and booze? Do they want to sell the bulk to Bayland? You already have a supplier. Does Philly intend to muscle them out? I'm not going to jeopardize what the German community has worked out," he said, shaking his head.

"All valid questions," Hubert said, neither confirming nor denying any active bootlegging at the park. He stretched out in the mayor's desk chair. "What's most worrisome here is not so much what the bidders are saying, as what they don't say. And the use of port. Tarkington's group is straightforward about its use. Obviously, they're interested in smuggling along the coast and bringing liquor in by boat. He's decided to show his whole hand. Not a bad strategy, considering the competition. But that can't be unique to them. What's appealing and profitable to one has to be true for the other. So you have to ask, what else will be going on that we *aren't* clued in to yet?"

"Exactly," Jackson said, taking the chair at Hubert's elbow and leaving Prentis to sit across the room. "Very well. Unless I hear some compelling argument to the contrary, I'm inclined to go with Tarkington. It's almost as if he already knew what we wanted to hear. And I think I can stomach him. I don't like that woman, and there's no doubt in my mind we would rue the day we ever got in bed with John J. McClure."

"Agreed," Prentis said with a sigh of relief.

"And I have nothing more to add," Hubert said.

Jackson picked both documents up and returned each to its envelope. "Now that's settled, there's just one final consideration," he said, studying one of the envelopes. Miss Lally is staying at the Bayside Hotel. How are we going to let her down easy? Prentis?"

"Don't even think about sending me. We don't want to invite any further discussion or attempts at negotiation."

"Fine. I'll call the postal courier back and have him deliver a note that is polite and to the point. Hubert, I'm sure you're good at writing that sort of thing. May I ask your assistance in drawing up both responses?"

"On one condition."

Jackson and Prentis exchanged a glance. "Go on," Jackson said.

"Relax," Hubert said with a chuckle. "It's not all that difficult, gentlemen. All I ask is the assurance that once *production* has commenced, the Bayland Partnership can continue the enterprises it currently has in place concerning product. We don't want to be forced to cut ties with any existing business partners."

Jackson nodded. "Understood. Nor would we want to put our local brewers out of business. We'll put it in our acceptance to Tarkington." He turned to Prentis. "Reschedule our appointment with Nathan. Let's get this over with."

CHAPTER TWENTY-EIGHT

My Sweet Jenny

The yellow-winged biplane came out of its loop and swooped earthward from the cloudless spring sky. As it approached the model T sitting in the field, it tilted slightly to the left and then righted itself just before it hit the ground hard, hopping along like a jackrabbit until it slowed enough to taxi back around. The pilot and a passenger, both in khaki jumpsuits and leather aviator helmets, climbed out.

"Stay here, Jackson," Prentis said. "I didn't say anything about Nathan bringing company."

Jackson watched as they met halfway and had a brief discussion. There was a nodding of heads, and Prentis waved him out of the car. As Jackson drew close, the pilot pulled off his leather flying helmet and smoothed back his hair. It was Nathan Tarkington, flush-faced and beaming.

"Good to meet with you again, Mr. Mayor," Nathan said, shaking Jackson's hand. "I was delighted to hear that we'll be collaborating. What do you think of my Jenny?" he said, turning to admire the airplane. "Isn't she a beauty?"

"Curtiss JN-Four? So, you were in the Air Service."

"The Hundred and Thirty-Ninth Aero Squadron in France. Swore if I ever got back to the States, I would fly one without ducking air fire."

"Where'd you borrow this from?"

"Oh, it's mine. They're all over, cheap as cars." He walked around to the front and patted the fuselage. "My best mate, Jerry Cooper, and I trained at Kelly Field, Texas, in this girl. Too bad he never made it home again. When I shipped back home and got myself settled, I went back out to Texas and found her right there waiting for me. Forked over the money on the spot and had her shipped by rail all the way back east. If you want, I can fix you up with one. The military's practically giving them away."

"Oh, no, I couldn't," Jackson said, running his hand along the plane. "What on earth would I do with it?"

"As Jerry Cooper said to me over a pint right before we shipped out: 'Freed from the confines of the earth, his spirit soared with God's winged creatures and discovered life's true delight.' A true loss, that man."

He was silent a moment and then motioned to the other flyer. "May I introduce to you my friend here, John Moore-Brabazon, who knows far more than I when it comes to flying. Be careful what you say around him. He can make pigs fly." Tarkington looked at the Jenny again and beamed like a new father. "Take you up?"

Jackson let out a long breath and shook his head. "Nice plane, but no thanks."

"Another time, perhaps."

Tarkington took two stakes from his gear, pounded them into the ground, and tied off the plane's tail section while his traveling companion handled the front end. "Everybody's raving over cars, but trust me. I own several beautiful Pierce-Arrows and Peerless roadsters, but flying's the future, my friend. It's going to fashion a new tomorrow. Envision an air mail service that will get a letter to your elderly mother in New York in a day, the ability to seal a deal in California in less than two. Or simply transporting goods in and out of inaccessible places—"

Jackson threw a quick look his way. "Like smuggling?"

Tarkington laughed. "A package is a package, isn't it? Or simply throw your cares to the wind and soar with the eagles. Chicago, Saint Louis, out west. There are pilots out there right now making money just entertaining people with the beauty of the machine. Two hundred smackers and I can set you free. Just holler."

Jackson would keep the tip about cheap planes, but he hoped their dirty business would be quickly concluded, and Nathan soon too far away for him to yell at.

"I hate to interrupt all this camaraderie, but we'd best get started," Prentis said. He pointed across the field to a solitary corrugated-metal building. "It's a little dirty, but there's a table and some chairs and it's private. Mr. Brabazon good out here?"

"He'll be right here when we get back. "Let's go."

Once inside, before Jackson or Prentis could even sit down, Tarkington got right to business. He turned to Prentis and said, "After I cleared my schedule to meet with you and the mayor, I was a little surprised at the hoop-jumping of the past week."

Jackson looked at Prentis and took a seat at the table.

Prentis shrugged. "And we were a little surprised at the additional interest in Nevis's economic potential. Just consider the end result, and let's move on. Where do we stand?" He sat down next to Jackson.

"Prentis and I talked briefly, Mr. Mayor," Tarkington said. "Do we need to recap?"

"Prentis has kept me informed. Nevis's liquor policies have been pretty clear and consistent. We're an insular little place, and as long as things stay quiet and inconspicuous, we'll have a no-questions-asked policy."

Tarkington smiled broadly. "If I had a nickel for every time I've heard that, my sweet girl and I would be halfway through my quest to circumnavigate the globe." He pulled up a chair, swung it around backward, and sat down. "So Nevis is dry, at least on paper, but the townsfolk, most of them, still want to imbibe. Stills are nestled off back roads in seemingly inaccessible places throughout the surrounding woods, and yet, you can't keep them up and running, and people are blaming the mayor for not ensuring their right to a nip. Why is that?"

"Because . . ."

"Because you can't lock up the Carrie Nations of this world," Tarkington said. "They'll be voting in this fall's elections, and Prohibition has become a public-relations nightmare. It's bigger than you are, and not what you do best. That's where my group, Delaware Valley Investment, will save you. This is the only meeting I expect to have with you. If you need to know, ask it now. Otherwise, we stay out of your way, and you out of ours."

"Millman's?"

"Couldn't stop the sale. I might eventually be able to sell it to you."

"The German brewers?"

"We will abide by the terms laid out in your written agreement. As you might have surmised by now, we already provide spirits for Bubbles, the park speakeasy. If Bayland wishes to increase its business association with us, we'd be more than happy to accommodate them, but our main objective is not to be a provider of Nevis' beer supply. My associates—"

"I'm not interested in knowing anything about your associates," Jackson snapped. He shifted in his seat and wiped the perspiration he felt popping out above his upper lip. "So you'll tell your people to stop demolishing our stills?"

Tarkington chuckled. "Now that we have your attention, I don't think you need worry about that anymore. There's no harm in individuals operating their own little enterprises out in the middle of a swamp somewhere. And I'm sure you don't need me warning you about the danger of poisoning the whole town if Mr. Flanagan wakes up on the wrong side of the bed one fine morning and loses his focus."

"So, you'll bring in enough hard stuff to keep Bayland prosperous?" Prentis asked.

Tarkington winked at him. "But let's refine what you said. Without a doubt, I could bring it all in, but there is a much easier way. We'll make it right here in Nevis. And what we don't use, we'll ship elsewhere."

"Hold on," Jackson said, rising. "You want to ship booze *out*? The intent is to keep this local and low-key."

Tarkington leaned forward and rapped with his knuckles on the small table. "You need two things to be truly successful in bootlegging: denatured alcohol and a good chemist. The government requires companies to add methanol to industrial alcohol to render it undrinkable. The methanol can be removed easily enough if you know what you're doing. Any good chemist knows how to strip it back out again, and voila, you can produce vats of excellent brew. Much more efficient than scattering stills willy-nilly across the landscape. Feds won't expect that kind of activity in a little burg like Nevis. We'll be fine."

"So that's the interest in Millman's," Jackson said, beginning to glimpse daylight. "It's not the location; it's his shipments of denatured alcohol." His mind raced to put the pieces together.

"Millman's would never have the amount of alcohol needed to support what we envision, but the presence of denatured stuff on the premise would never have to be justified. It's a cover beyond compare. There is so much industrial alcohol floating around for use by DuPont that it's practically free for the taking. So, we're going to take it and send it to Millman's. Easy stuff."

"And where are you going to find a chemist willing to break the law?" Prentis asked.

"I'm a chemist, Harvard trained, class of 'fourteen."

"Just looking for a little cash, are we?" Prentis asked.

"A little? Think again. People in the Delaware Valley are getting rich."

"Then why aren't you up there getting some of it?" Too many feds?"

"The Valley is crawling with enforcement officials, although it might surprise you to learn that there are more cops on the take for bootlegging than there are feds available to stop it. Happily for us, cops are woefully underpaid."

Tarkington looked out the shed window toward his plane. "This works best when all parties buy in. You need to get over the buyer's remorse. Shoreside communities such as your town offer splendid opportunities to expand business. There are worse things in the world than the production and sale of illegal liquor, and there's no need to worry about Nevis becoming a little Chicago." He turned back around. "Now, I have another engagement, gentlemen. Walk you back?"

"I've heard enough," Prentis said, getting up. He looked at Jackson, who seemed lost in thought. "Jackson?"

"I know a better place."

Prentis's expression tightened. "We're not going through all this again. Nevis has already committed itself."

"Parkers Wharf. It's the perfect place to move Millman's: secluded, deep water."

A sound somewhere between a sigh and a hiss escaped Prentis's lips. "But the steamboat doesn't go there anymore. And furthermore, that's an impossible sell to Father McGee."

"The church doesn't own *all* the land down there. I bought property along the shore when Camilla and I . . . Never mind. It has access to the wharf." He turned to Tarkington. "Swap land parcels with me— Millman's for the parcel down next to the church at Parkers Wharf.

As I'm sure you're aware, they're already running an efficient operation there. You'll end up with a more secluded area."

Tarkington gnawed on his lower lip. "I've been down there. Good location, but no *Chessie Belle.*"

"There's already business down there," Prentis said. "They've quietly figured it all out, but you're going to draw unwanted attention to them."

"No," Jackson said, shaking his head. "I don't want this activity in the center of town. It's Parkers Wharf or nothing. The *Chessie Belle* comes into Williams Wharf, a stone's throw away."

"Mother Mary," Prentis mumbled, closing his eyes. "You're going to take Father aside and explain it all?"

"Yes. He'll be relieved we're striking out on our own and not throwing our lot in with his."

They heard the *thump* of something hitting the outside of the shed. Tarkington put a finger to his lips and crept to the window. Yanking it open with enough force that the frame made a loud pop, he poked his head outside, remaining motionless for a moment. Then, apparently satisfied, he pulled the window shut again, offering only a shrug in explanation.

"I accept your offer," he said, sitting back down at the little table.

"And this Lally woman," Jackson said. "We're sure she's going to fade into the woodwork?"

"Don't give her another thought," said Tarkington. "We connect like this all the time. I'll take her to the Bayside and we'll discuss it over a nice dinner. Then she'll move on to the next opportunity, which will work to her favor because I'll be busy here. All you need concern yourselves with are the normal demands of government. Think of all the drinkers you'll be protecting from bad hooch, and get on with life."

"Then I'm satisfied," Jackson said. "Keep your activities down in the foggy bottom, and keep it discreet. After the property exchange, I don't want to see or hear from you again."

"Understood." Tarkington offered his hand, which Jackson ignored. "You have strong principles, Jackson. Definitely not your father's son."

"You knew him?" Jackson was beginning to think everyone but him had had a relationship with his father.

"Everybody knew Chance Dwyer, and everybody has a great story or two about him."

"So what's yours?"

Tarkington glanced out the window again. "Got to go. Weather's changing and John still has to fly north."

—•—

Prentis glanced at Jackson as they drove away. "So, you get Millman's and we're in less of a pickle now than before. Some risk comes with it, but nothing we can't handle. I'd say it was a productive trip."

Jackson stared out the roadster's window and over the green field to the puffy clouds coming in from the west, then decided it would provide the perfect mug shot for a nosy reporter—someone just like that Shoemaker fellow, lurking out behind a hedgerow somewhere. He looked the other way, at Prentis. "You're out of your mind. Somebody's going to nose it all out. We've got too many people involved. Too many moving parts and too many mouths."

Prentis nodded sagely. "Yes, but you see, they aren't *our* moving parts. Drinking isn't illegal. Furthermore, the courts are lenient about people moving it around. Before, the feds might have nailed us for production, and there was an outside chance they would frown on our gentlemen's club. But now they can't tie us to anything: no production, no transportation, no sales. As the courts would say, our connection to liquor is casual and slight. We're scot-free."

"Except for our agreement with Tarkington."

"Possibly, but they'd need tangible evidence to hang that on us. Where are the written bids?"

"They're locked away in my new file cabinet. In my lockbox. *Safe.*"

"Get rid of them. Immediately."

Jackson nodded.

"I do mean *right now,* Jackson."

"I heard you. I'll relax when you can keep the *Evening Star* and our chemist friend out of my office."

CHAPTER TWENTY-NINE

Playing the Field

Tate Shoemaker assured Tanner that he would be more than happy to check out the afternoon arrival of the *Chessie Belle,* and all the associated hoopla. But somewhere between the pressroom and the wharf, he made a wrong turn and ended up on the veranda of the Bayside Hotel—a good career move depending on who was paying attention. The Bayside was no hash house. Anybody who was *anybody* stayed there, and he hoped this Nathan Tarkington and Miss Lally fell into that category. Unlike many of the Bayside's patrons, his aim was to see and not be seen. He graciously accepted a table to the rear of the terrace and hid his face behind a menu.

"More fish in a barrel?" a young voice whispered in his ear.

Tate jumped in his chair, fumbling his menu. "Son of a gun, Jack!" The boy was covered nose to toe in dirt. Tate shrugged at the staring waiter and said to Jack, "When's the last time you had a bath, son?"

Jack grinned, slid into a chair, and pushed a small black ledger across the table. "Here's the mayor's appointment book. Look at it here. I gotta take it back quick because Fannie knows it's missing, and she's coming home at lunchtime to turn the house upside down."

Tate covered the book with his menu, then slid it off the table. "Have I made you a partner yet? How did you know I was here?"

"I know where everybody is. It's what I do. Like yesterday, the mayor's office traipsing down to meet in the shed where those airplanes fly in. The book says it was for flying lessons, but they didn't even go up for a ride. That make sense to you?"

Tate began thumbing through the blue-lined pages in his lap. "*Who* met? What'd they do?"

"I just told you. They met in the old shed. Mayor Dwyer, Mr. Gant, and the pilot. The fourth guy musta' just been along to fix the plane. He stayed in the field. When they got done, a car picked up the pilot. I followed him back here." The boy nodded toward the opposite side of the veranda. "Him—in the gray checkered jacket."

It was the man he had seen leaving the courthouse—Nathan Tarkington, he presumed. And the lady having coffee with him? The same woman he had seen leaving ahead of him. *Hello, Miss Honora Lally.*

"You didn't by chance hear any of their conversation, did you?"

"Not really," Jack said. "The only thing I heard before I fell off the bucket was 'Parkers Wharf.'"

Tate raised an eyebrow and waited.

"It's the only way I could get up to the winder. When I fell, there weren't nowhere to roll but under the shed. I couldn't let 'em make me, now, could I?"

Tate smiled. There had to be a way to bottle this. He sneaked another look at the couple, who appeared to be in the midst of a lovers' spat. She was tapping the table with her finger as he leaned in with a polite but pinched expression, no doubt waiting for her to take a breath so that he might get a word in edgewise. "Parkers Wharf, you say?" Tate pushed the menu, with the ledger beneath it, back across the table. "Jack, you're a peach. Meet me down at the bathhouses in five minutes."

He raised a forefinger, and the penguin-suited waiter glided over. "I hope you can help me out of a most embarrassing predicament. The gentleman in the checked jacket—I'm afraid to admit I've forgotten the man's name. They're newly betrothed and I'd like to send a note of congratulations."

"Ah, yes," the waiter said, looking toward the couple, who were now leaning back in their chairs glaring at each other. "That's Mr. Tarkington, and the lady is Miss Honora Lally."

"Yes, of course," Tate said. "Much obliged."

Miss Lally left in a huff. Tate placed a dime on the starched white tablecloth, and was about to slip out of the dining area via the back stairs when Tarkington welcomed a second woman to his table. Heavyset and matronly, she was known to all as Camilla McClelland, but to see her out and about . . . No stiff, formal introductions in this meeting. If there was one word to describe Mrs. McClelland's demeanor, it would be "*glowing*" . . . like a schoolgirl.

Tate ordered a Klondike Fizz and then settled back in and watched the sipping and chatting. Mr. Tarkington was charming, and Mrs. McClelland coquettish. Did she know he was two-timing her? Or maybe it was *she* who was stringing *him* along, gathering information before her next assault on liquor in Nevis.

—•—

Tate could already see his young confederate outside the women's bathhouse, twirling around the flagpole as the white fair-weather nautical flag wafted in the light breeze. The kid was a natural snoop with skills far beyond his years, but eventually, running the streets wasn't going to serve him well. Nevis wasn't the zenith of Tate's aspirations. He wondered how difficult it would be to take Jack with him when he went back to Philly. It was only fair, considering the legwork the boy was doing on a story only steps away from breaking big.

"Let me go through that book, lad," he said. "Then I'll tell you what our next steps should be." He stepped between the men's and women's bathhouses and scanned through the ledger. As he had suspected, N. Tarkington, H. Lally, and H. Carr had all met in the mayor's office the week before. There had also been a previous meeting with Lally, but it did not appear that the mayor had ever met with Tarkington before. The information about the recent flying lesson also panned out. He gave back the book and said, "Jack, you continue to amaze me. Do you think you can get it back home before Fannie catches you? I'm off to Upper Marlboro, and I'd like to concentrate on things other than how bad your sister will light into you. Then you should get back to school before Officer McCall catches you playing hooky."

Jack shoved the schedule underneath his shirt and tucked his shirttail in. "Been thinking on that. The best approach with my sister is to meet her head-on. I'm gonna take it to her at the mayor's office."

"Oh, no, you don't." Tate grabbed for Jack's shirt, but the boy darted away.

"Gotta trust me, Shoe," he yelled over his shoulder, already halfway to the boardwalk. "Who knows what else I'll see." He ducked into Mackle's fish shack as the Nevis paddy wagon rolled past on First Street.

CHAPTER THIRTY

Same Old Path

If God had told Jackson that the only way to save the world was to put Nathan Tarkington and Camilla McClelland together, he would have laughed in the Almighty's face. But there they were, bootlegger and Prohibitionist, tête à tête on the Bayside veranda, sipping tea together. The end-time must be near.

Catching Camilla's eye as the waiter seated him, Jackson nodded politely and left her to her own devices. Was she courting jealousy? She knew him well. Or, perhaps, seeking conversion of a lost soul? That would be the day. If she ever made good on her promise to join him for dinner, he might find out. After the fiasco at Oscar's, nothing was certain, but he felt that things would go right this time.

Apparently, her machinations were well under way when he arrived, because she concluded her meeting with Tarkington—who left without acknowledging him—and joined him almost immediately.

"Starting lunch early?" he said, tipping his head toward her departing companion. "Should we wait to order?"

"Oh, that," she said with a shrug of one shoulder. "A cup of tea and a little business."

"Really? I must say, I'm a bit surprised. Do you mind my asking what business you have with him?"

"Yes." The eyes flashed.

"Okay," Jackson said, hands raised in feigned surrender. "Just know that he may not be what he seems. I would suggest steering clear."

"Yes, Jackson. Let's both steer clear, shall we? And have a pleasant lunch?"

Her eyes softened into the ones he had fallen in love with. He motioned for the waiter. "Certainly. I've been looking forward to it since that day I came out to see you at the farm. In fact, this might be the highlight of my week."

She reached out and patted his hand. "And that's when you promised we could talk about local options."

"I've introduced a bill to consider them. It's a tough council, though. I can't promise anything."

The eyes danced. "I knew I could count on you. An effective mayor who feels strongly about supporting Prohibition should be able to influence the council."

Jackson glanced around the crowded veranda. Conversations hummed, and china rattled as waiters bustled between tables. He hoped Camilla would mind her temper in so public a place. "Yes, well, I'm trying, but it's complicated. It's not just about what *I* want. In a democracy, all these separate interests get a voice."

Jackson knew the hard look on Camilla's face well enough to wave off the approaching waiter. "We'll be a minute," he said.

"Well, if that's the way you want it," she said. "But if you were truly dedicated, you could make this happen. I've been counting on you."

"It's not a question of *if I want it*. It's a question of *how it is*, Camilla."

"You'd risk your political career for a drink? Well, at least some things never change."

"Let's take a walk," he said, standing. Guiding her by the elbow, he escorted her off the veranda and onto the walkway that meandered among orange hibiscus until it reached the boardwalk. "Madam," he said when they were a suitable distance from the other patrons, "I have not had a drink in years and do not plan on starting. That said, unlike you, I don't make it my life's mission to tell people what they can and can't do."

She pulled away. "Jackson T. Dwyer, I never expected anything from you but to be a good man—a decent, hardworking, *sober* man."

He grabbed for her hand, but she hid them both behind her back and looked away.

"You could have had two out of three and helped me with the third. It would have worked. Why do you have to keep singing 'The Lips that Touch Liquor Shall Never Touch Mine'?"

Laughter floated off the veranda. He glanced toward the boardwalk and wondered if it would be more private up there somewhere.

"No good man needs a nursemaid. And you're still the namby-pamby I thought you were."

Down the same old path. Jackson took a deep breath and blew it out. "Yes, Camilla, I guess I am. An old fool who thought we could have a nice lunch. An old fool who thought there was something good between us. An old fool who put aside his pride and decided to give us one more shot."

Now he felt his own expression harden. "What do you want? In all this time, I've never spoken ill to you, but I'm going to put the niceties aside and get right to it. You're the most miserable creature God ever made. Why are you making it your life's mission to make sure I'm miserable, too?"

"You're weak."

"I am. We all are. I've lived in that dark little corner of my heart, and I've lusted and I've coveted and God knows I've profaned. Yeah, I've sat down at that table and partaken of the forbidden fruit. Even enjoyed it. And do you know what? *Everyone* has."

Just as in old times, he watched her forefinger begin stabbing holes in him.

"Because you're a lazy sot and you're breaking the law. I'm going to do everything within my power to drive your wicked soul out of office. And that sneaky Prentis Gant—birds of a feather!" She stopped poking at him and instead tore an orange petal from one of the hibiscus.

"Oh, Camilla Foster McClelland, this started long before Mr. Volstead ever came along," he said, laughing. "It's been thirty-some years of nonstop sniping sabotage and venom! It's time to let go and stop being so self-righteous, don't you think? Jesus drank! He even *made* wine, or did you skim over the part about the wedding feast? Do you recall that passage?"

"Don't call me anymore," she huffed. And for the barest instant, he saw in her eyes a wounded look he had never seen before. She pushed past him and stalked away toward the park and the crowds.

He let her go. Or she let him go. Perhaps they were the couple the good Lord should put together, because they were never going to do it by themselves.

CHAPTER THIRTY-ONE

Spurious

The gentle sway of the rail coach, and the warm sun streaming through the window had yet again lulled Jackson into a sleepy haze—the best thing about his trips to Baltimore. He awoke a few miles outside Nevis as the train rounded the great curve. He gave his face a vigorous rub and straightened his tie.

The McClelland homestead was out there somewhere. He found it across a half mile of rolling landscape and then watched the specks on the horizon grow into barns and corncribs and a decent-size house with a broad front porch and red roses clustered about. He wasn't a farmer and would never choose to be one, but that farm was everything he ever wanted. And where was the mistress of the house? The bliss from his nap evaporated.

He had been gone only a day, attending a mayors' meeting that quickly disintegrated into endless harping on the pitfalls of Volstead—an issue that he and Prentis had successfully taken off their plate—so he was shocked to see a full railway crew engaged in tearing up the

McClelland property where it met the Chesapeake right-of-way. They had already laid the clear beginnings of a rail bed hugging the northern edge of the pastureland. They must have worked all night! He pressed his face against the glass, but the scene too quickly retreated into the distance.

— —

Jackson glared at Sean Murphy and then lit into the rail rep like a badger on a dog. "How is it that we have expansion of the railroad, and the mayor's office hasn't been informed?"

"It's . . . it's all new, Mr. Mayor. I just found out myself yesterday afternoon." Murphy held out a bulky business envelope. "Proper signatures throughout. The town council approved it yesterday morning. I would have thought . . ."

"I'm out of town one day. How *convenient.*" Jackson fumbled with the envelope a moment before tearing it diagonally across the front. It looked legit. "Make sure all the 't's' are dotted," he said, handing it off to Prentis. "This is all most inappropriate. Clearly not normal business. Give it to me in a nutshell, Mr. Murphy."

"Well, as I said, I had no inkling. Negotiations must have been conducted pretty far up the Chesapeake Railway Express chain of command. They're going to lay a spur across the northern boundary of the Archi—er, *Camilla*—McClelland property to connect with Williams Wharf Road. Then they'll beef up the landing at Williams Wharf and build warehouses for international tobacco auctions. With the spur, they can ship by boat *and* rail." Murphy looked from Jackson to Prentis and swallowed. "You know, Mr. Mayor, we've had a good honest working relationship, and I'm not joshing you. Swear on my dear mother's grave, that's the truth and all I know."

Jackson sat down with a huff. "I don't believe this! Does that all look in order?"

Prentis tossed the packet back on the table. "It's all here. Sam Hinton signed on behalf of the Nevis Town Council in the mayor's absence. Thanks for bringing the packet over, Sean. Would you let us know if something new turns up?" He showed Murphy out and walked over to the town map on the wall.

Jackson joined him. "Of course, illegal as hell since I was quite contactable. Which may explain why the railroad went hell's bells to start construction. Thoughts?"

Prentis traced his finger along the proposed track as it crossed Camilla's farm and intersected with Williams Wharf Road, then followed the road south to its terminus at the wharf on the bay. "Huh," he said, and retraced back up Williams Wharf Road until his finger crossed another notched road. "Parkers Wharf," he said, tapping the second road. "Pretty sneaky. If I didn't know better, I'd swear it was just as easy to use this new connector to ship things out from *Parkers* Wharf."

"Tarkington," Jackson said.

"Or I'm the queen of Holland. Him, a whole lot of money, and a wheelbarrow full of promises. He and his boozy associates just got the railroad to build them an overland access to Parkers Wharf without ever mentioning it by name. It's too late to stop, but you need to put the council on notice—Hinton in particular. He owns prime real estate on First Street. Take it under eminent domain—extend the boardwalk for commercial use, put up a new post office building, or even a monument to your late father. Doesn't matter what. He's been holding that parcel for years waiting for the value to skyrocket. We can pop that little balloon for him."

"No monuments," Jackson said. "Maybe a boardwalk extension. You're obviously familiar?"

"How do you think we got Harley Dugan's land? Your father despised him. That land had been in his family for generations, and now it's got a schoolhouse on it."

"Hinton's a thoroughgoing son of a bitch. Draw it up and make it clear that any opposition will be dealt with in a similar manner. And Tarkington—how do we put him in his place? Calling him in and cussing him out won't do much."

Prentis grinned. "Oh, we certainly need to do that."

"Unless . . . ," Jackson said, brightening.

He got up and walked out of the mayor's suite, turned left, and followed the hallway that bisected the upper floor of courthouse, until he reached the head of the stairs, and the windows that overlooked the rear of the building. Beyond the silhouette of town roofs, he studied the ribbon of track where it trailed off into the distance.

"That's what we do," he said, tapping the windowpane. "What good is a rail spur if a town ordinance prohibits the train from stopping there? Where is that executive order, dated *yesterday,* that put a moratorium on new train stops pending a thorough review of Nevis's transportation?"

"You do realize you're baiting a viper, right? A whole den of 'em. Maybe it would be better to let them have this one."

"Do it."

"Yes sir," Prentis said, shaking his head. "I'll get right on it."

"And get Tarkington in here while I'm hot. I need to whittle his conniving ass down a couple of sizes."

A squeaky stair tread behind them turned both men around.

"Gentlemen," Tarkington said, coming up the courthouse stairs. "Whom have I offended now?"

CHAPTER THIRTY-TWO

Beginning Jitters

"Sneaky bastard," Jackson said, moving toward Tarkington. "I should toss you right back down those stairs."

Tarkington put up his fists as Prentis slipped in between the two men. "No blows here," he said, staying each with a hand to the chest. He turned to Tarkington. "I seem to recall you wanting to make yourself scarce. We had an agreement, sir, that there would be no meddling."

"And so, I haven't meddled," Tarkington said. "I've just now heard what happened." He looked down the corridor as one of the office doors squeaked open and a gray-haired man stuck his head out and glowered. "Civilly, please, and in a less public place?"

Prentis nodded toward the mayor's office and walked between the other two until all were seated back in Jackson's office: Tarkington in the chair nearest the door, Jackson at his desk, and Prentis right beside him.

"I still run this town," Jackson said, stabbing at Tarkington with his fountain pen. "I'll have the feds in here so fast, you'll think I had them waiting outside the door!"

Tarkington scowled at him. "Let's not be rash, or we'll all be sitting in the pokey. If that's your intent, this conversation is a waste of time. I will gladly leave town and let you deal with the mess by yourselves. Which, if you'll recall, you weren't handling so well the first go-round."

Prentis leaned forward, gently took the pen from Jackson's hand, and returned it to the marble pen holder on the desk. "Civil, remember?" He addressed Tarkington. "What the hell are you *doing*? Right out of the gate, you're meddling with the town council."

"Fair assumption," Tarkington said, "but I haven't. Obviously, I don't control everything that goes on with Delaware Valley Investment. Everybody's got a boss, or bosses, and for whatever reason, mine have decided to get involved. Trust me, there's nothing I'd like better than to work without their interference. We don't need the rail spur. It draws unnecessary attention. But I don't control the purse strings, and I don't make all the final decisions."

A smirk crept across Jackson's face. "Then you'll be relieved to hear that earlier this week, I signed a moratorium on the expansion of railway stops along the Chesapeake line. The backroom antics while I was out of town were for naught."

Tarkington's eyebrows arched. "You did *what*?"

"That's right. And any little buddies you've cultivated on the town council won't be there long. Either you deal with me . . . or we all go to jail," he added in a rush.

"Nobody's going to jail," Prentis said. "So why are you here, Nathan?"

"To clear this up. I don't want bad feelings souring our deal."

Jackson gave him a hard look. "As far as I'm concerned, this deal has already gone south. As mayor, I'm washing my hands of this mess. You're on your own, Mr. Tarkington. Don't expect any favors from anyone here. Evidently, we should have been dealing with someone farther up the trough."

"I'm afraid it's a little late for that," Tarkington said mildly. "We've all got to hang together here."

"Or separately?" Prentis muttered.

"Exactly. You have to understand, this isn't a one-sided deal with you making all the rules. You need to give a little. The Delaware Valley Authority feels it needs a railway spur, has paid handsomely for a railway spur, and has been told it has a railway spur. Do you really think you can arbitrarily sweep all that away with a simple mayoral declaration? Haven't you been watching Chicago? We're all expendable."

Jackson slammed his hand down on the desk. "You said this wouldn't end up like Chicago."

"Because we were all willing to play nicely," Tarkington said, sliding to the edge of his seat. "Now you're not."

For the first time, Jackson saw hairline cracks in Tarkington's smooth facade. The smile was gone, and he looked a little wan. "Are you at risk here?"

"No one is irreplaceable," Tarkington whispered. "Everyone needs to stop and breathe deeply. It's the beginning jitters. That overwhelmed feeling and the impulse to run away? That's normal. You need to turn around the way you're thinking about this. What we're doing here isn't a destructive thing. We're making a positive effort. Come on, let me make it up to you. Let me show you the good side of things."

Jackson pictured Tarkington lying in a heap at the bottom of the courthouse steps. Now *that* was the good side of things. And yes, the impulse to run away was a normal, never ending consideration, and one that was growing stronger every day.

─ ─

Fanny Byrne glanced at the mayor's closed door. The voices were subdued. Apparently, whatever had caused the commotion in the hall was settled. She returned to rolling up the morning's *Baltimore Sun,* opened to Mencken's column, and the *Washington Post.* The mayor liked them placed side by side on the far right corner of her desk, where he could scoop them up as he passed. She paused, her attention arrested by an article right below the fold on page one of the *Post:* DIVERSION OF INDUSTRIAL ALCOHOL TRIGGERS CONCERN IN CONGRESS. Curious, she read about industrial alcohol being diverted to make illicit booze. When she finished the *Post* article, she found something similar in the *Sun*—also on the front page, but this time above the fold. Before she could read it, the door rattled open and Tarkington emerged.

He flashed her a smile, and his gaze skimmed her desktop. "Pretty and smart, too," he said, eyes lingering briefly on the newspapers. "If she's as efficient as Mrs. Hasson, you've got a keeper, Mr. Mayor."

"Miss Byrne is a real asset."

"Miss Byrne," Tarkington said, turning short of the door, "would you be game for a bit of fun? Just an hour or so."

"Um, I'm afraid I'm a little too busy today, Mr. Tarkington, but thank you for your kind offer."

"There's no problem in her coming along, right, Mr. Mayor? The world won't come to an end if the office closes for an hour. My car is parked right outside on the curb."

She looked at Jackson and Prentis but found in their expressions no hint whether she should tag along. In fact, they looked a little shell-shocked. Something didn't ring true about this man. Even though the deal he'd struck with Danny had been a godsend, Fannie still couldn't wrap her noodle around why the terms should be so generous to her fiancé.

The outer door creaked open, and Jack's mischievous face poked in. He looked at his sister and smiled. Then he glanced at the others in the room, and his impishness evaporated.

"Jack! What's wrong?" Fannie asked, jumping to her feet.

"S-sorry, Fannie. Nothing's wrong, but I have an important message from Milo Peppers."

"Mr. Peppers?" It was the code name they had used to indicate that their mother was ready to lower the boom. Fannie pointed to the door and followed him out.

"What have you gone and done now?" she asked, looking him over from head to toe. Her eyes settled on the strange square bulge in the front of his shirt.

Jack took out the ledger. "It was tangled up between your bed linens and the footboard. I didn't want you to get in trouble."

"You're lying, Jack Byrne. Why did you take my calendar?"

He shook his head. "Honest, Fannie. I know how much you love your job. Now, if you'll pardon me, I've got to get back to school before Officer McCall throws me in the pokey for truancy." He bolted.

Fannie flipped through the book. It looked to be intact, but Jack was lying—except for the truancy part. Her brother was a habitual offender with erratic focus and little discipline. Whatever his true motivation at the moment, she would accept his loyalty at face value—for now. She tucked the book under her arm and returned to the office. The least she could do was show a little loyalty of her own. "All right," she said. "I'll come, but only for an hour."

"Excellent," Tarkington said, holding the door open. "A good time will be had by all."

Fannie prayed it would be so. They got in, and as the car roared off at an alarming rate of acceleration, she dug her nails into the seam of the window frame. Much like Jack, this Tarkington fellow was too slick and worldly for her liking, and an odd confederate for a decent, hardworking man like Mayor Dwyer. She needed to pull her head out of the beach sand. There were things going on here that weren't right, and she had a job to keep and a precocious brother to protect. Out of the corner of her eye, she caught Tarkington smiling at her.

"I promise," he said. "Back in an hour. Just a little quick business with Mr. Merkle. All you have to do is sit back and enjoy the ride."

CHAPTER THIRTY-THREE

Snips and Snails and Strange Outings

Jack scrambled out from the concealment of the courthouse azalea bushes. *School, schmool* he thought, watching the green roadster rumble down Main Street. It was the same man Shoe was interested in, and this character had no business dragging Jack's sister into shady activities. He took off at run for the *Evening Star* building, skidded to a stop at the rear entrance, and sneaked in the back door.

"You!" Perkins said, stepping away from the linotype. "Out!"

"Yes sir." Jack made a dash for Tate's cubby. Empty. "Where's Shoe?" he asked the linotyper, who was closing on him fast.

"Upper Marlboro. Now, go chase yourself before I run you head-first through that press over there."

As Perkins reached for him, Jack ducked, and scooted through the pressroom and out the front door. And he didn't stop running until he stood outside Trott's Produce Market.

"Jack Byrne! Why aren't you in school?"

It was Shoe, at the gas pump topped with a red star, on the sidewalk outside Spitler's Auto Supply. Jack dodged a delivery wagon, darted across the road, and jumped in Shoe's car. "Got to come right now."

Shoe chuckled. "Whoa, slow down, bud. Everything jake?"

"Fannie's gone off with the man from the Bayside," Jack said as he got back out and tried to grab the gas nozzle.

Shoe pushed him away. "Quit, now. Are you talking about Nathan Tarkington? That wouldn't surprise me. He's a ladies' man. Look, scamp, we got a good thing going here, but there's nothing I can do about who Fannie keeps company with. She's a big girl—"

"Not with *my* sister. I don't care if the mayor's along for the ride or not. You got to get me down to Mr. Merkle's car lot."

"The *mayor's* riding around with Tarkington?" Shoe pressed four dimes into Jack's palm. "Run inside and give this to John Bernard. Tell him two gallons."

By the time Jack returned, Shoe had already cranked the pump twice and watched the gas drop two hash marks through the blue glass cylinder. "Thought you were in a hurry," he said, replacing the hose on the hanger. "What took you so long?"

Jack climbed back in the car. "Mr. Bernard thought I was up to something, but I wasn't going to take anything . . . No respect."

"Well, don't take anything next time, either, and he might." Shoe rolled through the intersection of Main and Bayside and accelerated toward the outskirts of town.

"Normally, that would be funny," Jack said, giving Shoe the stink eye. "But right now, I just hope this Tarkington is respecting my sister. Can't you pick it up a little? They're probably long gone."

"Relax," Shoe said. "The mayor's a good man. It'll be all right."

As the auto dealership came into view, Shoe geared down, turned into a gravel lot across the street, and eased behind a farm wagon unloading a haymow. Tarkington's tall, thin build was easy to identify in the middle of the lot. The mayor, his assistant, and Fannie sat nearby in his car.

"What are we waiting for?" Jack asked.

"Sit still. Your sister isn't going to appreciate us dropping in. Furthermore, I'm aiding and abetting you skipping school. So if you don't mind, I think we should just watch a while. We can rescue her if she needs rescuing."

That don't make no sense," Jack grumbled, but he stayed put.

"Lots of things don't make sense right now. That's why we watch and maybe learn something.

— · —

Jackson breathed a little easier as he sat in Neely Merkle's Ford dealership, next to one of Mr. Ford's latest mechanical wonders: a glistening black 1921 touring car with curved low-top hood. How much trouble could they get into here, right out in public view? A sprightly middle-aged man with tufts of red hair sprouting over each ear bounded toward them, polishing his round pince-nez spectacles as he came. "Mr. Tarkington," he said, sliding the cheaters back up on his nose. "Was I right?"

Tarkington climbed behind the wheel of the new car. "If she's as fast as you say, I think she'll do just fine."

"Oh, she'll fly, all right. Get 'er out there on the flat and push 'er up to forty-five. She'll purr like a kitten. Wouldn't take it much above that, though. Not like ya gotta outrun the wind, right?" He ran his hand over his gleaming head. "Mr. Ford will make you any color you like so long as it's black. But let's be honest about it. Does anybody really care about color? Versatility—that's the thing. Fred Simpson's reinventing his into a tractor, and Parker Wyatt needs something to run a portable conveyor belt."

"Now, isn't that smart," Tarkington said, running his hand along the mirror mounted on an arm outside the driver's window. "Nice work. Were the other two picked up this morning?"

"First thing," Merkle said. He trailed Tarkington to the other side of the car, followed closely by Jackson, Prentis, and Fannie, who had joined in the admiring comments.

Prentis studied the side mirror. "New one on me. What will Mr. Ford think of next?"

Tarkington shook his head. "Probably that. It's a postfactory addition by a local blacksmith. Extraordinarily helpful in seeing what's coming up behind you. Climb in and do me the honor of being the first to ride in my brand-new car."

"Somehow, I thought a man in your position would drive something with a little more zing," Jackson said, stepping back to take it all in.

"Actually, in my business, flash is not a good thing. Better to not stand out in a group."

Jackson's eyes wandered over to the motorcycles parked outside the sales office. The ones he had seen the day he committed to running for mayor? That fateful day when he let his life veer off on a path he had sworn he would never take? It was hard to believe someone hadn't snatched them up already.

"Can't go wrong with one of those, either," Tarkington said, following his gaze. "Reminds me of a Chance Dwyer story. Hop in and I'll tell you the best yarn you'll ever hear about him. Miss Byrne, you'll get less wind if you're up front with me."

Jackson checked his watch as Tarkington sat for a moment, going through an apparent checklist of concerns over the car's instrumentation, although it was ludicrous to think that Mr. Ford would ever change much of anything in his automobiles. Thankfully, their hour would soon be up and he could be rid of the scoundrel. Fannie appeared to feel much the same. She hadn't made a peep since they left the office. Even Prentis was uncharacteristically quiet.

Finally, to Jackson's relief, Tarkington seemed satisfied and pulled out onto Southern Maryland Boulevard for the inaugural spin.

— —

Tate Shoemaker drove out onto Southern Maryland Boulevard and let Tarkington put a comfortable distance between them.

"Where do you think they're headed?" Jack asked.

"From this side of town? There are only so many worthwhile places: Washington where Southern Maryland Road becomes Pennsylvania Avenue; Upper Marlboro, the next county seat; or more distantly, Bowie. Hopefully, Upper Marlboro—it's close by and exactly where I'm supposed to be. Two birds, one stone."

What Tate couldn't quite grasp was why the mayor was permitting himself to be entertained—even in a nearby town—by a slick operator like Nathan Tarkington. Jackson Dwyer guarded his reputation with vigilance. Surely, Tarkington's connections preceded him. Prentis Riley had to be in the know. There was no access to the mayor except through him. As Tate understood it, you had to pay handsomely to play in Nevis, and you didn't even get onto the ball diamond if you didn't pony up some serious moola to Prentis. Which of the two politicos actually ran things was a little murky.

"Keep up; you're losing 'em."

"Relax, kid. I'm more worried about you skipping class." He glanced at Jack, who had his hand out the window, cupping it against the force of the wind rushing past them. He was the handful—a habitual liar, truant, and apparent thief—but Tate wouldn't trade him for the mayor, his assistant, and a no-limit membership at Mumbles. "What's the upshot of you not being where you're expected?"

"*Pfft*. Nobody has high expectations. Mom has her hands full with the diner."

"Dad?"

"Never met him. He died five months and twenty-two days before I was born, but who's counting?"

Tate gave him a quick look, but he was still playing with the air. So, that's what made Jack tick. It was about *dads*. Some boys wanted to fill those big old shoes, others didn't want any part of them, and then there were those like Jack: forever searching for something to fill a void they couldn't quite come to grips with.

"Something intriguing is going on here, Jack. If I haven't said it yet, great lead."

A smile crept across Jack's face, and then he quickly grew serious again. "I've only got one sister. Step on it."

CHAPTER THIRTY-FOUR

The Jaunt

Jackson shifted forward in his seat. Tarkington had them miles outside Nevis, on a seemingly endless journey northward. "You've got the kipper's knickers here. Turning about soon?"

"Soon," Tarkington said, and he gestured toward a black and white lettered sign: "Upper Marlboro, est. 1706, pop. 385." He turned onto a paved thoroughfare fronted by stately brick homes. An immediate right onto Water Street and across the broad, sluggish creek brought them into the heart of town. Tarkington didn't stop there, but drove to the end of Main Street, where he made a bootleg turn in the shadows of the tobacco warehouses and pulled to the curb. Jackson breathed with relief as the car that had been trailing them since they left Nevis stopped following them and pulled into the nearby courthouse lot.

"We have arrived, Miss Fannie. Relax, this won't take long. You, too, Mayor," he said, looking at him in his side-view mirror. "A once-in-a-lifetime experience."

So is the gallows, thought Jackson. Beside him, Prentis slid down in his seat and muttered a string of profanities.

"So, where was I?" Tarkington asked as he pulled the hand brake lever back and took the car out of gear.

"Mayor Jackson's father," Fannie said.

"Heading for home," Jackson threw out hopefully. He watched the lazy flow of the Patuxent River tributary as it meandered past in its silted-up bed, long past accommodating ocean-going ships like the *snows* of colonial times. He braced for one more cringe-worthy story about his father cheating someone. Fool that he was, he had thought he'd heard them all.

"Yes, of course, Chance Dwyer," Tarkington said. "I'd never heard of Nevis before I came to meet him. Amusement parks—they're everywhere, you know? I'd been to Coney. Nice, plain-spoken New York town steaming along under its own manic power. But Nevis? It bustled with small-town warmth and Southern charm. Love at first sight. I was working for Mr. McClure at the time. He and Mayor Dwyer had been developing a cooperative agreement, and I was to deliver the final draft. I wasn't privy to what was in it. My role was more one of hand-holding, smoothing ruffled feathers. I won't bore you with the specifics, but Mayor Dwyer felt the agreement was unfairly weighted to favor John J., and refused to commit. Chance, not unlike McClure, was a force to be reckoned with, and knowing McClure as I do now, he was probably right."

Tarkington stopped and checked his side mirror, chuckling to himself. "Or it might have been another case of beginning jitters. Anyway, I read the paperwork, found a way to make some small concessions that would make Chance happy without inflaming McClure, and, thank God, everyone signed off on it. Probably the first time I felt like I was earning my keep. I was king of the world. I think Mayor Dwyer felt the same. Gave me a couple Indian motorbikes to thank me for my help. Lovely shade of blue they were."

Jackson felt his heartbeat accelerate. "New ones?" he asked.

"No, his own personal ones. Damnedest thing I ever saw. You'd think he was giving me a bag of gold eagles. I didn't want to be rude, but I had no use for them. Kept 'em in a barn up in New Castle. I think they were eventually buried in a hole with a bunch of farm trash."

"*Our* two blue Indian bikes?" Jackson said. "That son-of-a-bitch bastard!" He motioned at Prentis to get out. "I've heard enough."

There was a growing hum in the distance, like a swarm of droning honeybees, and in seconds, the sound morphed into the roar of an approaching car bearing down on them with a ferocity that Jackson had never heard before. He gripped the back of the seat as the Lizzie, trailing a cloud of dark smoke, skidded to a halt beside them.

"Coming fast," the driver called to Tarkington. "Behind us?"

"Beat it," Tarkington yelled over the rumble, and the beast sprang away. Working levers and foot pedals, Tarkington fell in behind the other car and quickly climbed into high gear. Fannie reached for the door handle, Prentis grabbed his hat, and Jackson lurched forward in his seat.

"What the hell are you doing?" Jackson shouted. "There will be police—"

"Behind us," Tarkington said, gesturing over his shoulder.

Jackson and Prentis twisted around. Through the cloud of smoke shot a second car, and it was flying, too—definitely upward of forty miles per hour.

"Good, Lord, you're going to try to outrun them?"

"No sir. Without a doubt, I *am* going to outrun them." He looked over at Fannie, whose knuckles were white on the door handle. "Good girl. Hang on tight, now."

"No, no, no!" Jackson screamed. "I have a reputation to maintain. For God's sake, pull over. Those are police officers!"

"God's not getting involved in this one!" Tarkington yelled back. "And no, those are dicks—*federal* officers, whose time would be better spent harassing real criminals, not a few southern Maryland boys out to sell a little hooch. We'll give 'em a little runaround, lose 'em, and then hunt up a drink."

Jackson smacked Tarkington's hat off. "Stop now and let me out. Now, sir, or I will personally tell those gentlemen where to find you. Stop. This. Flivver!"

"That's it!" Tarkington swerved right into a narrow alley, gunned the car to the end, and turned left onto the next block. "*Flivver,*" he mumbled, jerking to a stop. "Out, out, out! Tell 'em we went *right*."

— —

Jackson pelted out one side, and Prentis the other, but before Fanny could do the same, Tarkington took off again. "Don't worry, hon," he said, giving her a wink. "I'll circle back around and pick them up in a few. Just as soon as we ditch the pursuit."

Fannie scrunched down in the seat and covered her eyes. "Why?"

"We slow down the pursuit long enough for the lead car to lose 'em."

"But they're criminals."

"Not really. We're just having a bit of fun. Aren't *you* having fun?"

Fannie gave him a wilted look and checked the pursuit. "They turned left. Might want to speed it up a bit."

"Excellent," he said, checking the side-view mirror. "No need for them to walk away from this with a sense of failure *and* inadequacy." He slowed down. The first car stretched its lead, and the feds closed the gap behind Tarkington's car.

On the outskirts of town, the lead car made a quick left onto a side street and disappeared in a cloud of smoke and a shower of gravel. Tarkington did likewise, and they soon found themselves bouncing along an unpaved wagon track.

Fannie unclenched a hand. This man was crazy, and they both were going to die. She grabbed her thumb and began reciting the rosary—a finger for each bead. She had worked her way to the third finger when she heard the car whine and the engine labor. She opened her eyes. They were back on the outskirts of Nevis, at the bottom of Steed's Hill—a steep ascent before the land gradually dropped away toward the bay. The engine sputtered and their speed dropped.

Tarkington muttered something under his breath. "Hang on, Fannie. We'll never make it up with what's left in the tank. He slowed to a crawl, swerved across the road into another three-point turn, and began backing up the incline.

Fannie resumed her two-handed death grip on the dashboard. "If we're not going to make it—"

"Oh, we'll make it up backwards. Fuel flows to the carburetor by gravity. Watch the coppers," he said, nodding downhill. "Model T— they'll be doing the same." Moments later, the unmarked black police coupe made a similar maneuver and continued after them in reverse. "One has to admire their tenacity," Tarkington said, laughing. "Even if it is misplaced."

At the top of the hill, Tarkington swung the car back around and made an immediate right onto a narrow, overgrown farm road. Dense brush screeched and scraped against the doors and side mirror of the Ford. About a hundred feet in, the path opened onto a broad pasture with an overgrown shed. He bounced through several potholes and swung behind the dilapidated, vine-covered building—bumper to bumper with the advance car already hiding there. Cigarette smoke rose from the driver's side, and the passenger's feet stuck out the opposite window.

"Isn't that the—"

"*Sh-h-h.*" Tarkington pulled Fannie's hand loose from the dashboard. She latched on to his and held it like a vise.

They listened as the police car drew closer. At the sound of crackling stones and thrashing foliage, Fannie dug her nails into his hand and beseeched him with wide, panicked eyes. She would never live down an arrest.

"*Ouch,*" Tarkington whispered, shaking his hand free of her grip. He made a circular motion with the uninjured one. Within seconds, the federals' car had apparently turned itself around, and the engine noise was soon lost in the distance, replaced by the bucolic sounds of birdsong and the low hum of insects.

Tarkington hopped out of the car. "Sorry about the hill. My fault. I thought I'd have more fuel than that. Sit a minute, okay?" He jogged up to the driver's side of the other car, handed him something, and, after a few words, had Fannie join him. "Come on. We're taking this one."

The other two men, dressed unremarkably in brown caps and dungarees, hopped out and switched cars. With a cigarette pressed tight between his lips, the driver jumped in; then the other man joined him up front. By the time Fannie had climbed in their car, the men were gone.

"Now, how about a drink?" Tarkington said, navigating out of their hiding place.

"We need to pick up the others."

"Already taken care of." He pulled onto the road. "On these little jaunts, there's always another car trailing at a discreet distance behind the lead car. In this case, it's Mr. Fields, the car dealership's assistant manager. He took one of the new cars out to a *prospective* buyer who lives north of Upper Marlboro; only I'm pretty sure it wasn't a serious buyer. On his return trip, he won't have any trouble recognizing and assisting our roadside companions back to town." He shifted the lever and foot pedal and took off in the same direction they had been heading before their detour.

"Jaunt?" Fannie glanced over her shoulder. "Wouldn't it be more prudent to backtrack and meet them than to follow after the police? What if they're sitting up here waiting for us?"

"Nah, when the adrenaline starts flowing, all they understand is pursuit, pursuit, pursuit. They're probably in Nevis by now, creeping up and down alleys and wondering where in tarnation we disappeared to. I think you've been reading too many G. K. Chesterton novels, Miss Byrne. Whatever happened to a quiet afternoon with Emily Dickinson?"

"She's at home with my cross-stitching," Fannie muttered. "I want you to know I don't appreciate your dragging me all around the country, almost getting me arrested. It's not at all gentlemanly."

He gave her a quick look and chuckled to himself.

"And how is it that you know so much about *jaunting*?"

Tarkington tapped his head. "Because I get around and I pay attention. Ever been to Mumbles?"

"The bar? Hardly."

"Oh, don't say it like *that*. I'll bet all your friends have; they just aren't admitting it. Or maybe they're open about it and you're sitting at home alone, pretending you're a good girl."

She huffed and studied the landscape.

Another chuckle. "Why, Miss Byrne, we have to bring you into the modern age, and there's no better place to start than Mumbles. High-class, private, and the finest spirits this side of Baltimore."

"You sound so positive."

"I ought to be—I keep them stocked well enough."

"You're a . . . *bootlegger*?"

Tarkington whooped and gave the steering wheel a good slap. "Tell me you're not really that naive. My dear Fannie, what do you think this outing has been all about? You can now tell your friends that you are officially a rumrunner for Premier, the best booze makers in all Baltimore."

"Mother Mary! Stop at once and let me out!"

"Sorry. That would make Mayor Jackson, your surrogate father, very angry. And exactly what sort of dishonorable man would I be if I left a lady in the middle of the road? Settle down, and I'll make sure you get back safely."

"I'm not drinking with you. Take me back to the office right now." She unlatched her door.

"Dear God, woman." Tarkington brought the car to a skidding halt in the middle of the road. "Let's not be doing that."

"I've had enough of you," she said, sliding out of the car. "I'll meet Mr. Fields halfway." She took off in the opposite direction down the road.

Tarkington put the car in reverse. "Please get back in, Miss Fannie," he said, idling along beside her. "The mayor will be more than displeased should something happen to you."

"As he should. You're nothing but a common criminal," she said, wiping away a tear with one hand and waving the other at an approaching car. The car stopped, and the driver got out. To her surprised relief, it was Jack and Mr. Shoemaker, the young journalist she had met on the *Chessie Belle*.

"Don't get in a strange car just because you're mad at me," Tarkington said, getting out.

"Are you all right, Miss Byrne?" Shoemaker asked, stepping between her and the advancing Tarkington.

"No," she said, tears now flowing freely. "Would you please take me home?"

"What did you do to her, you scoundrel?" Shoemaker asked. But before Tarkington could answer, he swung a clean right hook that laid the bootlegger flat. "Get in the car," he told her, and they were gone before Tarkington could stagger back to his feet.

CHAPTER THIRTY-FIVE

A New Alliance

Tate parked on the north side of town, near Sollars Wharf. Miss Fannie Byrne refused to go home. She didn't look beat up or disheveled, but something unpleasant had happened. He and Jack were out of their depth. Mary Pickford never gave him any such puzzling behavior, and Jack had no earthly idea how to be nice to his sister.

"Wanna talk?" Tate finally asked.

She shook her head, then nodded.

"Did he hurt you?"

"Only my pride," she said with a sniff. "That man is nothing but a grifter and a ne'er-do-well."

"Yes, ma'am. Jack and I, we've been watching that one. Would you like me to take you home now, or should we sit here a bit?"

"Sit," she said and smiled at Jack. "The mayor needs to know who he's dealing with."

Tate arched an eyebrow and tried to calm his accelerating heartbeat. "Yes, ma'am. And exactly what is it that we need to say?"

"That Nathan Tarkington is a no-good, sneaky rumrunner. Right in front of the mayor. Why, if Mayor Dwyer hadn't stepped out of the car, he would have been right in the middle of it all. Imagine, a car full of demon drink, and the police nabbing that dear man for bootlegging."

"The mayor had no clue?"

"None. Mr. Prentis, either, from all I could see."

"Tarkington admitted he was bootlegging?"

"He most certainly did. He even went so far as to invite me for a drink. *Alone.*" Jack patted her shoulder as her eyes welled up.

"Miss Byrne, I'll be perfectly candid with you." Tate stopped a moment as a car approached. He doubted Tarkington would follow them, but the guy was a bad apple. He breathed a sigh of relief as the unfamiliar driver continued past them. "I'm desperate to nail this guy. At least run him out of town, at best throw him in the clink and protect the innocent citizens of Nevis. Will you help me?"

Jack nodded like a Babe Ruth bobblehead. "Yeah, Fannie, we've been working hard."

"You should be at school!" She wiped her nose with the handkerchief Tate had given her. "What could I possibly do?"

"There's a bootlegging operation at Parkers Wharf," Tate said. "It started out as German brewers tried to keep their heads above water, and then local bootleggers found it a safe place to create a liquor supply for Mumbles. That's the speakeasy downtown. But that's changed now. Little Nevis has caught the imagination of the out-of-state big boys, and they're going to squeeze out these locals and make the town a big-time operation. They play a hard game, ma'am. My greatest fear is that Nevis will end up just like Atlantic City—a city awash in tippling, high-roll gambling, and even more unsavory vices."

"Oh, dear."

"I know. It's a scary thing," Tate said, shaking his head. "You seem to think highly of Mayor Dwyer, and maybe he's just a good guy caught in an impossible situation. But as much as I hate to admit it, the mayor appears to be involved. If he's a weak link in the production chain, they'll boot him out and put in Nucky Johnson's twin brother to grease the skids." He reached out and put his hand on hers. "Miss Fannie, I can't do this alone. We need information, and you're in the best position to provide it. Think back. Has the mayor recently engaged in activities that you might now consider a bit odd?"

She slipped her hand free and left the handkerchief in its place. "Well, Mayor Dwyer has taken a number of appointments down at Parkers Wharf—a rather sudden and uncharacteristic interest in religion and Saint Raphael. And then there was that meeting a few weeks back with Hubert Carr from Bayland, Mr. Tarkington, and that hoity-toity woman from out of town. Mr. Carr was okay, but she was hard as flint and smelled of cigar smoke. Why, I never . . ."

Fannie's stream of consciousness was like Christmas and a birthday rolled up into one gigantic gift. Tate leaned across the seat toward her. "Honora Lally."

"Exactly," she said, poking a finger at the warehouse they sat next to. "And I should have listened to that little voice that told me to take a peek inside those envelopes. How often do we get mail delivered by courier—*two* special couriers, and all in the same day?"

"Why do you think the envelopes were connected to Tarkington and Miss Lally?"

"Because they arrived the day after they all met, and Mr. Carr reviewed them with the mayor and Mr. Prentis. They all seemed very pleased."

"Did you file them or any notes from the meeting."

"Oh, no."

Tate dropped back against the car seat. "Is that unusual?"

"Not at all. The mayor keeps a locked file cabinet in his office. There are lots of documents I never see."

"Key?"

"Only the mayor. Maybe Prentis."

Jack leaned over the seat and whispered like a dark angel in Tate's ear. "I could help her jimmy it."

"That isn't happening," Tate said. He pulled away and turned to Fannie. "You really need to take him in hand."

She gave Jack a hard look. "The good Lord knows my mother has tried."

"*Jeesh*," Jack said. 'If it hadn't been for me today . . ." He got out of the car and took off in the direction of town.

"You were my hero today, Jack," she called after him. "Dad would have been proud."

He dismissed her with a wave and kept walking.

"He'll bounce back," Tate said. "Would you like me to take you home now?"

"Oh, no. Back to the mayor's office. They'll be wondering where I am. If Tarkington's there, I don't want him telling any wild tales. And you could go to jail for assault."

"Aw, I'm not concerned. He doesn't strike me as the type who has much truck with cops. There's a lot of no-good under that slickness." Shoe looked deep into her big, sad eyes. Fannie had spunk, but he wasn't sure she had the survival instincts of her brother. "Work with me, Fannie. Help me nail this guy. I can if you feed me information about the mayor's activities—being discreet, of course."

She nodded with a gusto that scared him. He didn't need the dame to go off half-cocked or fancy herself a spy—just a little information.

"Okay, then," he said, and drove her back to the courthouse. He parked at the curb, and she sat a moment in deep thought.

"And you're sure the mayor is involved with what's going on at Parkers Wharf?" she asked.

"Nothing's sure without documents, but I saw him down there with my own two eyes, Fannie, and he wasn't praying."

That seemed to do it. She got out of the car without further discussion.

When she was safely inside the building, he swung back around to hunt down Jack and found him pouting down by the old pickle-boat houses. His offer of a ride was met with a scowl and the cold shoulder.

"Stop being a baby and get in, kid. We need to find a locksmith who doesn't mind a little moonlighting."

Jack's eyes lit up, and he climbed in.

"Where can I find the lowlife who taught you to jimmy a lock?"

"There's a guy down on the docks named—"

"Don't need a name, son—just an address and a little cash." He pointed the car toward the docks.

CHAPTER THIRTY-SIX

A Dame Half-Cocked

Jackson Dwyer was several inches shorter than Nathan Tarkington, but the taller man took a step back from the advancing mayor with thunder in his eye. "What do you mean, you don't know where she is? What the devil no-good have you been—" Jackson stopped and eyeballed Tarkington's bluish, puffy jawline. "Clocked you good, did she?" He picked up the telephone and dialed several digits before Tarkington reached out and bobbled the switch hook, disconnecting him.

"Hang up the damn phone. She's fine. Someone who works for the newspaper gave her a ride. Do you really think he would have let it go with one punch if something untoward were going on?"

"Dear God, you had *reporters* following you? Shoemaker?" Jackson hit his chair like a dropped rock. "Rum-running! How dare you put me in that position! What would people think of their mayor? Did you really not understand what I mean when I said we want nothing to do with your shenanigans? We had an agreement. You broke it."

"A bit of fun. I thought if you got into the spirit of things . . ." Tarkington shook his head. "Never mind. I wasn't being followed. Fannie's brother was in the car, and they offered her a lift. No harm done. Everybody's fine. Who is this Shoemaker?"

"A good friend," Fannie said, walking in. She went straight to Tarkington. "Are you all right?" she asked, grimacing as she raised a hand to his face.

"Dear God, Fannie, are *you* all right?" Jackson asked, though he could find no fault with her appearance.

"I'm fine. This has all been a terrible misunderstanding. Mr. Shoemaker thought . . . well, he misinterpreted, um . . ."

Jackson could see the relief wash across Tarkington's face. "No, Miss Byrne, it is I who should apologize. My judgment was poor, and I placed you in a most precarious situation. Although his swing at me was unjustified, I would have done the same in his position. Can you forgive me?"

"We shan't speak of it again," Fannie said. She shooed Prentis away from her desk and pulled out the mayor's schedule. "Now, don't we all have more important things to do than stare at me?"

"Well, then, er, back to business, I suppose." Jackson caught Tarkington's eye and tilted his head toward the exit. Then he and Prentis disappeared into his office.

— —

Nathan Tarkington stood in the middle of the anteroom, staring at Fannie. When she acknowledged his stare, he smiled sheepishly, hesitated a moment, and said, "About our little outing—I want you to know I don't do such things as a matter of habit."

"And your boast about supplying Nevis with liquor?"

He laughed. "Yes, that . . . It was a silly boast and completely untrue. The whole escapade started with a friend from Delaware who offered to set me up with some rumrunners. I thought it would be exciting, but it was an ill-chosen lark. Only now am I realizing how bad it would have been if I had gotten all of us arrested. The good mayor is understandably livid. I'm afraid I was afflicted with pretty girlitis. I haven't done anything to impress, have I?"

"I think there are better ways."

"And I actually know a few that are much more civil. I could treat you and Mr. Millman to an excellent dinner at the Bayside, if you'd like. Of course, I'd deeply appreciate it if you could find it in your heart not to mention my supremely awkward attempt to impress you. I do have my pride. It could be a congratulatory affair to celebrate the business deal with him. Then I could walk away knowing that we are on friendly terms."

"If I may be totally honest, Mr. Tarkingt—"

"Nathan?"

"*Nathan.* I've decided you were right. Not about everything, but I do read a lot of Emily Dickinson. It's time to put away the books and live my life instead of existing vicariously through the adventures of other people." Fannie took a deep breath. "I'm ready for that drink you offered."

"Alone?" Tarkington glanced at Jackson's closed door and moved to her desk. "One swollen jaw already far exceeds my quota. I'm not sure Mr. Millman would appreciate that."

"Oh." She put her pencil down in the seam of the schedule book. "And did you not give any consideration to him when you invited me out this morning?"

Tarkington chuckled. "Honestly?"

"Mr. Millman and I had a little fight . . ."

"Oh," he said, brightening. "Then very well, Fannie, if I may call you that. Are you free at the end of the week? I'll take you to Bubbles—the best Nevis has to offer. But this must remain a secret between the two of us. It's an exclusive place."

She mimed locking her lips and tossing away the key. "I'll plan on it. That should make us more than even."

"Would six o'clock Friday work for you? I can swing by your house."

"Seven-thirty? We'll be working late. I can meet you right outside."

"Perfect," he said. And with a dazzling smile, he bade her good evening.

— - —

At the end of the workday, Fanny hit the street. Tate Shoemaker watched as she stopped at the front window of Becker's dress shop. Then, with a quick look over her shoulder, she hurried down to the intersection of Main and Chestnut Streets and jumped into his waiting car.

"Nobody walking with you, right?" He craned his neck out the window to peek around the cars parked between his and the corner.

"Just me. Everything's swell. I have great news."

Tate studied the curlicues of hair that had escaped her hair clasp and were framing her face. She looked better than earlier in the day. A whole lot better. "Me, too," he said. "I don't have time to beat gums, so let's be quick about it. Fanny, I'll need a key to the mayor's office this Friday."

"I don't know," she said, frowning. "Why?"

"It's better you don't know. I promise, no one will ever know we were there. And forget I said that."

She stared at him as if gauging whether she could trust him, then nodded slowly. "Okay, but you need to meet me outside when I leave for the day. I've got an appointment with Nathan Tarkington."

He perked up. "Oh? He and the mayor meeting? I can get a photographer."

"No, just the two of us."

"For crying out loud, Fannie, you have a *date* with that scoundrel? Are you out of your mind?"

"*Appointment,*" she repeated. "You'll be thanking me when I help you crack this case."

His jaw dropped. "Crack? There'll be no cracking for you. What kind of twaddle is that dandy feeding you? He has girlfriends from here to Hong Kong."

"*Humpf!*" Her petite nose went up in the air. "I haven't gotten myself into anything. I'll give you the key, but I need something in return."

"I'm not making any deals with you. You have no earthly idea what you're getting yourself into. What are you up to, anyway?"

"You don't need to know the specifics. Didn't you ask me to trust you? Now I'm asking you to do the same."

Now Tate was beginning to see more of a family resemblance between Fannie and her brother. "Not until I know what kind of cockamamie scheme you're up to."

"Nathan Tarkington is taking me drinking at a very exclusive place—*Bubbles,* if you must know. When he trusts me, I'll get him to take me for a drink down at Parkers Wharf—"

"Oh, no, you're not—"

"And that's where you can have your photographer lurking nearby to capture it all on film. We'll have him red-handed."

"Did you stop to think that *you'd* be in the pictures, too? Surely, your fiancé hasn't approved this crazy plan."

Her face reddened, and he saw the fire in those lovely eyes. "Oh-h-h, why does everyone insist I need a man's permission to do things?"

"Because men are calmer, more rational creatures?" he shot back. "He's going to get you blotto and take advantage of you." As soon as the words roared out of his mouth, Tate wanted to suck them all back in.

She hopped out and slammed the door. "You think I'm some sort of sap, do you? Well, so was your old man. Seven thirty, outside the courthouse. Check the flower pots. I'll let you know when we'll be at the wharf. And since you have everything under control, I'm sure you don't need me to tell you that Mayor Jackson keeps his most important papers in a small metal lockbox. It's probably in the gray file cabinet closest to his desk." She stalked off.

Definitely Jack's sister. Move over Mary Pickford.

CHAPTER THIRTY-SEVEN

A Simple Plan

Fannie sat on the low marble retaining wall at the foot of the court-house steps and watched Tarkington park his green roadster near the courthouse steps. He was early, and Tate had yet to arrive. She glanced one more time in the direction of the *Evening Star* building and then looked back at Tarkington as he dodged two cars and came her way. What was she going to do with the office key? What was she going to do with *him*?" She took two deep breaths.

"Glad to see you didn't change your mind," he said as he drew near.

"Oh, not at all," she said. "I've been looking forward to it." She remained seated and checked the street once more. Tate had deserted her. Apparently, he was more vexed than she had realized.

He glanced over his shoulder. "Are you ready to go, or are we waiting for something?"

"No, just enjoying the marigolds and geraniums." She picked up her purse and slid off the smooth marble wall as a car pulled up to the nearby law offices of Barker and Surratt, across the street. Fannie prayed it was Tate, but the driver didn't get out. "Let's go," she said, and when Tarkington's back was turned, she dropped the key into the flowerpot beside her.

It was Tarkington who seemed distracted when they reached his car. As he opened her door, he paused and looked toward the law office, then closed the door before she could climb in.

"Legal problems?" Fannie asked, hoping Tate would stay out of sight. "I suppose we could have that drink another time."

He dragged his attention back to her. "No, ma'am. It's a nice warm spring evening. How about we walk?"

"Not far, I hope," she said, looking down at her narrow-toed pumps.

"No, actually. It wasn't what I had planned, but we can do quite nicely. There's a great place just down the street. I know someone who stocks it."

"Are you bragging?"

"And why not?" he said, grinning.

"As long as I don't get arrested for bootlegging."

He laughed, seeming genuinely in the moment again. "Oh, I don't think you need worry about that, although they say it's half the fun. Come on, you'll enjoy it." He took her hand and placed it on his arm, and they strolled to Mumbles, where he passed a membership card through the small window. Moments later, to the lively strains of Jolson's "Toot, Toot, Tootsie (Goodbye)," he swept her into the whirling, boisterous speakeasy.

— ◆ —

Just after nine o'clock, Tate unlocked the door to the mayor's office and ushered in his accomplice. He wasn't entirely sure he could trust Reuben Busby—he smelled half pickled—but Jack vouched for him, and, lame as it seemed, that would have to do. Jack knew the shady side of the wharf better even than Officer McCall, and his recommendation was likely Tate's best bet.

The plan was simple: get in with the key, pick the lock on the metal filing cabinet, find the lockbox or something else incriminating, then put everything back in order and get out. As Tate put it to Rueben, no gabbing, snooping elsewhere, or pilfering of so much as a paper clip.

Sure enough, Jack knew how to pick 'em. And so, apparently, did Rueben. Five minutes after they entered, Rueben handed the contents of the file's top drawer to Tate—folders, but no lockbox. Tate spread them out on the floor and started flipping and scanning under the illumination of a railway lantern Rueben had "borrowed" from the depot. "Personal minutes of formal meetings in Baltimore," he whispered. He gave them back and pointed to the next drawer.

Alas, the second drawer also had no box and no files pertinent to his investigation, although a few land-sale documents on eminent domain raised some red flags. Reluctantly he handed them back to Rueben, and they dug into the contents of the third drawer.

"Box," Ruben hissed. From the back of the drawer, he extracted a metal container about the size of a cigar box. A minute later, Tate heard the soft click of the lock, and Ruben handed the box over.

Tate rifled through personal belongings: motorcycle advertisements, a small leather diary, playhouse tickets, an aviator's watch, land documents, and two photographs, one of which was a recent formal portrait of Mayor Dwyer and a young man in military attire. Father and son? The second one was of a finely dressed couple standing in a field of daisies, gazing contentedly at the photographer. The young man bore a striking resemblance to the military man, but the style of the clothes dated it much earlier—probably Dwyer in his youth. He had no idea who the young woman was, but they had the look of love about them.

He put the pictures aside and continued leafing to the bottom, where he found a plain white envelope. The papers inside were puzzling: letters outlining bids of some sort, although it wasn't clear what the product was. New paper stock, modern English, and signed by George Washington, though not to be outdone by the one signed "*William Volstead.*" They carried the faint stench of dirty dealing.

There was something else: a sound so soft and ambient that Tate had ignored it at first. But it was louder now and less mellow. An unmistakable rustling. Tate froze. Reuben heard it, too, for he grabbed Tate's arm and tugged. They were not alone.

Tate put his finger to his lips, looking around the room in the dim red glow of the lantern. The desk chair was empty. No shadows lurked in the corners of the room. Nothing had changed since they entered. And then his eyes settled on the sofa and the dark form sprawled on it. There it was again—the unmistakable sound of snoring.

What kind of political figure slept in his office at night?

Tate eased the lockbox shut, thrust it at Reuben, and shooed him toward the door. He scooped up the rest of the miscellany from the floor and put it back in the drawer. Then he shot out the door behind Ruben as the snoring punctuated itself in a snort, a gasp, and a yelp.

— —

The wooden shipping crates full of oyster crackers were stacked twelve abreast and twelve high. Perched up on top, Jackson watched as the gray-haired temperance woman crept past, growling softly as she held her ax aloft. When she stopped directly below him, he tipped a box and sent it crashing down on top of her. A bloodcurdling scream filled the air, and he startled awake, sitting up on the sofa with a jerk. He flicked on the electric lamp. No warehouse, no Camilla, no ax—just a quiet office with nothing awry . . . except the drawers of his personal file cabinet. The bottom drawer gaped half open, and the corners of files poked out in all directions.

He dropped to his knees before the cabinet and, like a farmer delivering a calf, thrust his hands deep into the drawer. The lockbox was gone! He crawled to the door, shoved it closed, and locked it. Then he reached for his phone.

The voice at the other end was thick and slow, full of sleep. "Who is this?" Prentis asked.

"Your very irritated mayor. Standing in the middle of his ransacked office."

"Of course it is," Prentis mumbled. "Did you call the police? I'm a bit far away at the moment."

"Of course not. That invites too many questions. He's taken my lockbox."

"He who? If you know *who,* call the police. They'll make him bring it back with a nice apology."

"You're not getting it. He has my lockbox with very important papers in it. I'll not say another word over the phone. Suffice it to say, I'm—er, we're—in a very delicate position."

A sigh of exasperation came over the phone, followed by a long silence. "I told you that you put too much to paper. Get out of there in case they circle around and come back for more. Meet me at Mumbles in ten minutes, and in the meantime, figure out what it is they've taken. But for God's sake, *don't write it down.*"

Jackson hung up, dug his pistol out of the desk, and put it in his jacket pocket.

—•—

For his considerable weight, Reuben Busby could move. Tate hit the stairs at a dead run, but when he got to street level, his accomplice was long gone. Tate jogged a few blocks toward the water. He would be in one of the alleys, clutching the lockbox protectively and huffing like a steam locomotive.

After the third empty alley, Tate began to worry. Oh, Busby might just be protecting the box, but he was gone, and Tate had no clue where to find him before he fenced or bartered the contents. What, exactly, did the man think he had? Hell, if he just wanted more money, Tate would have negotiated. He put his hands on his knees, panting.

"Problem?"

Tate bolted upright. "No sir," he said, forcing a smile at the beat cop whose face was unfamiliar and whose voice carried an air of suspicion. "I thought I'd lost my money clip, but on second consideration, I believe it's at home. I'm headed that way now and no need of assistance. Good evening." Tate tipped his hat, but he wasn't feeling it, and the cop didn't seem convinced, either. Tate could feel his burning stare as it followed him down to the *Star* building, where his ride home sat.

Be damned if Reuben Busby wasn't sitting there, too, right on the running board. Tate double-checked that the flatfoot had moved on, and then rushed toward the locksmith. "Rueben, you're a sight for sore eyes," he said, grabbing him by the shoulders. "Where's the box?"

Rueben looked puzzled. "What box?"

"The metal box you were clutching to your breast right before we ran for our lives."

Rueben pulled at his pants pockets. "Nothing, man."

"You're joshing me, right?" Tate peeked into the car and then turned on his accomplice. "Have you been hitting the turpentine, Rueben? You're getting yourself involved in something really rough here. If the wrong people know you have those papers, they're going to come calling. Now, what did you do with the damn box?"

"Must have some pretty valuable stuff in there for you to get so worked up. Is that why we broke in there, to get the box? Seems like people should take better care of something that important."

Tate ran a hand through his hair. "Jesus, help me. How much, you miserab—"

"Hundred dollars."

"Hund . . . Are you out of your mind?" Tate wanted to throttle him. He walked to the other side of the car to put some distance between them. "I'm not giving you money. Give me the box back before you get yourself killed."

"That bad, huh? Two hundred, then." Ruben eyed him a moment and seemed to reevaluate. "Tell you what. Not many people carry that kind of cash around. I'll be down at the main dock tomorrow, doing some repair work on the landing. We can do business then. Eight o'clock sharp. And don't threaten me. I'm sure the coppers would love to hear who broke into the mayor's office."

CHAPTER THIRTY-EIGHT

Shedding a Bit of Light

The revolver felt like a lead weight in Jackson's coat pocket. He didn't need it here. In fact, as he looked around Mumbles at the swirling, festive crowd drinking and foxtrotting to the riffs and rhythms of "Hot Lips," he felt a bit foolish. He could never shoot anyone. Well, maybe Nathan Tarkington. Indian motorbikes, personal pictures, his hard-earned good name—what more could the man strip away from him? He watched a dour-faced Prentis maneuver through the crowd.

"What was in the box?" Prentis asked as he sat down.

"The liquor bids and all my personal documents, including the land swap."

"Are you sure you didn't just hide it somewhere else?"

"Don't be ridiculous. Tarkington's taken it all, the snake."

"How incriminating can it be for him to have a couple of documents signed by our first president and Mr. Volstead? He's not going to make waves. At most, he's protecting himself. In his shoes, I might do the same. You'd better hope to God it's him, Jackson. I told you to destroy those, didn't I?"

"You're not in cahoots, are you?

"Get a grip."

"It's not just the documents. It's the pictures and my personal diary."

Prentis drew back. "Please tell me the only thing of interest in your diary is your inexplicable lusting after Camilla, and the latest adventures of Ollie the oyster cookie."

"Cracker," Jackson corrected. He shook his head. "All of it, to the last detail."

"You jackass!"

Jackson stiffened. His eyes blazed as they lit on Tarkington, seated across the room with Fannie. "There's the bastard right there. But what the hell is *she* doing here?" He started to rise, but Prentis put a hand on his shoulder. Jackson sat back down on the edge of his chair, staring like a bird of prey.

"Sit and think about it, Jackson. He can't be two places at once. It's a great alibi, don't you think?"

"Don't be a sucker. He *knows* people." Jackson darted across the room before Prentis could react. "Mr. Millman about?" he asked a startled Fannie.

The color drained from her face, and she shook her head.

"Mm-m." Jackson turned to Tarkington. "May I see you outside?"

"Later?" Tarkington asked.

Jackson shook his head and walked toward the entrance.

"Sorry, be back in a moment," Tarkington said to Fanny. And putting down his napkin, he followed Jackson to the door. "Have your discussion with me right here. No reason to head out into the dark. What's gone so wrong that you had to hunt me down in the middle of a Friday night?"

"Outside."

Tarkington stuck his head out the door and looked both ways down the alley before stepping out.

"Where's the box?" Jackson hissed.

"Which box would this be, now?"

"The one you took from my office when you ransacked it this evening. I know it was you."

There was a sharp intake of breath. "What's in the box, Jackson?"

"Don't play with me."

"I've been with Miss Byrne all evening." Tarkington tipped his head toward Mumbles. "Ask her."

"Oh, I figure you know people."

Tarkington grabbed Jackson's arm and directed him down the alley, toward the back street. "Listen to what I'm saying," he whispered. "Something else is afoot here. I need to know what's in the box that may incriminate you, me . . . anyone."

It was too dark to read Tarkington's face, but his tone alarmed Jackson. "The bids from you and Miss La—"

"No names." Tarkington stopped as if listening, then took another quick look around them. "Both documents, no doubt, written in the most general terms. Unfortunate, but not damning. What else are you so worried about?"

"A journal describing my day-to-day struggles over the Nevis liquor crisis."

"How specific?"

"Names, dates, the reasoning behind certain decisions I've made."

"Christ." Nathan released his vise grip on Jackson's arm. "Why the hell would you write that down?"

Jackson rubbed his arm. "I had to work my way through the decision process to be sure I was making the right choices. I write down everything. Old habits—and, in this case, an unfortunate compulsion—die hard. I'm afraid the land swap documents are gone, too. Now they're out there and available for all sorts of potentially nefarious purposes. I certainly don't want my business connected to yours."

"Yeah, well, the feeling is becoming more mutual by the minute." Tarkington kneaded the back of his neck and gave Jackson a hard look. "You'd better see what you can do to fix it on your end." He started back up the alleyway.

"Where are you going?" Jackson asked, following him.

Nathan stopped at the door. "To finish my drink, escort Miss Byrne home, and then try to clean up what I can. In the wrong hands . . ."

"I know you're aware Miss Byrne has a fiancé, Millman. Stay away from the kid."

"Yes, I am aware, and I am ever respectful of that fact. She wanted to know what a speakeasy was like, and I agreed to show her. Whatever sordid suspicions you have about my intentions with Miss Byrne are without basis and, frankly, unworthy of you. Now, if you'll excuse me, there is a lovely lady sitting all alone in that den of vice and iniquity."

There was a *hiss* and a *crack,* and Tarkington fell back against the brick wall and collapsed. Jackson shrank against the building as a dark figure disappeared into the shadows. As footsteps pounded down the narrow passageway, and a flash of bright light dazzled his eyes, Jackson reached for Tarkington. The bootlegger moaned, and Jackson pulled back a wet, bloodied hand. "For God's sake, get a doctor!" he called out. "This man's been shot!"

"One more, Mayor." The cameraman raised his flash pan, and the alleyway lit up again as acrid smoke drifted over the scene.

CHAPTER THIRTY-NINE

Panning for Gold

The Pulitzer was so close, Tate Shoemaker could taste it. But if he didn't work fast, someone was going to scoop him. With Riley waiting on the dock, the last thing he needed this morning was an instructional session in the boss's office.

"You've begged, whined, and badgered for an assignment with teeth in it," Riley Tanner said, pointing an ink-stained finger at Tate. "So I give you one in Upper Marlboro, and what happens? I find out you've let me down. Upper Marlboro isn't that far. You thought it more important to step away for a quick nip and a bite to eat?"

Tate found the most comfortable line of sight to be a direct bead on Tanner's right ear. If he kept his mouth shut, the lecture would soon be over—brutal but quick. He smiled earnestly at Tanner and tried to look amenable. "No sir. I went to Upper Marlboro, but once I got there, a much bigger fish landed in my lap—a fish that could land us both a Pulitzer. What would you say if I told you our local government is up to its peepers in bootlegging? And that they're brewing right here in Nevis?"

"Bootlegging, you say? Son, we have a town full of German brewers."

"Not Germans, boss. Philadelphia and Delaware . . . with industrial alcohol. John J. McClure and his sort."

"You been sampling some of that alcohol, by any chance?"

"No sir, not a drop. And I can prove all of it."

Tanner's finger quit shaking and stood down. "I'm listening, but get to it quick. I don't have time for hunches and hearsay."

Tate launched into a condensed version, including activities at Parkers Wharf and the trip to Upper Marlboro. He stressed the primary players as best he could without specifically mentioning the mayor's office, fearing that if he made it *too* good, Tanner would assign it to one of his more seasoned reporters.

"Documented sources?"

"Not yet, but I'm close. Jack Byrne—he's just a kid—"

Tanner slid off the edge of the desk he had been ranting from. "Hit the desk back there or the highway. If I have to talk to you one more time—"

"But his sister, Fannie, is the mayor's secretary. She sees a lot."

"Stay away from the mayor. I've already got Wilson investigating last night's shooting outside Mumbles."

"No problem. I'm not working on an angle with the mayor. She's my source concerning other activities. I just need a little bit more time." Tate read the indecision in Tanner's eyes. The word of a kid and a dame wasn't going to be enough. "I have a source who has documents linking the players. I'm taking possession of those later today."

Tanner sat down with a huff. "Look, Shoemaker, your father was a great journalist. One of the best. Your passion reminds me of him sometimes, but your caboose always seems to be out of the yard ahead of the hog. We're talking town movers and shakers here, and I'm not about to get sued for libel. Don't step on Wilson's toes. You get me dirty deeds in writing, and credible witnesses who will swear to what you're asserting, and I'll consider running it. A week. If you haven't got anything for me by then, you need to consider a different career. Clear enough?"

Tate grabbed his hand and shook it hard. "Yes sir. I won't disappoint you."

Tanner yanked his hand free and pointed toward the door. "That weekly *Chessie Belle* report better not be lagging, either. And stay out of the courthouse!"

"Yes sir."

Tate hurried back to his desk and pulled out the two hundred dollars in an envelope taped under the second drawer—every cent he had to his name. His father had always told him to "Give it your all or don't do it at all," and he was seldom wrong. He hoped the information in the box would be enough to mollify Tanner for now. All he needed was a few more days.

Reuben Busby might be a double-crossing snake, but he knew how to keep an appointment. As Tate approached the waterside, he saw immediately that one of the workmen couldn't keep his attention on the plank he was cutting. Their eyes met before Tate ever stepped onto the wharf. Busby put down his saw, picked up the knapsack at his feet, and met him halfway down the landing. There were no courteous salutations.

"Money?"

"Box?"

They swapped, each eyeing the goods suspiciously. Tate was surprised the man didn't insist on counting the dough before handing over the lockbox. Tate popped open the box and poked through it as Busby counted his ill-gotten profits.

236

"Two hundred?"

"Yes. Did you remove anything?"

Busby shook his head. "Doesn't matter to me what's in there." He shoved the wad of bills into his pocket. "Nice doing business with ya," he said, then turned and walked back to the plank he was cutting.

Tate beelined from the waterfront hubbub to a quiet bench on the boardwalk. Taking off his jacket, he laid it on his lap and upended the box's contents onto it. The picture, the folded documents executed my Messrs. Washington and Volstead, and the other mementos tumbled out. He couldn't make sense of the legal document detailing the land transfer, but that was easy enough to track down at the courthouse. He leafed through the journal. Jackson Dwyer appeared to be a dedicated diarist. The journal was nothing less than a day-by-day accounting of the mayor's activities. What better way to get a window into the mayor's mind? It felt invasive, but then, so was breaking and entering.

He riffled through the pages to the day in Upper Marlboro and read with increasing interest the detailed account of the trip, including Jackson's surprise and anger at being included in a certain *"T's rumrunning activities."* Tate put the journal down and considered the implications of the mayor's reluctance. That shot his story angle to hell. He scanned the whole account and several earlier pages. The man was a fool but not a damned fool. He had put pen to paper but was not so reckless as to name names. There were initials everywhere. "P" stood for "Prentis." That was easy, and it followed that in the unpleasant Upper Marlboro adventure, "F" was a reference to Fannie Byrne, and the "T" was for "Tarkington." The question, then, was whether the "T" discussed in a number of the other journal entries was the same man.

Tate stopped, his eyes darting as he assessed his isolated position. He had a gold mine here—stuff Wilson could only dream about. He dumped everything back into the box and hurried back to the *Star*. He needed transcriptions. And a meeting with Jackson. How would the mayor react to having his own accounts—obtained from an anonymous, protected source—parroted back to him?

CHAPTER FORTY

Reluctant Mayor Story

Officer Reagan puffed on the butt of a hand-rolled cigarette as he put one of Jackson's answers to paper. Jackson eyed the holding cells with dread. His visit to the Nevis clink was strictly administrative, or so he had been told, but the questions coming at him seemed anything but.

"Got any more of those?" Jackson asked. "I left mine at home." He lit the one Reagan offered, and took several puffs. "I feel you're trying to accuse me of something here, but if I were out to kill the man, why pay to have someone do it, and then stand right next to him knowing he's about to get shot? A little risky, don't you think?"

"We find you outside a downtown blind tiger with a piece in your pocket, and at least two witnesses have come forward to tell authorities that you threatened Nathan Tarkington at the courthouse last Tuesday. Do you deny any of that?"

Jackson shook his head. "I was angry. And I dislike men such as he, but kill him? Really, now. You ought to know me better than that." He brushed a fleck of tobacco from his lip. "No one will tell me anything. Is Mr. Tarkington dead?"

Officer Reagan glanced up briefly from his papers, then resumed writing without comment.

"I feared for my life in that alleyway."

"Is that why you were packing last night?"

"I always carry it when I'm out late, as do many others. Speaking of it, will you be returning it to me now?"

The officer shook his head.

"Well, do you have any leads on the culprit?"

"Mr. Tarkington refused treatment and left town."

Relief washed over Jackson like a tidal wave. "Not dead? That's good news—er, amazing, actually. Where did he go?"

"I thought you might be able to help us with that information."

Jackson put his hands out. "I hardly know the fellow. In fact, I've told you all I know. So if you don't mind, I'll be going. I have the town's business to attend to."

"We're done for now." Regan slid the sheet of paper over and had Jackson sign the bottom. "I would ask that you not follow his lead."

"Leave town? Where would I go? I practically live in the courthouse." As Jackson turned to go, it suddenly occurred to him that he should ask whether anyone had turned in a lockbox, but Officer Reagan seemed to be brimming with unanswered questions. Jackson left it alone.

— • —

Back at the courthouse, Jackson found Prentis standing watch at the window. "The crook has run off with my papers," Jackson said.

"*Left*, you say? How is that possible? I thought he was at death's door."

"Damned if I know. They think I know where he went. If they only knew how much I want to be rid of that scoundrel."

Prentis crossed the room and tossed a newspaper on the desk. "They must have stayed up all night preparing this." He tapped the front page, just under the masthead: MAYOR FRONT AND CENTER IN SHOOTING OUTSIDE SPEAKEASY. Below the headline was a picture of Jackson in the alleyway, kneeling over Tarkington's body.

Jackson snatched it up. "Good Lord, I was an innocent bystander! Get Riley Tanner in here. Tell him if I don't get a clarification on that headline, I'll sue. I'll set him back so far, he'll have to set up shop in Timbuktu. Is Fannie in?"

"I sent her home. She seems okay, but I figured she didn't need to be subjected to all the attention the office might get. A reporter type followed you back and is haunting the courthouse steps. I'm surprised he's not up here pounding on the door."

"One of Tanner's?"

"I wasn't paying that much attention . . . and he's gone now," Prentis said, taking another look out the window. "That won't be the end—"

A knock at the suite's outer door interrupted him.

"Get rid of him, whoever it is," Jackson said. He picked up the *Star* and began reading in earnest. But the visitor managed, without any tussling, to slip past Prentis and into Jackson's presence.

"Good morning, Mr. Mayor," Tate Shoemaker said. He removed his hat, took a seat near the desk, and nodded to the slack-jawed mayor.

"Sorry, Jackson," Prentis said. "Mister, if you don't take your carcass out of here immediately, I'll have Officer McCall do the honors. He's not known for his gentle manner."

"Yes, of course. But first, the *Star* would like a statement from you about last night—to set the record straight. It's your chance to clarify things before other, less sympathetic interests come knocking. What do you say?"

Jackson threw the newspaper in the reporter's lap. "Shouldn't due diligence occur *before* Tanner splashes me all over the front page of his tabloid?" He looked at Prentis, who nodded. Jackson sat down with a huff, and Prentis pulled up a chair.

"Here's your statement. As you might know—and could certainly verify with ease if you found a little time in your busy day to check your facts—I do not drink. I was at Mumbles to attend to a very delicate matter. My assistant, Miss Byrne—and I do hope you will refrain from using her name—was there with a certain fellow whom I deemed to be of questionable integrity. And seeing that Miss Byrne is formally engaged, I thought it best to inquire as to her wellbeing."

"Gallantry is not yet dead," Prentis added."

"Exactly. I invited this fellow, Nathan Tarkington, outside to have a word or two, and the next thing I know, someone's shot the poor man! As I understand it, he refused treatment and has left town. I say, good riddance. Nevis doesn't need his sort hanging about."

"How does this relate to rumrunning and your trip with him to Upper Marlboro?"

"I beg your pardon?"

"The bootleggers that Nathan Tarkington ran interference for with Miss Byrne. I was there. Very exciting, but even in a state that has so far resisted passing enforcement legislation, a strange pursuit for a mayor—or any other official, for that matter."

Jackson and Prentis exchanged a glance. "I'm afraid you've mistaken me for someone else. I haven't been to Upper Marlboro in months."

"You don't say." Shoemaker scribbled in his notebook. "And if I may ask about the land transaction between you and Mr. Tarkington—a swap of Danny Millman's waterfront for a place down at Parkers Wharf?

Interesting place, Parkers Wharf. A bit isolated." He pulled a folded paper from his book. *"Hopefully, none will be the wiser to any questionable activities of T."* Did I get that right?" He pushed the transcribed journal page across the table, along with the picture of Jackson and the young military man.

Prentis picked up the telephone. "You're out of here."

Jackson motioned for the phone and then smacked the receiver back onto the cradle. He fingered the photograph. "Breaking and entering is illegal."

"So, you're verifying these are yours?" More scribbling. "Wouldn't know about that. An anonymous source." He looked up. "So, you keep a journal, and the land swap occurred with this"—he checked his notes—"Tarkington *'of questionable integrity'*?"

Jackson's dislike for the needling, muckraking newsman was growing.

Shoemaker frowned at him. "Your relationship has soured, hasn't it? Must be difficult, what with your interests so intertwined."

"There is *no* relationship, no entwinement, and I'll not verify any rumors floating around amongst common riffraff. The land swap was handled by intermediaries. I didn't even know until the finalization that the other party was Tarkington. The documents are all proper. As I'm sure you must know by now, the property on the wharf is adjacent to mine. I have plans to rebuild my torched plant and expand. Nothing underhanded there."

"And the bids collected from Tarkington and Miss Honora Lally . . . Now, she's an interesting character. Works for John J. McClure. Personalities don't come any bigger than—"

Prentis, who had been sitting quietly and staring, stood up. "Not. Another. Word."

"—and I'm not sure exactly how Hubert Carr is involved in all this. The park gets a share of the white lightning? Anyway, I saw all these players leave the courthouse after your little bidding war."

Prentis walked out, his voice soon loud and clear on the phone at Fannie's desk.

Shoemaker leaned conspiratorially toward Jackson. "You're a very popular politician," he said. "The untainted mayor, reformer breaking away from the old backroom way of doing business—"

"Don't entertain him, Jackson!" Prentis yelled from the outer office.

But the young newshound was undeterred. "Does *everybody* have it wrong? Clear me up here, Mayor, and give me some facts, because right now it looks a lot like you're running a hooch game at Parkers Wharf, in partnership with a bunch of big-city East Coast racketeers. Don't waste both our time with the don't-know-from-nothing routine. I've already been given enough goods to run an intriguing story, but I have plenty of other questions. What's your cut? How much does it cost to get a parish priest to turn a church into a gin mill? Who did Tarkington work into such a lather that they decided to bump him off? Maybe he stepped on the toes of someone trying to horn in—this Miss Lally, maybe?"

A wave of nausea flooded over Jackson. "You don't understand."

"I'd like to. Honest, I would." Shoemaker sat back in his chair as if reassessing his brash approach. Then he whispered, "What we print is going to make or break you. Which will it be: reluctant mayor or chip off the old block?"

"Does it really matter what I say, Mr. Shoemaker?" Jackson nodded at the *Evening Star*. "What kind of honesty will repair the damage created by your innuendos in this little smear job?"

When the reporter didn't answer, Jackson heaved a deep sigh and said, "What do you *really* want? A nice wad of cash and you go away quietly? Political position to make your mother or sweetheart proud?"

"Jackson!" Prentis said, reappearing. "Please stop entertaining him. Officer McCall will be here shortly."

"Shut up and sit down, Prentis!" Jackson turned back to the reporter and said, "Because if you do, Mr. Shoemaker, you're hitting up the wrong Dwyer. That was my father, not me. Now, go print what you like. I'll stand behind my reputation."

"If that's the way you want it. Riley Tanner is waiting for my story, and if he balks, I'll contact Mr. Volstead myself if I have to." Shoemaker stood and put his hat on. "As for sweetening the pot in some sordid backroom deal? My aspirations extend far beyond the confines of this provincial little backwater. Good day, gentlemen."

Jackson wavered. Maybe Shoemaker wasn't a no-good son of a bitch just out to get him. He let him get as far as the door. "Wait." He picked up the transcribed journal page. "I won't deny it. This is an accurate transcription—"

Prentis sprang up. "Jackson!"

"—of the journal I keep. It was stolen from my office yesterday evening. Do you have more of it, or just this section?"

"The whole thing," Shoemaker said, eying Prentis as he came around the side of the desk.

Jackson pointed Prentis to an empty chair and continued. "Then you should understand the difficulty I've faced in enforcing a law that half the population despises. Why are you so dead set on upholding the Eighteenth Amendment? Are you one of those Bible-thumping teetotalers?"

The reporter tipped his hat back. "Certainly not. I try not to let my personal feelings color my reporting. Right is right, wrong is wrong, and it's my responsibility as a journalist to lay bare corruption wherever I find it. The story here is corrupt politicians who fail to live up to their civic duties and who trade political favors for fat kickbacks—not the local brewers and moonshiners."

Jackson beckoned for him to sit back down. "I've spent my whole life running from liquor. Please don't put me in the middle of all this bootlegging nonsense."

The reporter stayed where he was. "Aren't you already there?"

"As you get older, Mr. Shoemaker, you're going to find that nothing is quite so black and white. If there is any organized effort in Nevis to violate the Volstead Act, I suspect that the intention is to prevent needless deaths from bad booze and to keep illegal efforts on a small scale. None of which has put so much as an arcade token in my pocket." Jackson shifted in his chair. "Suppose this office could provide you with enough information to nail the *really* bad guys. Anonymous, of course. 'Snitch' has a bad connotation, and possibly hazardous consequences. What protection could you provide in return?"

Shoemaker's face brightened. He removed his hat and sat down again. "I think we can reach a mutually agreeable deal, gentlemen."

Prentis tipped his head back and stared at the ceiling for a moment. When he finally spoke, his voice was measured, his look penetrating. "You will immediately return the mayor's journal and other effects. Whatever information the mayor provides, he will expect the same degree of anonymity you would extend to any other confidential source. If your source leaks, we will run you out of Nevis on a rail, and I don't mean the Chesapeake. Understood?"

"Thoroughly."

Prentis reached over and picked up the receiver on Jackson's telephone. "Let me call off McCall; then we can proceed with the *reluctant mayor* version of events."

CHAPTER FORTY-ONE

Infallible Sources

For the first time in months, Jackson relaxed. The police had backed off on their inquisition about the shooting, and in exchange for details about operations at Parkers Wharf, Tate Shoemaker agreed that no *Evening Star* headlines would be screaming corruption at the highest levels of local government. Could Jackson trust him? As much as anyone else he surrounded himself with. Everyone wanted something. As Jackson saw it, the newshound had the promise of an even bigger scoop than what he could print now. Shoemaker would keep their agreement.

A courier from the *Star* returned the lockbox to the courthouse by late afternoon. Jackson promptly took out the watch and buckled it on his wrist, then inventoried the contents. Finding everything in order, he dumped the bids into the trash can and set a match to them. The journal, he secured in a breast pocket.

Prentis watched the show like a hawk, seething with irritation that was palpable. "If you had destroyed those bids when I told you to . .

. And burn the journal. Only a fool would write all that down. If I'd known, I'd have stolen it myself just to keep it in safe hands."

"I'll deal with it," Jackson said. "Everything's under control. Shoemaker's the best thing that ever happened to us. Dealing with these out-of-towners was a mistake. Now we have a chance to be rid of them."

"No, Jackson, *this* is the biggest mistake of your career. It's not smart to play the ends against the middle. I just hope I'm not with you when it's your turn to get plugged in a dark alley. We don't even know who shot Tarkington. Racketeer? Former associate? Jilted lover? Now that we've put the kibosh on the Williams Wharf railway spur, Tarkington doesn't need Camilla anymore. Maybe he jilted her. *'Heaven has no rage like love to hatred turned . . .'"*

Disgust swept Jackson's face. "You've always been wrong about Camilla."

"No, let me think. The smart money wouldn't be on Camilla. She's a hellion, but Honora Lally is a bigger one, and has a big backer in McClure. She had him plugged. McClure will be gunning for us now. Don't think baring your soul to young Shoemaker has solved anything."

"Architectural plans?" he asked as Jackson spread oversize sheets of paper across his desk. He put a hand on one edge to keep it from curling.

"For my building. I'm taking them with me to the meeting in Baltimore tomorrow. I want them finalized before I leave office."

"There's a year left on the rest of your father's term. You have plenty of time."

"Young Shoemaker is going to get me out of this mess, and then I'm going to concentrate on life without politics. You want to be mayor? Take it; I'm done. No more terms for me."

Prentis pulled his hand away and let the plans scroll back up. "Nice of you to tell me. What am I supposed to do?"

Jackson sighed in irritation and shoved the roll into his briefcase. "For the next day or so, why don't you see how you like running the place? Then I'd strongly suggest you find a brighter star to hitch your wagon to. If you need me—and I seriously doubt that—I'll be at the Belvedere."

— —

After tipping his hat to more friendly constituents than he had imagined he had, Jackson retreated to the rear platform of the train depot and lit up a Camel. The main rail crew was dragging back into town after what looked like a particularly grueling day's work. It was hard, honest work, and he admired them. They probably felt as connected to those endless ribbons of steel as he felt to his buildings on the dock. The railroads would be running long after the oysters were gone. Jackson studied the young Byrne kid for a while as he skulked about, up to no good. His sister Fannie, though, was a keeper. Unfortunately, this younger one was destined for the Big House.

At the distant blast of the incoming 222 from Baltimore, he crushed out his smoke and returned to a bench on the main platform. Once aboard, he would hide behind his copy of *The Innocents* and be done with his mayoral duties for another day.

The Chesapeake Railway was lightly traveled this late in the day, and the carriages quickly emptied. They carried an inordinate number of burly day-laborer types, which struck Jackson as a bit odd. Last off was a blonde in an expensive black dress and pearls. Jackson shrank behind another passenger and watched Honora Lally sashay off the platform and climb into a waiting lizzie coupe. Then he strode to a car at the end of the train. Halfway up the steps, he had to reverse course and move aside for a disembarking straggler—who suddenly grabbed him by the arm and turned him back toward the depot.

"Just the man I wanted to see," a dulcet voice murmured in his ear.

Jackson couldn't say the same. "Tark . . . You—you're well?" Jackson asked. He freed himself from Nathan Tarkington's clutch and looked him over.

"Superficial wound. There's something to be said for a good, solid whiskey flask in one's vest pocket." Tarkington herded Jackson across the platform and down the steps to the street. "We can swap war stories later. There's a bigger issue that requires immediate attention."

"Yes, I saw her. Miss Lally disembarked just ahead of you."

"Honora and I have joined forces."

"When did that happen?"

"Right after she shot me." Tarkington thumped the roof of a yellow cab parked at the curb, startling the snoozing driver. "Courthouse." Then Tarkington turned and said to Jackson, "I wouldn't enjoy the walk right now. Hop in."

Jackson hesitated. "How about somewhere less official?"

Tarkington shook his head, and refused to be drawn into further conversation until they were ensconced in Jackson's office and Tarkington had locked the door. Jackson stood near the door while Tarkington eased himself into one of the upholstered chairs.

"Don't you want to have her arrested?" Jackson asked.

"Nah, we have a history. Apparently, she thinks I have eyes for Camilla McClelland. I apologized. She apologized. It's easier to go with the flow than try to dam the river." He shrugged.

"So, she's left McClure and is working with Delaware Valley Investment."

"No, just the opposite. *Delaware* has been subsumed into McClure's business. Don't get in a lather, though. It was a relatively smooth transition as those things go. Nothing will change except whose coffers get filled."

Jackson shook his head. "*Everything's* changed. Nevis struck no deal with McClure. With the demise of *Delaware,* our exclusive agreement is null and void, and it couldn't come at a better time. Thanks to your gun-happy girlfriend, I have become uncomfortably familiar with the Nevis police headquarters. You're going to have to pack up and take your friends elsewhere. Nevis is now officially out of the moonshine business." He opened the door. "Feel free," he said, and sat down behind his desk.

Tarkington remained seated, pulled out a cigarette, and casually lit up. "She's not my girlfriend. And yes, your notoriety has become something of a problem, although local police seldom object to being paid to look the other way. The bigger problem here is that someone's digging around in our business, flapping their trap."

"You're not under the mistaken impression that it could be me?"

"Hope not. After all, we're in this together. Someone at the pier has been pedaling your box. And that young journalist fellow has been asking the wrong sort of questions. He's an accident waiting to happen."

Jackson blanched. "You don't intend on encouraging any *accidents* along the way, do you?"

"Not my job, but I can't vouch for anyone else. What I'm about is shutting down operations and moving product. Tonight. I have a source within the Bureau of Prohibition, and so far, she's proved infallible. Federal agents are hitting Parkers Wharf at the crack of dawn tomorrow. Our goal is to have the place cleaned out by midnight." He pulled a map out of his jacket and unfolded it on Jackson's desk. "I already have a crew headed there to load it onto boats and ferry it down to here." He indicated Cape Charles, near the confluence of bay and ocean. "We'll hand it off to the buyer, and our problems are over. Okay?"

"Are you *crazy*? No, not okay. There is no *our.* This is *your* venture, and I will disavow any knowledge of it. I'm not going anywhere near Parkers, where I might get swept up in a federal raid."

Tarkington exhaled a swoosh of smoke and tapped out the butt. "Let me make one thing clear, Jackson. It's not like I'm asking you for a favor. You're a major player, and I expect all my major players to be front and center. Be a champ, call up Prentis, and let's get things rolling. No need to lose good light. I aim to keep Honora in a happy mood. Nobody wants to be left behind as the sacrificial lamb, do they?"

Jackson unclenched his jaw. Rumrunning through swampy waters in the middle of the night to enrich the likes of John J. McClure? Tarkington should shoot him right here. *MAYOR DIES IN GANGLAND HOLDUP.* Surely, Camilla would shed a tear over that headline. His eyes flicked to Tarkington. The confident son of a bitch was studying him closely. If the man had a gun, he wasn't showing it off. Honora, however . . . He tried to fight the puppeteer's strings tugging on the backs of his hands, then finally picked up the phone. He dialed several numbers, depressed the receiver cradle, and started over. "Can't even remember the damn number," he mumbled. "Prentis . . . Yes, I know it's late . . .Tarkington's back in town. I'll tell you later. Feds are going to raid Parkers Wharf tomorrow morning. Everything's being moved out tonight. Meet me down there in half an hour." Unwilling to hear any argument, he hung up at once.

"Let's get this over with," he said.

— —

At the other end of the call, Tate Shoemaker was slower to hang up. Had he just been invited to a bootleggers' party? Accepted. He peeked over the partition to where Corbin, the photographer, worked. No one. He borrowed one of several Eastman Kodaks sitting on a side table, grabbed an extra roll of 116, and strode to the back door.

The rear door flew open, almost smacking him in the nose, and Jack burst in. "Mr. Shoe!" he said, latching onto his arm. "Come on, there's no time to waste." He pulled Tate toward the door.

"Whoa, there," Tate said, trying to peel himself loose. "Keep your britches on."

"No, *you* shake a leg, sir. There's a man at the train station asking for you."

"Damn it, Jack, let *go*! He's probably a news source. "Did you get a name? What's he look like? Old, young, scar running down his mug?"

Jack frowned. "Mean and ruthless like Lon Chaney in *Outside the Law*. He got off the same train as Nathan Tarkington and he has a gun. I saw the lump in his jacket. Come on, Shoe, trust me on this. Have I ever steered you wrong? I'm the best eyes and ears you got." He yanked again, planting his feet and putting his whole body into it this time. "Duck out until we figure out what he's up to."

"Son, I'm in the middle of the biggest scoop of my career. Now leggo." Tate tried again to shake the boy loose, but he held on like a limpet.

"*Shoe!* Come on. You're the only friend I've got that pays—"

"Tate Shoemaker available?" The inquiry at the front desk resounded clearly in the stillness of the office.

Tate ducked behind the linotype and pulled Jack with him. "That him?" he whispered.

Jack nodded. His precocious demeanor had vanished, and for the first time ever, Tate saw fear in those twelve-year-old eyes.

They bolted out the back door. Tate's head whipped right, down the alley. They could hit Main Street and head west toward the depot—which might be running toward trouble—or east to the pier, but getting past all the press building's big front windows would be risky. His head whipped left, to the rear alley. Once past the loading dock and a few fences, they might make the pier, but with no easy way to reach Parkers Wharf in a timely manner.

"Know how to start a car, Jack?"

"Yes, sir."

"Perfect. I'll crank. You do the rest. And, Jack, no matter what happens, don't stop." He pushed him to the right, and they ran as if their lives depended on it.

CHAPTER FORTY-TWO

Swamped

Jackson sent Tarkington to the car and made a quick second call to Prentis. Then, as the lowering sun set the high, wispy clouds aflame in a burst of crimson and orange, the three men took off down Three Notch Road to Parkers Wharf.

At the wharf, relocation was in full swing. The new Millman's Glass and Varnish building, hastily constructed out of poles and corrugated steel, as well as Jackson's former house—salmon-colored brick laid in Flemish bond—seethed with the comings and goings of laborers rolling barrels and carrying crates of white lightning. The scent of honeysuckle hung heavy in the air, and grunts and muffled cursing drowned out the late-day birdsong. Tarkington nudged them toward the house and then went off to find the foreman.

Jackson and Prentis threaded their way to the far side of the house. "In a nutshell," Jackson said, "Honora Lally shot Tarkington, McClure's running the show now, and if we don't get out of this we'll be wearing stripes." He surveyed potential avenues of escape: the swamp behind them, or the tall-grass meadow with a stand of trees in the distance.

"Settle down. If we pitch in, we should be out of here long before the feds show up."

"*Pfft*. Do you really want to trust your lot to some snitch down at the Prohibition bureau?

Prentis turned toward the meadow. "That would be the best choice, but it's an open dash. Somebody would see us."

Jackson's gaze swept that area. Where was Shoemaker? Was there still enough light to take pictures on the sly? Had the reporter even understood what Jackson was asking of him?

In an instant, Armageddon was upon them. A blinding light arced into the sky. Prentis pushed Jackson through a stand of cattails into the swamp as gunfire reverberated through the trees.

Jackson resurfaced, dripping swamp muck and a pollywog or two. Through a screen of cattails and cord grass, he could see them—a yard full of government men. Fedora-wearing, overcoated hulks wielding sawed-off shotguns and flare pistols. Bootleggers scattered in every direction.

Prentis surfaced beside him. "Infallible informant? We're cooked. Dry land with our hands up, or deeper into the marsh, where we'll either drown or get snakebit?"

Jackson closed his eyes and swept away the memories of Camilla that haunted this house. He pushed his awareness beyond the mayhem outside its doors and let his mind's eye move across the landscape to memories of a daylit meadow and black-eyed Susans. He knew that field well and the sanctuary of St. Raphael just beyond it.

"My choice, then!" Prentis grabbed his arm and struck out into deeper water that quickly rose above their knees. Jackson pushed him off. Paralleling dry ground, he sloshed through the reed-filled water, toward the church. Prentis muttered a few choice words but let him go.

The next minutes felt like a slog through purgatory. Jackson flailed, he stumbled, he blasphemed, until he reached shallower water, bald cypress knees, and the rising bank of the shoreline. He clambered halfway up and collapsed.

CHAPTER FORTY-THREE

The Good Father

Jackson awoke in darkness. He took off for the yellow glow at St. Raphael, praying that it was friendly and that Father McGee was up to tending a wayward member of his flock. As Jackson neared the church, the beckoning soft glow brightened into the light of a lantern that swayed along in rhythm with the gait of someone walking—a robed figure. Jackson prayed it was not the great disciplinarian, Father Piper. He couldn't survive a fiery rant at the moment. With relief, he watched the figure recoil as he ran toward it. Father Piper never backed down.

"Father McGee!" Jackson said as he barreled past, "I'm in need of confession. Do you have the time? If not, simple sanctuary will do."

The priest raised his lantern. "Jackson? Slow down, son. God has time."

Without pausing to chat, Jackson yanked open St. Raphael's double doors, slowed to a respectful trot, darted down a side aisle to the confessional, and disappeared behind the heavy maroon curtain on the far side. In the pitch dark, panting heavily, heart thumping, he dropped to the kneeler and shrank into the corner.

Soon, soft footfalls approached, lights came on in the nave, and someone entered the confessional booth from the other side. The wood panel between the two booths grated open, and the silhouette of the good father appeared, ear to the mesh screen.

"Bless me, Father, for I have sinned," Jackson said, shivering in his wet clothes and smelling like pond scum. "It's been years since my last confession. These are my sins. I . . . er . . ." He stopped and cleared his throat, then began again. "Father, I have so many sins, I have no idea where to begin. And I'm sorry for them. All of them."

He stopped a second time, and the tension in the confessional felt at odds with the calm, holy quiet of the nave beyond. What was he doing?

"Son, we all have sins, and happily, most of them are not so serious that they will damn us to eternal perdition. Unburden yourself of the egregious, damning things you have done, and then, if you wish, we can discuss the rest. I have been a priest for almost thirty years, and I don't think there's anything you could say that would shock me."

"I'm overwhelmed by all this liquor business," Jackson said. "I have tried to be a good steward of the office of mayor, but I've made a mess of it all by trying to please too many people. I've been vain and overly concerned about what others think of me; I've broken laws and allowed bootleggers to run rampant through the area. But what I detest most of all is that I've put my trust in people whom I knew to be of bad intent."

"Were you down by the wharf?"

"Yes, Father. It's full of revenuers busting up the stills. They might very well find yours hidden in the woods. I'm sorry—"

Jackson stopped as the massive church doors squeaked open on their ancient hinges, and heavy steps echo through the church. They approached and stopped near the confessional, the tips of spit-shined dress shoes peeking beneath the bottom of the velvet curtain. To his horror, Jackson watched a puddle of water from his dripping clothes inching toward them.

"These are serious matters, my son. Is it so hard . . . Excuse me." Father McGee's chair creaked, and light washed over the booth as he swept his curtain aside.

"Do you realize that it is most inappropriate to be standing here?" Father McGee said. "The sacrament of confession is confidential. Now, I would be happy to hear your confession this evening, but you must wait over there."

The shoes rotated toward the priest. "My apologies, Father." The voice was deep, measured, full of confidence but no real remorse. "I'm Federal Agent Leonard with the Bureau of Prohibition. Were you aware of the bootlegging operation at the wharf across the way?"

"Sacramental wine is exempt under the conditions of Volstead. We have no need for bootlegging here."

"There was no accusation in that, Father . . ."

"McGee."

"Father McGee. We're searching for anyone who might have eluded the dragnet, and figures were seen running in this direction. Have you seen anyone lurking about?"

"No, the evening has been rather quiet until the last hour or so. Lots of commotion over *there,* but nothing amiss here."

Jackson glanced at the wet floor again. The puddle was coming dangerously close to the tip of the agent's shoe. Moving slowly and cautiously, Jackson leaned over and tried to sweep the water back with the edge of his hand. The puddle responded by spreading out to almost the length of the shoe and gave no sign of halting its advance.

"You should probably return to the rectory for the night, Father. These are criminal types who may be desperate. Do you mind if we check around? Respectfully, of course."

"Not at all, Agent Leonard. I would assist you, but as you may have surmised, I am in the middle of a confession. I would appreciate your respecting that and moving on with your business as quickly as possible."

The shoes pivoted again toward Jackson.

"*Over there,*" McGee repeated.

The puddle reached out and latched onto the shoe's tip. Jackson held his breath as water dribbled from his hair into his eye.

"Have a good evening, Father McGee." The shoes turned and disappeared.

Jackson exhaled and drooped his head against the lattice screen. Light flashed again, and the priest resumed his listening position. "Now, where were we, son?"

"Between a rock and a hard place, but sincerely sorry," Jackson said.

"Ah, yes." McGee's silhouette gently nodded on the other side of the screen. "A good start, but are we truly finished? Say a good act of contrition for me, and then I want you to kneel here and say twenty Our Fathers. The Father is loving and forgiving to those who are sincerely sorry and want to change for the better. Spend some time reflecting on that. Then you might want to consider coming back another time, when there's less, um, *urgency.* You always come here in a rush."

"Thank you, Father. I will."

Father McGee slid shut the grate between them.

"Father," Jackson called before the curtain on the other side swept open.

"Yes?"

"What about *your* stills?"

"Don't worry. God's hands. And the agents will have their hands full busting up yours. I can't imagine they'd suspect more than one operation going on down here, and we're deep in the woods on the other side of the church. Now, get busy thanking your loving Father. And if you don't mind, throw in a nighttime prayer for me. I'll snuff the light when they leave. Pull the front doors tight when you go."

CHAPTER FORTY-FOUR

Puckers and Partnerships

Tate's fingers tightened around the binoculars' leather grip. He was too far away to take pictures, so he would have to sear it in his memory. In the battle down at the wharf, the federal men appeared to have won. There had been some gunplay—from which side, he wasn't sure—but it all ended with disappointing speed. He watched now as the feds—easy to pick out in their intimidating long coats and fedoras—loaded up the paddy wagons.

He pulled the binocular strap free and turned to Jack. "See if you recognize anybody down there. Mayor Jackson, Gant, Tarkington."

While Jack scanned, Tate double-checked their hiding place. He wasn't so worried about the revenuers. With his press credentials, he could eventually talk his way out of arrest. It was the gun-toting Lon Chaney type who concerned him. Evidently, the racketeers had learned of Tate's snooping around. His press badge and gift of gab would do him no good there. Dead men told no tales.

"Tarkington."

Tate pulled the binoculars free. "Sure enough. And if I'm not mistaken, that's Prentis Gant standing right next to him. Jiminy. The man doesn't have a lick of sense." He watched as the two men stepped up into the last of the police wagons, and the doors thumped closed.

"In the car, Jack. With a police escort right behind us, I can't see the man from the depot fooling with us. If he got this far and saw what happened to his friends, I'll bet he's skedaddling back to town. You need to get home, and I need my typewriter."

They took off just before the lights of their escort turned up the hill.

— —

Fanny intercepted them at the Byrnes' front porch. Rounding the hood of the car, she stuck her head in the driver's side. "Word's all over town. It's Parkers Wharf, isn't it?" She looked past Tate to Jack, sitting on the passenger's side. "Did you drag him down there?"

Tate opened his door, backing her up. "Jack's been with me, but he was safer than anywhere else. Feds are down there busting up stills. Look, Fannie," he said, touching her arm, "I need a favor. This story needs to break big, but it isn't going to get a fair shake here. I'm going to Washington to peddle it to one of the larger papers, probably the *Washington Star*. There might be some bad sorts in town looking for me so I need to get in and out fast without calling attention to myself. Will you drop me off at the newspaper so I can grab my things?" He looked into her big, trusting brown eyes. "Can you do that?"

She elbowed him out of the way and pointed to the other side of the car. "Get in. And you, Jack, in the house."

"I'm with him," Jack said, jerking a thumb at Tate.

Fannie got in the driver's seat and shoved him hard. "We're not going anywhere till you get out."

"Uh, yes we are," Tate said. "We can discuss this later."

She folded her arms across her chest and glared at him.

"Mother Mary," he mumbled. "*Go* or both of you get out."

After some huffing and a few choice looks, Fannie put the car in gear and turned it back toward town. Atlantic Street and Bayview was impassable, clogged with paddy wagons, feds, and uniformed officers spilling out of the jail and into the lamplit street. Fannie bypassed the mess, turned down the next block, and pulled into the *Star* building alleyway from the opposite direction.

Tate hopped out. "Take the car home and bring it back tomorrow morning on your way to work. No one will miss it. I'll work my way back to the depot and catch the midnight mail express to the District." He checked his watched. "In ten minutes."

Fannie cut the engine. "We're going with you."

Tate heaved a deep sigh and walked around to her side of the car. "No, you can't. Take your brother home."

Fannie leaned out the window and bussed him full on the lips. "Who's gonna stop me?" she asked.

Tate pulled back, sputtering. "M-M-Mr. Millman."

"Danny's a good man, but maybe just a little too settled for me. We've all but said our goodbyes." She got out of the car and motioned for Jack to do the same. "You've got eight minutes. We'll go get tickets."

"Your mother will be worried—"

"They have telephones in Washington. Go!"

Tate darted inside, scooped up the portable Corona, and slipped his father's picture into his shirt pocket. Then he leaned forward and planted a big smooch on Mary Pickford. He left the building and, with five minutes to spare, trotted toward the train depot and, with luck, his Pulitzer.

CHAPTER FORTY-FIVE

North

Jackson swept past the police station once more, walked a hundred feet or so farther down the street, and then made an about-face. He needed to spring Prentis, but what would people think? If it proved advantageous, his honey-tongued assistant could without a doubt be pushed to provide details about the Parkers Wharf affair. Maybe he wouldn't incriminate anyone in the mayor's office. After all, what would that accomplish?

On the third attempt, Jackson dug deep, pushed through the door, and went inside. Prentis, looking bedraggled and insignificant, peered through the bars of the nearest holding cell. Officer Reagan glanced up disinterestedly from his desk duties. "Help you?"

"I'm here to arrange the release of Prentis Gant."

The officer shuffled through his stack of paperwork and shoved a form at him. "Three hundred dollars and he's yours," he growled.

"And Mr. Nathan Tarkington?"

"Gone." He consulted his paperwork. "As long as you're paying, got three more back there. Hayes, Bacon, and Tuttle. Want them, too?"

Jackson shook his head. "I'll be back shortly for Mr. Gant." He locked eyes with Prentis and mouthed the word *bank*.

— · —

At the First National, Jackson slid a note underneath the bars of the bank teller's cage and looked about him to be sure he couldn't be overheard. "I'd like to close this account," he whispered.

Mr. Hamilton's bushy salt-and-pepper eyebrows arched gently as he read the slip, silently mouthing the words as he went. "*All* of it, Mayor? If our services haven't been satisfactory—"

"Oh, no. You've been excellent. It's just that . . . I have plans."

"I see. The amount—it's rather large. Would a check suffice?"

"Split it in half. One check, the rest in cash, please."

"Yes, of course. I'll need you to step over to my desk. This will take a moment." He hung a sign from the top of his window—*next window, please*—and led Jackson to a nearby office with a handsome mahogany desk and a nice, unobstructed view of the bay. "And your other account—will we be doing anything with that today?"

Jackson frowned. "The other account?"

The enormous gray eyebrows knitted together. "Yes, sir. The joint account set up by Mr. Gant."

"Uh, well, that's a good question," Jackson said. A better one: *What in heaven's name are you talking about?* "Give me the amount banked, and then I'll decide."

"Certainly, sir." Hamilton pulled a ledger from his drawer, thumbed through it, and scribbled figures onto a new slip of paper. "There you are. Accurate as of Mr. Gant's deposit yesterday. Something to consider while I proceed."

Jackson almost choked. The account contained just over ten thousand dollars. How did a civil servant do that on a salary of eleven hundred smackers a year? "And the amount of that last deposit?"

"Five hundred dollars."

Jackson crumpled the paper up in his fist and took a deep breath. *That conniving rat was on the take. Tarkington? Lally and McClure? Does it really matter?* "Let's close that one, too."

"Yes, sir. Paid out the same way as the other account?"

"No. One check will do. Make it out to me, please."

— —

With his mind reeling, Jackson left the bank and walked aimlessly, eventually finding himself at the intersection of the boardwalk and the great pier that seemed to run until it bumped into the horizon. As if by instinct, he followed the pier and, reaching the end, turned around. Before him stretched a panoramic view of the Nevis waterfront: Nichols's boathouse, the warehouses, the old Millman's Glass and Varnish, and all the quaint neighboring storefronts and dives. How did it all survive in this ruthless, shifty world? And then there was his empty lot. He imagined the oyster plant still there. He had built it, and all that he had, to impress Camilla in the foolish hope that she would forgive the poor decisions of a misdirected youth. But it hadn't turned her head, not a bit. If he had never become mayor, would the plant still be there? Or would he just have found another way to destroy it all? Maybe fate had rolled the dice on him long before and decided that despite his best efforts, it would drag him down to dear old Dad's level and do him in that way. Perhaps Prentis was right—maybe it was all in the blood.

Money talked, and Prentis had used him. Was there any other tie besides power and position that bound them? He had never really needed Prentis except to direct his wayward feet down a path he swore he would never trod. Was Prentis worth it?

When at last he had his fill of what-ifs and might-have-beens, Jackson trudged back up the hill to town. When he got there, he walked right past the jail—only once—and returned to his office, which, thankfully, was as quiet as a tomb. He sat at his desk and put up his feet. A moment to think before he acted.

For the moment, his reputation was intact. The feds could suspect him, though they wouldn't charge him. No, but they would watch him until he slipped up, and then they'd have him. He was way past "beginning jitters," as Tarkington liked to call it. He could tender his resignation immediately, buy an Indian motorbike, and take off, but he would look guilty as hell. Camilla wouldn't like that. Or would she think him an innocent, wiping his hands of the whole sordid mess?

He tipped back in his chair. If he didn't stick it out, even his bottom drawer would be disappointed in him. He slid it open, and the bottle of bourbon gave him a welcoming look—his anxiety medicine from the good doc. Hell, his anxiety was through the roof! He pulled the bottle out and set it in the middle of his desk. He had been saving this, though for what exactly, he wasn't sure. The repeal of the Eighteenth Amendment, perhaps? The end of his term? Camilla finally forgiving him? A *toast*, not a *drink*—that, of course, would be foolish. But Volstead was alive and well, Camilla still despised him, and his moral compromises on liquor proved he was just a chip off the old block after all. He slid his feet off the desk, uncorked the whiskey, and poured two fingers.

He fished around in the drawer for his personal note paper. His hand bumped the 1911-model Colt pistol he had confiscated from Prentis the day Alice told him she ran off and got married. It came out with the box of stationery. There was a round in the chamber, but the safety was engaged. He released it, dropped the hammer, and placed the half-cocked pistol next to his drink. Then he walked across the room and centered the whiskey bottle on the windowsill.

From the stationery, he chose a buff-colored envelope and, in a strong hand, addressed it to *Mrs. Camilla McClelland*. After a moment's reconsideration, he ripped it up. She was another one who only saw him as an opportunity to get what she wanted. He pulled two more envelopes from the box. The first he addressed to Fannie, with the name "DREXEL" in capital letters under her name. On the second, he wrote "Mrs. Prentis Gant" and "The Johns Hopkins Hospital." He stuffed each with fifteen hundred dollars and propped them against Fannie's telephone.

He returned to his desk, picked up the pistol, and felt the heft of it in his hand. He weighed it against a life of good intentions but some pretty bad choices, a future that seemed incapable of getting him where he really wanted to go, and an oyster cracker who would never have his due. So many missed opportunities. Camilla was right. He would never amount to anything. He cocked the gun and fired, showering the room in glass and whiskey.

"A smart man never forgoes an opportunity when it presents itself." Prentis had told him that the day his father died. Maybe the problem was that he just wasn't smart enough to act on the possibilities that came his way. He looked at the mess on the windowsill and floor. He might not be too smart, but his aim was pretty good. As the banging on his office door grew louder, he shifted the gun to his left hand, wiped his right hand down his pant leg, then shifted the gun back.

If anyone had potential, it was Ollie the oyster cracker. Ollie, a star in the making; Ollie, the only one who had never done him dirty; Ollie with, unfortunately, no brain at all. Opportunity was practically pounding the door down. Ollie was ready. He was ready. Was it possible for them to handle it together?

He thumbed the safety back on the Colt, sat back a minute and stared at the cracks in the ceiling. Then he picked up the phone.

"Mr. Merkle, I'm ready to take you up on that deal you offered the other day . . . Yes, the red one . . . Excellent . . . What's that? Oh, north, I suppose. I hear New England is lovely this time of year."

Made in the USA
Middletown, DE
15 December 2021

55783388R00168